THE LONG
ROAD
BACK

JASON K. KOOP

THE LONG ROAD BACK
Copyright © 2025 by Jason K. Koop

Soft cover ISBN: 978-1-4866-2658-8
Hard cover ISBN: 978-1-4866-2659-5
eBook ISBN: 978-1-4866-2660-1

Word Alive Press
119 De Baets Street Winnipeg, MB R2J 3R9
www.wordalivepress.ca

WORD ALIVE
—P R E S S—

Cataloguing in Publication information can be obtained from Library and Archives Canada.

ONE

THE TEXAS SUN drifted behind the city skyline, igniting the sky in a painful rouge. A blue pickup truck sat silent yet warm in an empty parking lot. Windows rolled down, its occupants didn't share a word as the scalding air passing through slowly cooled. A German shepherd whined as the phone on the dashboard rang out a song that had once brought a smile to his new master's lips. Now it only made him look away.

The incoming call eventually dropped and the screen displayed three such missed calls and thirteen unread texts, all from the same contact: Susan.

Taking in a breath, he finally reached for the phone and read the latest messages.

Simon, the city hall offices close soon; you'll have to hurry to get those informal marriage papers.

What's with the dog food in the kitchen?

You should cancel the credit card you gave me: I can't find it anywhere.

Something primal stirred in Simon's heart.

Where r u?

Simon?

R u okay?

Y aren't u home yet?

Primal anger swelled within his chest and his fingers clenched into a fist around the phone.

Fingers shaking, he started to play one of the voicemails.

"Simon, I'm getting worried. Please—"

He hurled his phone out the window. The device broke apart on the pavement.

The German shepherd whimpered and dropped his head to the centre console as Simon ignited the truck's engine.

———————

Simon squinted his eyes open as the searing yellow of the overhead light bore down on him. He squeezed his eyes shut again, but the glare was burned into his vision. A pair of men laughed a short distance away and Simon clutched at his ears, their mirth like a jackhammer striking against his skull.

He knew what this was—the greeting of an old friend, the kind you never want to see, because he only ever shows up to remind you just how bad the night before went.

Metal shrieked on metal, the sound piercing through his hands and into his ears.

And then he heard his name.

"Simon Fletcher. Let's go."

Cracking one eye open, he saw a police officer leaning against the doorway to the drunk tank, bags under his eyes. One of those eyes was black. A moustache graced his upper lip, but more than a five o'clock shadow haunted his cheeks and jaw.

The cop was holding a pair of crutches out to him.

Simon cleared his throat and tried to stand up, then grunted as he dropped back onto the cold concrete floor. He glanced down at his left leg, noting that everything below the knee was missing.

Just as it should be.

Sighing softly, Simon raised himself up onto the bench behind him. The cop, though clearly fatigued, watched his every move as if waiting for the amputee to try something.

"Just give me a few minutes," Simon rasped. He reached up to touch his throat and took in a sharp breath as his fingers grazed the purpled flesh. "Please…"

The cop nodded and walked off, taking the crutches with him.

Eventually Simon's senses began to return to normal. A grimace took hold of him at the smell of alcohol and urine assaulting his nose. Memories of the previous night came back to him, followed by memories of the whole preceding day. The job site inspection, meeting new clients, adopting the dog…

When the cop finally returned, Simon met his gaze. "I'm ready."

With a nod, the cop handed him the crutches and gestured for him to follow. Simon hobbled after the officer down the hall. They passed other cops and a few perps until they reached the bullpen.

The cop sat down at his desk with a heavy sigh, then waved his hand for Simon to do the same.

"Where's Delta?" Simon asked.

The cop raised an eyebrow. "Your dog?"

Simon only offered a nod.

"We got a canine unit here. He's down in the kennels with the others."

Simon noticed the officer's nametag: Monroe.

"Now…" Officer Monroe shifted in his seat and sniffed, his brown eyes reading over a report on his computer as he lifted an icepack to his raccoon eye. "Do you remember anything about last night, Mr. Fletcher?"

CHAPTER ONE

His mind strained to conjure up something, anything, after he'd left the parking lot. The rhythmic pounding of his old friend returned, though, and he finally just slumped in the chair and shook his head.

"No." Simon glanced up at the officer, dread clawing at his voice. "What did I do?"

Officer Monroe yawned. "You sent a guy to the ER."

Simon's gaze fell again and he fidgeted, his muscular frame a stark contrast to the timidity that suddenly gripped him. "Is he going to make it?"

"He'll live." The man made a note in his report. "If the medical bills don't take him out."

Relaxing, Simon ran his hands down his face. "Why'd I do it?"

"He was yelling at his girlfriend to get an abortion." Monroe took a sip from his coffee mug, a brown stain circling the inside of the ring. He made a face and set it back down. "He started gettin' physical and you took exception to that. Tried to get him to leave, and he took a swing at you." A sigh escaped the officer's lips. "Least, that's what all the other patrons sober enough to answer questions said. It's all a little too rehearsed for my tastes. But if it's true, nobody will want to touch this case with a ten-foot pole."

Monroe took out a piece of paper and slid it across the desk to Simon, an expectant look on his face.

"From the girl."

Simon unfolded the paper and found the words *Thank you* scrawled in flowery handwriting with a heart next to it. He locked in on that piece of paper, as if there were more to see—if he only stared long enough.

Monroe leaned back in his chair and interlocked his fingers over his abdomen. "Now… when I showed up, you took a swing at me. I had to taze you."

Simon's gaze snapped up to meet Monroe's. "I'm so sorry."

"You got a mean right hook." The officer held the icepack to his eye again. "Mind telling me what you were trying so hard to forget?"

With a shrug, Simon turned his attention back down to the note. "It doesn't matter. There's no excuse for getting that drunk in the middle of the week."

Monroe leaned forward, his elbows on his knees. "Say there was."

Silence gripped Simon for what felt like an eternity, but he finally managed to break some words past his throat. "My girlfriend and I have been trying to get pregnant for the last year." He fidgeted. "I found a positive pregnancy test in the garbage, then found out through my bank that she'd gotten an abortion and tubal sterilization."

"And you…?"

"I drove off to an empty parking lot and sat there for a while." He shook his head. "Then I guess I went to a bar."

"This a regular occurrence, Mr. Fletcher?"

Simon took in a breath, trying to clear his head. "No. I drink socially, but I haven't gotten blackout drunk in… a decade."

"All right." Monroe stood up. "I'll go get that dog of yours. I called your emergency contact, by the way. He's waiting outside. Also, this…"

The man reached under his desk, then straightened and handed Simon his prosthetic leg. Simon started to affix it to his stump as Monroe placed Simon's keys and wallet down on the desk as well.

"Thank you," Simon said.

Monroe walked off while Simon worked on the prosthetic. His fingers shook and fumbled with the device and he finally struck his leg in frustration. His hands wouldn't stop trembling, but he kept at it until the leg was in place.

Hearing pawsteps on the floor, he glanced up to see Delta trot up and sit before him, resting his head on Simon's leg, his wide canine eyes peering up at him.

Simon gently petted him. "Sorry, boy…"

The dog whined softly.

As he rose to his feet, Monroe held out his hand.

"I'm sorry again," Simon murmured, surprised. "About the eye."

"And I'm sorry for your loss, Officer Fletcher."

Simon's muscles constricted for a moment before relaxing. "I'm not a cop anymore."

"Oh, I know." A chuckle rumbled in Monroe's throat. "Believe me. Hopefully next time we meet under better circumstances."

"Hopefully."

Simon turned and walked towards the exit, Delta at his side. He racked his brain, trying to figure out who his emergency contact was. All he could think of was his boss. A bolt of fear shuddered through him as he considered what this would mean for his job.

He's going to fire me…

He stopped at the doors and prepared himself for the worst. Taking in a breath, he stepped through.

TWO

SIMON HAD STEELED himself to see his boss, Winston, waiting outside the police station. He was also prepared to encounter either Carson, Eggsy, or Roman, his own righthand men at the construction company, Quincy & Sons. He would even have been okay with seeing Susan herself leaning against a taxi.

What he was not prepared to see was a vision of what he would look like in twenty-three years. His dad was leaning against a new pickup, arms crossed over his blue plaid jacket. Jeans hung off him, faded some time ago and tucked into leather cowboy boots that looked as worn as the man who wore them.

The man raised his icy blue gaze to peer at Simon from under a black Stetson hat. "Don't you look awful."

Once the shock had begun to fade, Simon descended the stairs. "It feels much worse, trust me."

Mark eyed his son, then opened the passenger door. "Well, get in."

The older man barely managed to hide his surprise as Simon wordlessly got in without remark or complaint. Delta climbed in after him and sat at Simon's feet.

Taking in a breath, Mark closed the door and rounded the vehicle to climb into the driver's seat. "No telling me to go to hell?"

Simon shook his head, his shoulders slumped as if the weight of the world were dragging him deeper into the seat. Delta rested his head on Simon's knee, looking up as his master absently petted him.

"That officer, uh… Monroe," Mark said. "He said your truck is still at the bar. Lira's, I think."

"Would you mind driving me there?"

"Not at all." Mark started the truck, his movements a bit stiff and unsure.

Simon reached into his pocket for his phone, but his fingers only found his keys and wallet. He started to panic, then went still as he remembered.

"Dad, can I borrow your phone?"

Mark pointed at the glovebox with his chin before pulling out into traffic and starting to drive towards the bar.

Simon took out the phone and found that it had no lock. He considered admonishing his father and then thought better.

"Hey Winston," he said into the phone.

"Simon!" His boss's gruff, booming voice exploded out from the phone's speaker, nearly drawing Mark's attention. "I've been tryin' to get ahold of you all mornin'!"

"Sorry." The word slipped past Simon's lips, dripping with unbridled shame. "I, uh... got in a scuffle at a bar. I'll get a new phone today."

"Are you in fightin' shape?"

Simon cleared his throat. "Yeah, no... I'm good."

"Your girlfriend called."

Silence throttled Simon's voice for a moment, but he managed to eke out a few words. "What about?"

"She was hysterical. Said you weren't answerin' her texts or calls, couldn't find you anywhere..."

Running a hand through his dark brown hair, Simon sighed. "Uh... if she calls again, tell her I'm fine and that my phone's broken."

"All right, Simon. In either case, take the day. I'll handle your sites."

Fear gripped Simon's heart and he straightened. "No, boss, I—"

"Take the day and set yourself right, Simon." Winston's tone made it clear there was no room for negotiation. "And look in on that little lady of yours before she has a heart attack."

Only two words slipped past Simon's lips, marking his defeat. "All right."

He hung up and stared at the phone for a good while before putting it back in the glovebox.

"Let's get some breakfast," Mark suggested.

Simon blinked a few times, then looked over at his father. "What?"

"I got called early this morning and drove about an hour out here. Didn't have time for breakfast and I'm assuming neither did you, what with being in the drunk tank and all. Know a good diner?"

Watching his father, Simon tried to discern an ulterior motive. But then his belly growled. Delta sniffed and barked.

"Yeah, I know a good place."

Over the next few minutes, he directed his dad towards an old-school diner in town he liked to visit from time to time. When they finally pulled in, Simon got out and glanced up at the name: Vera's Diner.

"You coming?" Mark asked.

Simon snapped out of it and saw that his father had already made it to the door. Simon followed him in, Delta at his side.

Mark took off his hat as they entered and settled into a booth, Delta laying down at Simon's feet. They sat in silence until the young waitress interrupted it.

"Twice in as many days?" She grinned at Simon, her pearly teeth gleaming. He noticed she'd done up her hair today and wore a subtle perfume. "You're making me feel special."

Simon offered a half-hearted smile in return, struggling to keep his eyes open. "I'll have a black coffee please. And a few breakfast sausages for my dog."

The waitress filled a mug right then and there before turning to Mark. "And for you, sir?"

"Coffee, black, scrambled eggs and bacon please."

She wrote it down on her notepad, then filled his mug. "All right, sir. It'll be just a few minutes."

Mark sipped his coffee, his gaze never leaving Simon. His wedding band clinked against the side of the mug as he lightly tapped his fingers against it.

"So why'd I get out of bed an hour early, just to wait three hours for you to wake up?"

Simon was silent but could feel his father's gaze. It felt like he was a kid again, shame and disappointment bearing down on him.

It took him a moment to find his voice. "It still doesn't feel... real."

"It was real enough for you to—" Mark stopped when he noticed the waitress returning with the plate of sausages. She set it down in front of Delta, scratched behind his ears with a smile, and straightened. "Your breakfast will just be a little while longer."

"Thank you, miss." Mark didn't take his gaze off Simon and the waitress decided to leave, feeling the tension.

"My girlfriend and I have been trying to have kids for about a year now." Simon's voice sounded detached, as though he were reciting some bit of trivia. His gaze was locked on the dark liquid in his mug. "Last night I found a positive pregnancy test in the bathroom bin."

"Congratulations." Mark mirrored Simon's lack of enthusiasm. "So you went out to party?"

A frown touched Simon's lips as his emotions swirled back in. "No. I got a call from the credit card company for suspicious activity. I cancelled the card, figuring she'd just lost it. But then I saw it on the counter when I walked in. She'd..." Simon took a few breaths, his chest heaving with the weight of what he was about to say. "She got rid of our kid, got sterilized, and used my money to do it."

A crack formed in Mark's expression, feeling his son's pain. "Oh."

Simon covered his face with his hands. Too many paths stretched before him, and all of them seemed to lead off cliffs. "I don't know what to do. She always said she wanted kids, and I asked her a good few times about it. It was practically a monthly tradition as soon as she was in the right time of the month."

He tried to pick up his hot coffee, his hands shaking. Some spilt over the edge and he cursed as he set the mug back down and grabbed some napkins.

"Miss?" Mark called to the waitress, his voice calm. "Could we get a rag soaked in the coldest water you've got, please?"

The waitress glanced over and her eyes widened. She swiftly wetted a rag in cold water and brought it over. "Are you all right?"

"Fine." Simon wrapped the cloth around his hand. "Thanks."

Lines etched in her face. "Are you sure? I can get some ice, or—"

"I'm okay." He noticed the anger in his voice and reined it in, barely. His voice softened. "Thank you."

A frown tugged at her thin lips, but she nodded. "All right. Holler if you need anything else."

Simon waited for her to walk away before looking at Mark. "It's some kind of practical joke, right?"

Sipping his coffee, Mark could only offer a shrug. "I'm sure she tried to call or text. Did she mention the credit card at all?"

"She texted me to say she thought it was missing and I should cancel it."

Mark watched his son for a long moment. "All right. We're going to—"

He stopped as the waitress returned with Mark's breakfast.

"Here you are." She turned her chocolate brown eyes to Simon and offered a small smile. "How's your hand?"

"Better, thanks." He removed the cloth, the skin still an angry red. He held the cloth up to her.

"Anytime." She glanced down at Delta. "Something wrong with the food, boy?"

He looked at Delta and noticed the dog had been staring at him expectantly the whole time.

Simon patted Delta's head. "Go ahead. Eat up."

Delta immediately set to the food and the waitress let out a soft whistle. "That's a well-trained dog."

"He is."

She looked like she wanted to say more but opted to turn back to Mark. "Enjoy your meal." She walked away.

"We'll go to your bank first," Mark said.

Simon blinked a few times and resettled his gaze on his father. "What? Why?"

Mark ignored Simon's question and ate, covering his mouth as he spoke. "Then we'll head to your place, gather things like your clothes and anything expensive of yours."

"Dad, wait—"

"Son, can you keep a level head around her?"

Simon went silent, his mind going back to how he'd thrown his phone out the truck's window after trying to listen to one of her voicemails. "I don't know."

"Then you're going to need a place to stay." Mark kept eating, already nearly done. "Which is why we're going to the bank. If she goes into panic mode, she may try to take what she can from your accounts."

"Dad..." Simon sighed. "She's not going to take my money."

"Does she have a job?"

Simon went quiet for a moment. "No."

"A car?"

He shook his head.

"Then as soon as you aren't there, she's going to think the worst. If I'm wrong, great, no real harm done. If she gets upset over being cut off, then that's just too bad. She used your money to kill your kid and sterilize herself, after telling you she wanted kids for over a year."

Simon's gaze dropped to the table. "Okay…"

Mark finished eating and leafed sixty dollars from his wallet before placing the bills on the table. "Let's go, son."

Mark stood up, but Simon didn't move from his seat.

"Simon, no matter what you're feeling right now, remember this: she betrayed your trust. You need to protect yourself. Has she added any money to that account in the last two years?"

Simon shook his head. "But, Dad, I don't…" He trailed off. "All right, fine. Let's get me a new cell phone, then go to the bank."

THREE

THE LOW DIN of tellers and clients filled the spacious main hall of Simon's bank as he and his father walked in. Mark sized up each teller until his gaze settled on one in particular. He got into her line.

Simon noticed her baby bump as they got closer.

She smiled at them warmly, one that would be infectious if Simon had been in any other frame of mind. "Good morning, gentlemen."

Mark glanced at her nametag. "Good morning, Felicia. You look absolutely radiant."

A laugh slipped past Felicia's lips. "Thank you. The little one doesn't help much at night, though."

"My wife said the same thing about my son here." He gripped Simon's shoulder good-naturedly. "How far along are you? You sure you ought to be working?"

Another smile graced her lips. "Thanks, but the hospital's only a couple blocks away and my husband's helicoptering me whenever I'm home." She leaned forward. "This gives me a nice breather."

"Boy or girl?"

She shrugged as she rested a hand on her swollen womb. "We want it to be a surprise."

"My wife couldn't wait to know. She asked about that before she even asked if he was healthy." He let go of Simon's shoulder and took a breath. "So, Felicia, we need your help."

Her eyes darted between them. "I'd imagine so, else you'd have asked for a withdrawal by now."

Mark smirked and glanced down at his hands. "Too true." He returned his gaze to Felicia's. "So my son here was going to be a father."

Felicia glanced at Simon. "Was?"

Anger bit into Mark's voice. "Yes. His girlfriend has lied and manipulated him for two years, just for his money, and to top it off—"

"Dad."

Mark paused at the sharpness of his son's voice.

Felicia looked between the two of them before turning to her computer. "Well, one option is to change the codes to your accounts."

Mark cleared his throat. "That'd be a great start. But she knows my son quite well, so she could answer security questions or spin some tale to a new teller. Not to mention, if she's got his chequebook, she can use that to forge his signature. Not that she necessarily would, of course, but I want to make sure she can't hurt my son any more than she already has."

"Honestly, the best option is to close your account and switch banks if she's that much of a concern," Felicia remarked.

"All right." Mark rapped his knuckles on the counter. "I'll call my credit union and get the process started." He turned to Simon. "It's your choice, son."

Simon didn't move and no words rose up in his throat. It was like a brick wall in his mind was holding back everything that could push him forward.

Felicia's eyes narrowed. "Sir, I know a little something about being in that kind of relationship. They will hurt you, betray you, take everything they can from you, then make you believe it's your fault. The best way to move forward is to completely disconnect."

Her words chipped away at the mortar of the brick wall and it finally cracked.

Simon drew in a breath. "All right. Let's do it."

They went through the process, all the way up to the point at which all he had to do was sign. His hand hovered over the paper, the muscles in his arm refusing the move.

"Son?"

Simon's gaze flicked over to his father.

"Don't let her take anything else from you."

Simon fought against his muscles and rigidly signed the paperwork, his usually elegant signature rendered as little better than rough chicken-scratch.

"Is there anything else I can help you with today?" Felicia asked.

Mark shook his head. "No. Thank you so much for your help today, Felicia. Congratulations on the little one, and I pray the child's healthy."

A gentle smile touched her lips. "Thank you." She turned her knowing expression to Simon. "I hope everything turns out well for you. Whatever you do, don't give up on finding someone. I almost did."

Simon's gaze was locked on the piece of paper he'd just signed. "Thank you for your help today."

A hint of sympathy touched her eyes as she bid them goodbye.

Simon and his father left the bank.

As Mark got back into the truck, he noticed Simon hesitate by the door. Delta looked out the window at his master and whined.

"Son?"

"What if this is all some big misunderstanding?"

Mark sighed. "She used your credit card, then told you it was missing after you saw it on the counter with your own eyes. She's tryin' to hide what she did, Simon, because she knows it'll hurt you."

Simon's new phone started to ring and he took it out. He stared down at the familiar number.

Mark's eyes darted between the phone and Simon's face. "Text her you're busy. After we've got your truck, tell her you'll meet her somewhere. We'll get your stuff while she's out. You don't want to be getting your stuff while she's there."

The phone rang until it finally went to voicemail.

Simon wrote up the text and sent it off, then got into the passenger seat. Their next stop was to retrieve Simon's own truck, after which they drove together to his condo.

He walked up to the door and tried the handle hesitantly, letting out a sigh of relief when he found it locked. He took out his key, unlocked the door, then went in. As he followed, Mark raised an eyebrow as he took in the sink full of dirty dishes, the discarded rags, and generally unkempt space.

"I don't remember you being this messy."

Simon ignored the comment and went to the bedroom to grab his gym bag and suitcase. He began to stuff clothes into them.

Mark stopped at the bedroom door. The room was seemingly split down the middle. The floor on one side was barely visible under a few layers of clothing, the dresser drawers pulled partway out and overflowing with women's clothes. A few other paraphernalia were scattered about.

Simon's side of the room was clean and organized, everything in its place.

As the relationship dynamic began to become clearer, Mark shook his head. "Did she at least cook?"

Simon's silence was more than enough of an answer.

Mark walked in and patted his son's shoulder. "I'll pack your clothes. You get keepsakes and valuables."

After a brief hesitation, Simon nodded and grabbed his few suits.

Mark grunted as he knelt next to the dresser and started packing. "And by valuables, I don't mean the TV, by the way. I mean things like watches and rings."

Simon snorted, then began to collect items from around the house, including rings and necklaces, cufflinks and pins. He pulled out his dogtags, the two metallic pieces fused into a single unit of shrapnel. From the closet, he pulled out some hard plastic gun cases and a few tins of ammo. Next, he gathered his tools. All in all, it wasn't much, but he added it to the suitcase.

Mark finished packing the clothes and watched idly as Simon grabbed a wooden box engraved with a stag. The younger man opened it and looked over the knives inside.

"Am I taking too much?"

Mark shook his head. "Nah. Got any cologne or stuff like that? Hair products, trimmers, whatever?"

"Right…"

"Chequebook? Money lying around?"

Simon frowned as he set down the last few things on the bed. "I'm not going to leave her with nothing, and the chequebook is invalid now."

"Still gotta destroy it." Mark sniffed. "As for money, collect it together. Leave two weeks of groceries for her."

Taking in a breath, Simon did as his father suggested. He set the cash on the counter, then added a few more bills to it from his wallet before pinning it down with a paperweight.

He and Mark transferred everything into their trucks, which didn't take long. Delta watched the whole ordeal with mild interest, not fully understanding what was going on beyond the fact that everything smelling of his new master was on the way out.

Once they were done, Mark leaned against Simon's truck. "Now for the hard part, son."

Simon rubbed his eyes. "Finding a place to stay?"

Mark shook his head, his arms crossed. "No. Talking to her."

Simon went completely still. "What?"

"You said you'd meet her." Mark cracked his neck and winced. "You need to be a man of your word, even if she isn't a woman of hers."

"Dad, I—"

"She deserves to know what's going on." His father's uncharacteristically soft tone caught Simon off-guard. "I also recommend you record the conversation, just in case."

"All right. Could we drop my truck off at a worksite? I'd like you to drive me there."

"Of course, son. Don't need her doing something to your truck."

Simon nodded and then got into his truck.

FOUR

SIMON SAT IN his father's truck, staring out the windshield at the coffee shop just down the street. Everything within him raged against getting out. His instinct was to run and never look back. He felt a palpable sense of terror at where this conversation could lead.

"You have to do this, son."

Simon fidgeted with Delta's ears. "What if she convinces me to come back?"

Mark sucked on his teeth. "Give me your wallet."

Hesitantly, he took out his wallet and handed it to his dad.

Mark took out a twenty and gave it to Simon. "Phone. Keys too."

"How am I supposed to record the conversation without my phone?"

Mark reached past Simon and opened the glovebox. He rummaged around for a moment before pulling out an old audio recorder.

"This is older than I am, Dad."

Mark looked halfway offended. "It still works."

Simon eyed the device, then pocketed it.

Mark pointed towards the coffee shop with his chin. "If she convinces you to come back, you can both walk home."

Simon's gaze snapped to Mark, and the older man's expression hardened.

"I'll drop off your wallet and phone at that job site, don't worry."

Simon's fingers curled into fists, but he finally nodded. "All right."

He got out of the truck and Delta made to follow him, but Simon stopped him by closing the door.

"No," Mark said. "Take him with you."

A frown touched Simon's face, but he held the door open and Delta hopped down. Together they walked towards the coffee shop.

He stepped in the door and immediately spotted Susan's dark brown hair from behind. She was sitting at one of the tables along the far wall.

CHAPTER FOUR

He drew a deep breath, started the recorder, then walked over and sat down across from her. Her eyes immediately went to Delta and shifted away from the German shepherd. Delta happily stared back, panting with his tongue out.

"That explains the dog food," she murmured.

Simon nodded as he tried to figure out how to broach the topic of her deceit. "Yeah. A buddy from the military needed someone to adopt him, at least for a while. So I offered."

She looked ready to bolt. "Dogs don't like me much."

"Delta seems fine with you. Delta? Shake."

Delta immediately lifted one paw up to her. She slowly reached out and shook his paw. And when Delta barked, she immediately recoiled as if bitten. But the dog didn't move; he only dropped his paw and tilted his head in confusion.

"So you wanted me to meet it?" Susan asked. "Doesn't seem like something worth ignoring me all yesterday evening for…"

Simon was still trying to work out how to say what he needed to. "No. I'm…"

She watched him expectantly. "You're…? Is this about losing the credit card? Did someone make a big purchase with it or something?"

"That's part of it." He looked her in the eye, still woefully unprepared for the bomb he was about to set off. "I'm breaking up with you."

She remained eerily still. "What?"

He stared at her for a moment, shock flashing across his eyes. Why wasn't she screaming at him?

He pushed his advantage before he lost the momentum he'd just gained. "The credit card company called and told me it was used at an abortion clinic. One that offers sterilization. I found the pregnancy test in the bathroom garbage. And I saw the credit card on the counter."

With each word, guilt and shame clawed for primacy on Susan's face. "Simon, I can explain—"

As his eyes hardened, any words she could have mustered died swiftly in her throat.

"You said you wanted kids." Simon felt rage rising from his belly. "I asked you a few times over to be sure. But now I'm starting to think it took so long because you were preventing it. Then when it happened, you—"

He cut himself off, desperate to keep his wrath from spilling over. He managed to keep a lid on it as he spoke these next four words, the accusation he'd needed to level against her ever since finding out what she'd done.

"You killed our child."

She leaned forward, her hands pressed tightly into her lap. "I did want kids! It's just that when it actually happened, I… I got scared."

Something inside him snapped, but then he remembered the recorder and tried to keep his voice even. "But why did you get yourself sterilized then?"

She flinched as if struck. Tears started to build up at the corners of her eyes. "I didn't really listen to what they were saying… I didn't realize what it all meant until after."

Simon quietly watched her break down. He started to feel sympathy for her, but he couldn't let that stop him—not in the face of what had been lost.

Delta's ears flattened against his head. He was starting to feel Simon's anger and pain.

"I can't trust anything you say, Sue. Your first response was to destroy your pregnancy and then hide what you'd done." His hands clenched into fists and the nails dug into his flesh. "You trusted a complete stranger instead of coming to me. You used my own money to kill my child... because you got scared?"

She looked off to the side, indignation carrying her voice as she muttered her own attack. "It's not like you haven't killed kids."

Her eyes widened as she realized what had just slipped through her lips. She met his gaze to see a seething storm of rage brewing, reflecting a wound so deep that she almost fell apart.

He rose to his feet. "I've already packed. I only took the stuff that's mine. I left two weeks of grocery money on the counter. You have a month before I list the condo."

The storm inside him threatened to take control. He walked away before he did anything he'd regret.

She reached desperately for his arm. "Simon, I'm sorry. Please!"

Before he could say or do anything, Delta barked and growled. She recoiled from the animals. The other patrons who hadn't already been gawking at the exchange now joined in on observing the spectacle.

Simon snapped his fingers. "Come."

Immediately calming, Delta followed after Simon, leaving Susan to break down alone, her eyes squeezed shut as she covered her mouth to stifle her sobs.

Each step felt heavier than the last, like he was dragging a chain. And when he finally made it back to the truck, he got in with Delta and slumped into the seat cushions. The dog whined and Simon started to pet him, soothing them both, if only a little.

"How'd it go?" Mark asked.

With a shake of his head, Simon looked out the window. "Just go. I need to find a place to stay."

"No you don't." Mark started up the truck.

"Dad, I can't live out of my truck."

"I'm not saying you should." Mark pulled into traffic and started driving back towards the worksite where Simon had parked his truck. "You've still got a bed back home."

Simon blinked a few times as he processed what his father had just said. "You want me to...?"

"Did I stutter?"

Simon shook his head and stared at him.

With a long, drawn-out sigh, Mark continued. "Son, you need to be around people who care about you. So let's go home."

FIVE

A CLOUD OF dust kicked up behind Mark's truck and hung low to the ground as Simon followed behind him down a familiar driveway in the farm country of Coyote Flats, about forty-five minutes south of Fort Worth. Delta looked around in curiosity as they passed under a large archway that bore the sign *Fletcher Ranch*. The arch had been recently painted and the fences fixed up. An old but sturdy barn stood off to one side, its red paint faded and peeling.

They pulled up in front of a sprawling farmhouse, built with a stone base, plenty of log-work, and a few chimneys. Mark was already out of his truck and walking to the house when he noticed Simon standing on the step of his truck, staring up at the house.

Catching his father's gaze, Simon got down from the truck. "Delta."

Delta jumped out of the truck while Simon grabbed his duffel of clothes. He looked down at his shaking hands and closed them into fists a few times, desperate to calm himself. He finally gave up, gripped both bags, and walked up to the house.

He stopped again as he was about to take the first step onto the porch, his gaze locked on the wood beneath his foot. He steeled himself then and ascended the steps with Delta.

Simon reached the front door just as it opened. The smell of vanilla, fresh baking, and a hint of lavender filled his nose, bringing back years of memories. He instinctively dropped his bags and accepted his mother's warm embrace.

"Welcome home, sweetheart."

Simon held tightly to her. "Hey Mom."

Shelby pulled back, her deep brown eyes taking him in as she held onto his arms, as though he might bolt at any moment. "Let me look at you. Have you been eating well? Oh, you're skin and bones!"

He half-smiled despite himself. "I'm lean, not skinny. I go to the gym regularly and eat well."

She raised an eyebrow, judging his words for a moment before accepting them. "Well, come on in, sweetie. Your room is just the way you left it."

Delta barked and Shelby's gaze darted down to take note of him. "Who's your friend?"

"Delta."

The dog looked up at Shelby, tongue out as he panted while Shelby gave him some attention. "Well, if you're as well trained as my son, you're welcome inside."

Delta whined as Shelby stood back up and went inside.

Simon picked up his bags and followed her into the house, noticing a lot more grey hairs amidst her once blonde mane than when he'd last seen her. A pang of regret stabbed into his heart, but he pushed those feelings aside.

Kids toys were scattered about the rustic interior and confusion crossed his eyes.

Shelby noticed and smiled. "We have a goddaughter, Hailey. She's with us now."

"Ah." The word passed his lips in a murmur.

He made his way through the house, observing some of the modern upgrades.

Upstairs, the walls of his old bedroom were lined with the same band, sports, and motivational posters. He set his bags on the bed and lifted the bottom of one poster to reveal another one hidden underneath, this one depicting a woman in only half a bikini. He shook his head and repinned the poster.

Turning away, his gaze settled on a framed photo lying facedown on the bedside table. Delta nuzzled Simon's hand, pressing his shoulder against Simon's knee.

"Just as you left it," he muttered.

He snapped out of it just in time to see Mark leaning against the doorway, arms crossed. "That's what Mom said. Remember the house rules?"

Simon nodded as he turned his attention to unzipping his duffel. "No getting drunk or showing up drunk here. No unmarried sex here. No smoking anything or smelling like it here."

"We'll lift the smelling of cigarettes," Mark said. "I imagine there are a fair few guys at work who do it."

"Thanks." Simon stiffened, his response having come out far more sarcastic than he'd intended.

Mark narrowed his eyes at his son's tone but let it go. "A new rule too: no swearing around Hailey. I'm sure she'll be hearing all kinds of things on her own, but she isn't going to be learning it here."

Simon cleared his throat, more mindful of his tone. "Got it."

He walked past his father and descended the stairs, mindful to look away from the family photos on the wall, as if their still gazes would cut through him.

"Anything else I should know about Hailey?" Simon asked.

"She's eight. And I'm not sure there's much else to say."

"What happened to her parents?"

"Car crash," Mark said as they made it back outside. "She was in the car with them. Somehow she came out without a scratch. She's still fine riding in vehicles, thank goodness."

Simon grabbed some of his gun cases from his truck, and Mark grabbed a few more. "How's the farm running?"

Mark shrugged as they walked back into the house. "The cowboys keep it going. I try to get out there whenever I can, but your mother doesn't like me riding much anymore."

CHAPTER FIVE

Shelby called from the kitchen. "That's cause when those boys get bucked, they get back up. When you get bucked, we have to fly you to the hospital."

"Yeah, yeah, I know," Mark grumbled as they ferried Simon's things inside. "Can't do nothin' these days…"

They continued until Simon's belongings were all put away.

"Mark, dear," Shelby said, coming out of the kitchen. "Could you pick up Hailey?"

Mark glanced down at his watch. "It's that time already, huh?" He turned to Simon and the look in his eyes conveyed that the next words weren't a request. "See if your mother needs any help, huh?"

Simon found himself nodding. He felt like he was back to age seventeen. "Will do, sir."

A flicker of regret passed over Mark's eyes, but he wordlessly left.

Snapping his fingers, Simon went to the kitchen and knocked on the door, Delta at his side. "Anything I can help with?" he asked.

Shelby glanced up, then returned to what she was doing. "Absolutely, sweetie. And—" She grabbed a bowl, filled it with water, and set it on the floor out of the way. "This is for you, Delta."

The German shepherd looked up at Simon expectantly.

"Go ahead," he murmured.

Delta lapped at the water while Simon filled the dog's food bowl and set it beside the water.

Shelby spoke while he washed his hands. "Could you dice the peppers?"

He wordlessly set to the task.

"So what do you get up to these days?" she asked.

Simon shifted his weight off his prosthetic. "Work, mostly. I'm a site manager for Quincy & Sons."

"You were always a natural leader." There was a wistful tone to her voice. "How long have you been at it?"

"Seven years at the company, three as site manager."

She nodded. "So only four years before they put you in charge of things? That's quite the feat, sweetie." She glanced back at him. "Do you know how long you'll be staying with us?"

He shook his head and set aside the diced peppers, then started cutting up some other vegetables. "Not yet. Dad kinda pressured me into coming back."

"Well, you can stay as long as you like, honey. Just let me know if you'll be here for dinner on a regular basis or not."

"Will do."

Shelby started talking about the last ten years since they'd last seen one another. He listened to her, sometimes offering a comment. Eventually she took a step past him and accidentally hit his prosthetic leg. He dropped the knife on the counter and gripped the edge as she grabbed his shoulder.

"I'm so sorry, honey. Are you all right?"

Letting out a breath, he nodded and straightened. "I've got a bad habit of keeping my weight off it."

She couldn't bring her eyes down to the metal and plastic limb that had replaced the lower half of her son's leg. "We'd have taken care of you back then." Her voice was soft and low, filled with regret and longing. The pain was evident in her eyes. "You know that, right? You didn't have to do it alone."

He leaned against the counter, his hands gripping the edge. "What did Dad say?"

She swallowed. "About your leg? Only that you lost it in Israel. I saw the incident on the news, but—"

"I mean this time around."

"Nothing. Just that you were coming home for a while." A gentle smile touched her lips. "But you know I'm always here for you, dear. No matter what."

He couldn't hold her gaze any longer and looked away, knowing that the pain in her eyes had in no small part been inflicted by him. "I'll keep that in mind."

She watched him for a moment, trying to find some way to connect, but decided to give it time. "Well, thank you for your help. I got the rest from here." She nudged him. "You should finish unpacking."

"I don't think I'll be here too long." He regretted those words the moment they slipped past his lips and he saw Shelby's shoulders drop almost imperceptibly.

She opened the fridge. "Okay, sweetie. Like I said, we're more than happy for you to stay as long as you like."

Simon noticed Delta's ears perk up. He looked out the window in time to see Mark's truck approaching. "The last time Dad and I talked…"

She glanced at him. "He did invite you to come back."

"I know, but how long is that going to last?"

He walked out of the kitchen, Delta following close behind, and then climbed the stairs to his room, where he took out his phone.

"Hey Winston. I got things sorted out and will be back at work tomorrow."

"Tomorrow's Saturday," his boss said.

Simon blinked a few times, mentally kicking himself. "I mean Monday."

"All right." Winston's voice betrayed his concern. "And Susan?"

"We're not together anymore." He heard a young girl's voice prattling downstairs. "If she wants to know where I am, or anything really, don't give her the information please. Pass that on to the office staff."

A barely audible sigh came through the phone speaker before Winston replied. "Will do. I want you to focus on the Torringtons' job next week. They gave the green light. They've got a lot of good connections that'll mean more work. I'll help manage your other sites in the meantime."

Anxiety tugged at the back of Simon's mind, but he ignored it. "Yes, sir."

Simon hung up and tapped his phone against his lower lip. *The commute's going to be a bit longer,* he reasoned. *But if the home gym is still intact, I don't have to spend time driving to the gym anymore.*

He sighed, then looked around at his stuff. He started by taking down all the posters and threw them out, ensuring in the process that the hidden one remained hidden. He started dusting the room while Delta lay in the middle of the floor.

The dog sneezed, then looked up at Simon.

"Sorry, Del."

Delta dropped his head and Simon continued to clean until he heard a knock at his door. He turned to see a young girl, half-Hispanic, staring up at him, her dark brown eyes alight with excitement.

"Are you my brother?"

Simon blinked a few times. "Uh… I'm Simon. Mark and Shelby are my parents."

She bounced on her feet. "They're my parents now too. I'm Hailey. May I come in?"

He nodded and cleared his throat. "Sure."

"Are you living with us now?" She stepped into the room and looked around.

"For a bit, yeah."

She looked down at Delta, who watched her keenly. "What's his name?"

"Delta."

"May I pet him?"

"You may."

She knelt and ran her hand along his fur. Delta soaked up the attention and rolled onto his back for a belly rub.

"What happened to his eye?" Hailey asked.

Simon looked back at Delta. "He was in the military. He got hurt and then a really good friend of mine brought him to me to take him in."

"Where's your friend?"

He took a moment. "Somewhere overseas by now. He's still in the military, so he couldn't stay."

She looked up at him. "What's his name?"

"Don."

She returned her gaze to Delta. "I'll pray he stays safe."

He kept himself from challenging her as his own past reared its head in his mind. "Thank you."

She giggled and complied. "Wanna play?"

He paused. "Uh… not today. I've got some things I need to take care of."

"Okay." Her voice dropped in volume, but her disappointment was loud and clear. "May I play with Delta?"

He thought for a moment, then looked down at the dog whose eye had lit up at the p-word.

"Do it outside," he said. "And stay close to the house."

"Really?"

He sat on the edge of his bed and nodded, giving a dismissive wave of his hand. "Yeah, knock yourself out."

"Thank you!" She ran up and hugged him. He went completely still as she turned and fled back into the hallway. "C'mon, Delta!"

Delta looked to Simon. "Go ahead, boy."

The dog stood and followed Hailey out as Simon flipped through his phone.

"You might not get that dog back."

Simon glanced up to see Mark leaning against the doorframe, an all too familiar sight.

"Yeah, well... I'm sure he'll be well loved and taken care of."

A smirk tugged at Mark's mouth. "Probably."

"She's pretty polite. She didn't even ask about my leg."

"Yeah, she's a good kid," said Mark. "And we've got a few amputees at our church, so it's not new to her. Anyway, dinner will be ready in ten."

Simon nodded without meeting his father's gaze. "Thanks."

Mark pushed off the doorframe and turned while Simon stared at the downturned picture frame on his bedside table.

"It's good to have you home, son."

"Thanks."

Mark nodded to himself, then left Simon to his thoughts as he sat alone in the room, his gaze held hostage by the picture frame on the bedside table.

SIX

THE MIDDLE EASTERN sun beat down as Simon and his squad posted up outside a house, preparing to breach the door. The air was thick with dust.

Simon adjusted his shemagh and readied his rifle before nodding to his men. He held up three fingers, curled each one in, and the man opposite him kicked in the door.

A swarm of bullets took down his comrade, catching him in the chest, neck, and jaw as the loud report of the AK-47 screamed. Simon shot blindly through the open door, hoping to slow the torrent of bullets. It worked and one of his squadmates grabbed their injured comrade and dragged him back to safety.

Covering the doorway, Simon glimpsed the shooter on the floor inside, blood soaking into the dust. The AK-47 lay still in his dead hands.

Simon was about to signal for them to continue when movement caught his eye. He pointed his rifle down the hallway in time to see someone pick up the automatic weapon.

He froze for a split second, and a split second was all it took. The muzzle of the AK-47 ignited with flame as it spat lead at him. The aim went wild, but a few shots struck Simon's vest. Hitting the ground, he shot back at his assailant, the bullet hitting the enemy's neck and dropping him.

Simon groaned and rose to his feet, stumbling forward and keeping his rifle up as the rest of his team followed him in to clear the building.

He stopped when his eyes adjusted to the dark and he saw the second assailant. Blood bubbled in the young boy's neck and his body shook as they reached for the AK-47 once again. Simon kicked the weapon away but couldn't look away from the eyes of the boy who glared up at him with pure, unadulterated hatred seething in his fading eyes.

Simon lurched forward, nearly launching himself out of bed. Cold sweat drenched his shirt and shorts, making them stick to him like an uncomfortable second skin. His chest heaved, his lungs bursting at the seams as he tried to force air in. He finally managed to sneak some air through his constricted throat, and each breath became easier. His leg ached and he reached for flesh that wasn't there.

His thoughts were interrupted by Delta's soft whine. The German shepherd was having a nightmare of his own.

He was about to get out of bed, but he stopped himself. *I don't wanna get bit.*

Simon took off his shirt, balled it up, and tossed it at Delta. The dog jumped to his feet and growled wrathfully as his ears flattened against his head.

"Delta. Come."

Delta went still and peered up at him in the dark. Simon leaned toward him and patted the bed.

"Up."

The German shepherd jumped up and lay beside him, pressing his body against Simon. Simon lay his head back and scratched Delta behind his ears absently, his eyes wide open as he stared up at the ceiling.

Delta eventually dozed off and they remained in that position for a while…

Until Simon's alarm went off. Delta perked up at the sound and Simon slapped the alarm. He sat on the edge of his bed, resting his elbows on his knees and staying there for a moment. He ran his hands down his face.

Delta took the opportunity to duck under his arm and press against his side. He hugged the dog.

"C'mon, boy. Ready for a run?"

Simon affixed his prosthetic and stood, stretching before they quietly made their way through the house. The familiar creaks and whispers of the old wood caressed his ears with each and every step.

He frowned as he looked down at his feet, silently cursing his prosthetic, as that was the only foot causing the floorboards to creak.

When he and Delta stepped out the front door, they were greeted by a pink sky. The sun was nowhere in sight, but the horizon's blush spoke of its nearing arrival.

Simon did some stretches and then started to jog out into the fields. He followed a path inspired more by his heart than his mind or the ground beneath his feet. The cool morning air whispered through his clothes and hair, kissing his skin and bringing some small token of comfort from the night's terrors.

All he heard for a while was Delta's panting and his own heart pounding in his ears. Eventually he wiped the sweat from his forehead and slowed to a stop. He leaned forward, hands on his knees, and glanced at his wrist; there was no watch to be found.

He was about to start running again when the sounds of hoofs thundering against the ground filled the air, accompanied by ornery mooing. He crested a small rise in the direction of the noise and encountered a group of mounted cowboys herding cows. An Australian shepherd dog circled the bovines and barked. He watched as they wrangled one of the cows and got it down to examine it.

Just then, one of the men spotted Simon and approached at a decent clip.

"'Scuse me, sir, but are you lost?"

Simon shielded his eyes. "In some ways, but I know where I'm standing."

"Then you know you're trespassing." The cowboy rested his hand on the revolver at his hip.

"Hold up there, Chip."

Chip looked over his shoulder to see an older cowboy with a silver Mobius moustache ride up, the Australian shepherd trotting alongside him.

"Hey Clyde," Simon greeted as the second man approached.

"Simon." Clyde lifted his hat a bit, then rested his arms on the front of his saddle. "Welcome home, sir."

Chip frowned and looked back at Clyde, his face skewed in confusion. "Simon?"

"Mr. Fletcher's prodigal son," Clyde explained. "Go on back to the boys, Chip."

Chip eyed him before turning his horse and rejoining the group. Meanwhile, the two dogs got acquainted with each other. Delta wanted to run off after the Australian shepherd, but he looked back towards Simon for permission.

"Go ahead, boy."

Delta took off running. Simon watched them go until they disappeared.

"What's the dog's name?" Simon asked.

"Daisy," Clyde replied. "Yours?"

"Delta."

Clyde sighed and took off his hat to wave away some flies. "It's been a while."

"Ten years." Simon placed his hands on his hips.

"Dang… you're making me feel old."

"Silver before gold, Clyde."

A smirk shifted Clyde's moustache. "My hair ain't gon' turn gold anytime soon. So what brings you back home? You're a little less…" His dark brown eyes drifted down to the prosthetic. "…whole than when I last saw you."

"I—" Simon's words died in his throat.

Clyde sucked on his teeth. "C'mon, Simon. You used to tell me everything. I'm still good for it."

Weighing the words of his old friend and mentor, Simon finally took in a breath and laid out the events of the last forty-eight hours.

Clyde listened intently and whistled at the end of it. "That's some heavy stuff there. May I make a suggestion?"

Simon nodded, a spark of hope in his eyes as he remembered the years of wisdom he'd gleaned from this old cowboy. "Sure."

"Whenever I'm having trouble figuring things out, I talk to Jill."

The spark faded and a frown tugged at the corners of Simon's mouth.

"I know what yer thinking, but there's comfort in talkin' to the dead," Clyde assured him. "I find I'm able to express myself much better when I know they're just there to listen, without judgment or response."

Simon struggled with the advice, but all he could do in the end was nod quietly and say thanks.

He whistled and Delta and Daisy came running back.

Clyde noted Simon's hollow response but let it go. "Anytime, Simon. You know where to find me. Hyah."

With that, Clyde turned his horse and rejoined the other cowboys along with Daisy.

Simon and Delta resumed their morning run.

When Simon returned to the house, he climbed the front steps and went straight to the kitchen. He poured a glass of water and noticed a bouquet of flowers on the kitchen counter, wrapped with a blue ribbon.

Shelby walked up behind him, smelling of fresh dirt amidst the usual floral scents she kept up with.

She started to wash her hands as she spoke. "Those are for you."

"What for?"

"Clyde called and said you'd need them." She gave him a side hug and kissed his cheek. "So I picked them. They're the right colours, right?"

Simon looked down at the reds and whites. An obligation stirred within him to follow through, despite his dismissal of Clyde's advice. "Yeah, they're perfect."

She smiled and started to busy herself around the kitchen. "Are you staying for breakfast?"

He shook his head, his gaze still on the flowers. "Thanks, but I don't have any appetite right now."

"Okay." Her shoulders dropped, but she wasn't going to let her voice betray her. "Lunch will be at one, dinner should be at six. I'll call if it isn't." She paused. "Your number's probably changed."

He stepped across the kitchen and opened a drawer to find a pen and notepad. She smiled to herself, a hint of hope at how naturally he'd done so, like he belonged here.

He scrawled out his number, then ripped off the note and held it out to her. That's when he noticed her hint of a smile and her slightly narrowed eyes.

"What?"

She shrugged and accepted the note. "It's just really good to see you again. When you decide to leave again, please keep in touch."

His gaze settled anywhere else so it wouldn't have to meet hers. "Dad's been great with what I'm dealing with, but... I'm not so sure—"

Shelby reached up and cradled his jaw, trying to bring his gaze back to her, as if it'd bring him with it. "Your father loves you. You both hurt each other very deeply that day. And while the wound isn't healed, it is something he wants to heal. Otherwise you wouldn't be here."

Simon tried to keep his eyes off to the side, his words fumbling in his mouth as he tried to get them out. "I... I don't—"

The sound of heavy footsteps on the stairs interrupted his stuttering. His whole demeanour changed as he straightened.

"I'll see you later, Mom."

Shelby fought tooth and nail to maintain her smile. "See you, Simon. I expect you home for dinner. And don't forget these." She reached over and grabbed the flowers.

His fingers curled around the stems, as though he were holding a small bird. "Thanks. I'll let you know if I can't make it."

He walked out of the kitchen just as Mark made it to the doorframe. His father stepped to the side to let him through.

"Morning, sir."

"Good morning, Simon." Mark walked past and made himself a cup of coffee.

Simon went upstairs, got changed, and then left with Delta.

———————————

From the porch, Mark watched his son drive off before returning to the kitchen. He sat at the table.

"I see he spoke with Clyde this morning."

Shelby nodded. "Yeah."

He took a sip of his coffee. "You got the flowers?"

She nodded again and finally allowed her voice to betray her. "He still hasn't told me what's going on."

Mark grunted. "Well, it's his place to say it."

"I can't help him if I don't know what's going on with him!" Shelby said, crossing her arms.

"I know." His voice gave way to his fatigue. "But you also can't help someone who doesn't want it. He'll open up if and when he's ready."

Her lips trembled and her voice cracked, yet there was a determined fire in her. "I'm not losing him again."

"I'm not either." He let out a breath. "Which is why I'm not breaking his privacy and telling you."

She blinked a few times, her posture loosening.

"He's my son too, Bee. All we can do right now is be there whenever he's ready to work through it with us."

SEVEN

ROW UPON ROW of gravestones cropped up from the verdant field, waist-high wrought iron fences providing a border around these grounds of dreams and memories lost. Simon's prosthesis tried to slow him down as he marched on with Delta, grim determination carrying him through the growing dread. The feeling in his chest only grew tighter, like his heart could explode at any moment.

He finally reached his destined chunk of granite and stared at the hunk of stone, rage boiling in the pit of his stomach at this piece of rock that could never do justice to the woman who lay beneath it. He gritted his teeth, set the flowers on top of the stone, and forced himself to sit down on the grass.

Silence gripped him, no words visiting his mind to pass through his lips. His fingers curled into fists as they trembled, his nails digging into his skin. Delta whined as he leaned against Simon, yet his presence went unnoticed.

This is stupid. Heather's not here. She's not anywhere.

His breathing quickened as the rage boiled over. The tears clinging to his eyes betrayed the source of the internal flames that ignited his wrath.

Delta's ears perked up and he yelped, nuzzling Simon, who went completely still to mask his turmoil as best he could. A man about Mark's age was approaching, though this man was smaller and hunched over.

Simon recognized Neil, Heather's dad, but the man gave him a slight wave of his hand.

"No, no, Simon." Neil knelt beside him, his eyes on a nearby marker. "Heather wouldn't want you goin' on my account."

Eyeing the man, Simon slowly settled back onto the grass. He watched as Neil set down his own bouquet of white and red flowers next to his daughter's final resting place.

The older gentleman placed his hands on his knees. "I was just visiting Veronica." He gestured across the cemetery.

Simon couldn't meet his gaze. "Veronica's...?"

Gone, he wanted to say.

CHAPTER SEVEN

Neil nodded solemnly, the weight on his shoulders dragging him towards the ground that had swallowed the two most important women in his life. "She never really recovered after Heather... passed."

Guilt danced with shame in Simon's heart. "I'm sorry, Neil."

A frown touched Neil's lips. "Thanks."

Silence gripped both men for some time, broken only by Delta's occasional panting.

Eventually Neil glanced at Simon's prosthetic. "I get that you needed to grieve in your own way, Sye... but I wish you'd stayed to grieve with us."

Simon closed his eyes, fists clenched as the dancing emotions within him threatened to break him in two.

"I didn't grieve." Simon's voice came out quiet. "I still haven't. All I've done is run away."

Neil reached out and gripped Simon's shoulder. "You still had flowers delivered at least, every year on the anniversary. That's meant the world to me, did to Veronica, and I'm sure it does to Heather too."

No words could make it through Simon's throat.

"It's not the anniversary now," Neil remarked. "If you've been running from this, it's a little strange to come back without some sense of obligation."

"I didn't know where else to go." Simon's gaze never left the headstone. "Clyde mentioned that he talks to his wife, so I thought I'd give it a try. But Heather's not here."

Neil's bright blue eyes gauged Simon, who finally let his hand fall back down to his knee. "I am."

Simon blinked a few times, fidgeting, not sure what to do. He finally opened up and recounted his experience with Susan.

Once all was said, Neil let out a pained breath. "I'm sorry to hear that, son. The loss of a child..." He shook his head, the sorrow clear in his eyes. "Well, I went through something similar with Heather, as I'm sure you can imagine."

Simon spoke quickly. "I wouldn't say they're the same. I mean, you had Heather for seventeen years, and would've gotten more attached, and Heather... herself..."

"I'd say it's pretty similar. Someone you love killed your child, and you couldn't do anything to stop it. The pain here..." He pressed his fist against Simon's chest. "It'll hollow you out if you let it. That's what happened to Veronica."

Neil pulled his hand back and Simon looked down at where it had been. "How did you make it through?"

"One day at a time." Neil sniffed. "Every morning and night on my knees, talking to the big man upstairs, asking him to pass along my love for my girls."

Simon swallowed. "And if I don't believe in him anymore?"

A smile tugged at the corners of Neil's lips. "Then I'd say you didn't believe in him to begin with. Which puts you in the perfect place to start."

Neil grunted as he struggled to his feet, and Simon swiftly rose to help. The older gentleman took out his wallet and handed Simon a business card.

"Don't be a stranger, son. If you ever need to talk, or just want a place you can sit down with someone who understands and cares, my door's always open. I don't do much these days, so I'm home most of the time."

Simon pocketed the card.

Neil held out his hand, but Simon instead leaned in and embraced him. Neil stiffened for the briefest moment but then felt his own eyes mist up as he returned the embrace, as if Simon were his own lost son.

"I'll try to carve out some time regularly," Simon whispered.

Neil smiled as they broke the embrace. "I'd like that, Sye. See you."

Simon watched the man walk away, then looked back down at the gravestone. "I'm sorry, Heather. I'm sorry I wasn't there to stop you, that I couldn't show you just how much I love you."

He reached out and touched the top of the stone, Delta watching the ritual with curiosity before following Simon out of the cemetery.

EIGHT

PULLING UP TO a small one-story house in an equally small lot, Simon got out of his truck and leaned against it, Delta hopping down to wait at his side. He crossed his arms, his eyes unfocused as he heard the screams of phantom gunfire echo in his mind. It started as a whisper and built into a raging storm.

"Mr. Fletcher?"

The voice cut through the inferno and ripped Simon back to reality. He snapped his head up to see a beautiful woman on the front porch of the house, an infant in pink swaddling bouncing in her arms. Bethany's blue eyes watched Simon with a hint of concern.

He forced a smile and straightened. "Good morning, ma'am."

"You look about how I feel. Everything all right?"

Simon tilted his head and offered a professional smile. "Perfectly fine. Just waiting on the guys." He glanced down at his watch. "I moved over the weekend, so I misjudged the travel time."

"Want some lemonade?"

"I'm good, thank you." Simon glanced at his watch again, but out of the corner of his eye he noticed Bethany fidget. He was about to speak when a few other trucks rumbled up.

Simon approached the first truck and a slender man with dirty blonde hair hopped out.

"Mornin', bruv."

Simon took in a breath. "Eggsy." He looked back at his two other coworkers as they got out of their trucks. He turned back to Bethany. "Things are about to get pretty loud, so you may want to be offsite for Annabelle's sake."

Bethany shifted her weight from one foot to the other. "My car's in the shop right now."

"And Mr. Torrington is…?"

"At work."

"Gotcha." He drew in a breath. "Is there someplace I can take you?"

She thought for a moment. "You don't need me here?"

He shook his head. "No, ma'am. I've got the list. If there are any questions, I know how to contact you."

Her gaze dropped to Annabelle and she finally nodded. "I'll get my purse."

Simon turned to Eggsy. "I've texted you the list. Don't do anything that's not on it, and try not to cause any extra damage. Spot-check the pipes and wiring. And watch for asbestos. You can probably go under the house, but make sure you wear a respirator."

Eggsy nodded. "You got it, bruv."

The man turned to the rest of the guys as Bethany came back out of the house with Annabelle in one arm and a baby seat in the other. She walked over to Simon's truck and started setting up the baby seat. After fastening in Annabelle, she climbed in.

Simon opened the back door and Delta jumped up onto the seat, watching Annabelle with curiosity. He sniffed her but didn't get close enough for her to grab him.

Simon got in as Annabelle started to coo and babble at Delta.

"He's good with kids, right?" Bethany asked.

"He's one of the best-trained dogs you'll ever meet." Simon glanced in the rearview mirror. "I trust him with my life." He buckled in. "So where are we headed?"

"Foundations Church," said Bethany as she watched the two in the back for a moment longer. "Corner of Renfrew and Halliday."

"All right."

Bethany turned her gaze to him as he drove. "How long have you been in the business of fixing people's homes, Mr. Fletcher?"

"Simon," he replied. "And it's seven years at this point."

"That's quite a while."

"Raising a kid'll take much longer," Simon remarked as he glanced in the rearview mirror.

Bethany giggled. "Yeah. And I have to take my work home with me too, huh?"

He smirked as they pulled into the small church parking lot. "All right. You still have my number?"

"I do," Bethany said as he got out and opened the door for her. "Thank you. I'll probably be here until Ray's off work."

"All right. We'll be finishing up around four p.m. for the day. I'm going to focus on the bathroom so it's up and running as quick as possible."

She got out and retrieved Annabelle and the car seat from the back. "Thank you. We'll come home around four so you don't have to worry about locking up."

"Much obliged."

Simon returned to the site, took in a breath, and got out of his truck. He worked with his guys through to the end of the day, loading up a trailer full of the materials they'd just ripped out.

At the end of it, Eggsy approached Simon with his phone in hand. "So the insulation's all right. There's some wiring that's utterly shagged underneath, though."

"Rats?"

Eggsy ran a hand through his hair and nodded. "The bloody wankers chew through everything."

Simon sighed and looked down at the list in his hands. "Then that's tomorrow's focus: get our sparkies here. I'd rather not have the house burn down before we even get the chance to properly start the job."

"Consider it done, Sye."

Simon made a note. "And the pipes?"

"Definitely old, but they'll hold." Eggsy showed Simon some pictures of the piping under the house.

Simon took some notes on his phone. "Okay... demo went smooth. I want to focus on getting the bathtub installed and working so they have something to clean with, since that'll be their main source of water in the house. Let's get the plumbers out here to take a closer look at the piping and get that started as well. I also want the boiler removed tomorrow, cause we didn't get to that today. Otherwise everything's going to be roughly in the usual order... sound right?"

Eggsy shrugged. "Right as rain."

"Then you're off. See you tomorrow."

Eggsy didn't move and Simon glanced at him.

"Was there something else?"

"You all right, bruv?"

Simon put the clipboard into his truck before he started typing a message on his phone. "Just another day. Why?"

Leaning against the truck, Eggsy crossed his arms. "I don't know. Something just seems off."

Simon's thumb twitched and he mistyped on his phone. "Going through a bit of a rough patch."

"Susan?"

"Yeah. We broke up. Turns out she didn't want kids."

Eggsy clicked his tongue. "Sorry to hear that."

Simon finished typing out the message. "Some things just don't work out."

"You doing anything this Sunday?"

"No. Why?"

"Swing by my church."

With a sigh, Simon scratched his head. "I haven't stepped in a church in over a decade."

"So?" It was practically a challenge.

"I don't believe in God anymore."

A smirk tugged at Eggsy's lips. "You don't have to believe in God to receive a little hope. I'm not even sure I believe myself, but it feels good to be there."

Simon eyed him, everything within him screaming at him not to do it, but a small voice whispered yes.

He finally spoke. "What time?"

Eggsy took out his phone and fired off a text, making Simon's phone chirp. "There. Time and place. See you tomorrow."

Eggsy left and Simon started firing off texts to the various trades.

Delta's ears perked up at the sound of a vehicle approaching, and Simon looked back to see Bethany roll up in a minivan with a large bald man with skin the colour of dark chocolate. He got out and smiled warmly.

"It's good to see you again, Simon." Ray went around the van and opened Bethany's door. "So what's the damage?"

"No asbestos," Simon said. "Pipes look like they should be fine, but I've got my plumber coming in tomorrow to confirm, and we'll get the furnace out tomorrow as well. I've also got sparkies coming in to replace the wiring beneath the house."

"What's wrong with the wiring?" Bethany asked.

"Rats like to sharpen their teeth on the metal," Simon explained. "Wires seem to be a favourite. So power'll be off while we're working on that. The stove is gas, though, so you'll be able to do some cooking. We won't replace it until the new appliances come in. Follow me."

The couple followed him into the house. Bethany hesitated as she saw the missing components of her home.

"You'll want to keep your shoes on inside," Simon said as he gestured to the subflooring. "The toilet's still in and working, but be mindful of the pieces of tile still underneath it. We'll break those out when we get the new flooring in here. Also, we haven't found any concerning mould yet, but I'm going to do a thorough check tomorrow, especially around the boiler. That will mean putting a few holes in the walls, but we'll take care of it. You won't even notice it once the paint's on. Do you have any questions for me before I head out?"

Ray took in a breath. "No. Looks like you guys are making some great progress already. One of my coworkers said the demo at his condo took three days, and his condo's about this size."

"Condos are trickier," Simon said. "More specific work hours, building rules, waste disposal is a nightmare..." He smiled. "This is a walk in the park."

"That's good to hear." Ray draped an arm around Bethany's shoulders. "Well, I think we'll bid you good night, Mr. Fletcher."

"Good night, Mr. Torrington."

Simon walked out of the house and opened the back door of his truck. Once Delta had jumped up and in, Simon drove off.

His phone started to ring and he answered it through the truck's Bluetooth. "Hey Winston. What's up?"

Winston's gruff voice came through. "Just getting an end-of-day update."

Simon rattled off the report and could almost hear Winston nodding along. "So I figure I'll be able to call up the city building inspector... uh, Ryan. I should be able to get him in there early next week."

"Good, good," Winston muttered. "The other sites are going well too. I've got a few others in the works as well, but I think my sons can handle those for now."

"I'm all good, boss."

"Just focus on the Torringtons for now, Simon. Once they're far enough along, we'll talk."

Talk about what? he thought, confused.

"You're the boss," Simon replied. "Is there anything else?"

"Not tonight. Keep up the great work."

Simon hung up, then struck his steering wheel. What had Sue said to him?

Delta whined from the back seat.

"Come on up here, bud."

The dog climbed up to the front passenger seat and sat, looking at Simon expectantly.

Simon scratched him behind his ears. "At least I know you're on my side." He paused. "Until Hailey gives you a treat, huh?"

NINE

SIMON STARED DOWN at the dark ring where the hot water tank used to be. Powdery black mould stared back at him, a direct mocking challenge.

"What's the plan, bruv?"

Simon took in a breath and glanced back at Eggsy. "Spot-check the walls. Focus on the kitchen and bathroom. If it's in there…"

He shook his head and waited as Eggsy went out to check.

Eggsy came back. "It's in the walls."

"Damn."

Simon took out his phone and dialled the city records office. He needed a history of insurance claims against the house, to learn whether there had been flooding claims or anything of that nature.

He hung up a few minutes later with the bad news.

"There was some flooding here last year," Simon said, nonetheless managing a smile. "Remember the hurricane that came further north than normal?"

Eggsy nodded. "Yeah. Why's that got you so happy?"

Simon flipped through his phone. "Insurance. But Ray's not going to be happy, and they'll have to get out of the house so we can do the full demo. I've got an idea, though."

He dialled another number and put the phone to his ear.

"Hey Mom, I've got a favour to ask…"

———————

Later that morning, Simon found himself in Winston's office. A full frown had taken hold of Winston's face, enough to give his wrinkles wrinkles.

"This is turning out to be a lot more complicated than we planned," Winston remarked.

Simon leaned forward, his anxiety gnawing at him, but he refused to pass up this opportunity. "I know, and I've got a plan. We can contact the previous homeowner's insurance company and have them foot the bill for taking care of the mould since the last contractors who came through only did a slap and dash. I can even leverage the fact there's a newborn here. If they don't cover it now, they'll be paying for the kid's medical fees in the future if she contracts any respiratory issues… not to mention the bad publicity. And I'll call Ryan and get him to write an official report of the problem. He's always been good about inspecting our sites."

Winston blinked a few times but slowly nodded. "See if you can get him to fluff it up a bit."

Simon shook his head. "Won't need to. Ryan's got a newborn himself."

"And the Torringtons?" Winston steepled his fingers. "Where are they going to stay? And their belongings?"

"I've got a travel trailer I can borrow for them. We can rent a cargo container for their things."

Winston raised an eyebrow. "And where will we put it? No cargo container is going to fit at any campsite."

"My parents have a ranch and all the necessary hookups for the trailer. We can set the container next to it."

Winston nodded. "All right. Run it by them. If they give the go-ahead, we'll get the ball rolling."

"Thanks, boss."

Simon swiftly got up and left for his truck. He drove to Foundations Church and walked up to the front doors, followed by Delta. But he hesitated before going inside.

The door suddenly opened, causing him to take a step back. A young woman looked up at him with a warm smile.

"What are you doing just standing out in that heat?" she said. "Come in!"

He entered and Delta came with him. "I'm here to talk to Bethany and Raymond."

"Of course!" She motioned for him to follow. "Follow me."

He entered and looked around at the simple interior.

"I'm Marion Alabaster," she said as she led him to the office. "But everyone calls me Mary. Here's Ray's office."

She knelt down and petted Delta. "And who's this handsome fella?"

"Delta. Stay."

Delta sat down.

"I'll keep him company," she murmured.

Simon nodded his thanks and opened the door to the office, where he found Ray on a call. He glanced back at Simon and held up a finger while gesturing for him to take a seat on the room's other chair. Simon eased himself down as Ray continued talking.

"No, Sal. I do understand. I've been there myself. What I'm saying is that if the two of you can't sort things out, then bring it to me or one of the deacons. We're all more than happy to mediate." There was a pause. "Yes. Suggest it to him, and remain calm when you do. Tell him that you want to resolve the issue and that you're having a hard time doing that. I know it means admitting you're part of the problem, and he may jump on that, but don't give in. Just suggest having me mediate, all right?" Another pause. "Sal?" Ray slowly smiled. "Good. Get back to me with the results. God bless."

He hung up and turned to Simon.

"What's the news?"

"It's a mixed bag," Simon said as he cracked his neck. "We found black mould around the hot water tank. When we checked the kitchen and bathroom walls… well, the insulation's just infested with the stuff. It's probably spread through the rest of the house. I called up the city records and learned your neighbourhood flooded last year. It looks like the previous contractors did a slap and dash."

Ray sighed and slumped in his chair. "Darn."

"But I'm confident I can get the previous homeowner's insurance company to cover it, since it was their contractors who screwed up in the first place. That'll mean no extra cost for you, and no higher premiums with your own insurance. It should actually bring down the cost for you."

"That'd be good, at least." Ray ran a hand over his bald head.

"If you're all right with me pulling the trigger on that, I'll get the ball rolling today."

Ray nodded. "Yes. Obviously we can't leave the mould as is."

"And if you don't have a place to stay, I've got a travel trailer that'll have everything you need until the house is ready again. We can also rent a container to hold your stuff offsite."

Ray raised an eyebrow. "Where's the trailer?"

"On a ranch outside Coyote Flats," Simon said. "It's about forty-five minutes south of Fort Worth. My parents own it."

"That's very generous." Ray reached over and took a sip of his coffee. "We wouldn't want to impose, though."

"I already got the green light. It'll be ready for you by the end of today."

Ray watched him for a moment, his eyes narrowing. "You're putting in a lot of effort for a small-time pastor."

Simon wore a smile. "Even Jesus accepted the hospitality of sinners."

"That he did, but he also recognized when people had ulterior motives."

"Did he question the boy who brought the bread and fish?" Simon asked. "Or the widow who gave all her coins?"

"No, but he did point out the wealthy man who had given little compared to what he had."

"He also stayed with tax collectors."

"Are you offering to be my next missions trip?" A smile spread across Ray's face when Simon went silent. "You'll have to forgive me, Simon. I don't get to verbally spar much these days."

Simon shook himself out of it. "Happy to help. So are you taking my offer?"

"I am. We'll start packing the necessities today and box up whatever else we can. When can we expect the container?"

"Tomorrow. Day after at the latest." Simon stood up and sent Ray a quick text. "There's the address, but you can follow me back at the end of the day if you like. The roads can get a little confusing if you don't know the area, even with GPS."

Ray stood up. "I'll take you up on that."

"And I'll start making calls."

He stepped out of the office and walked in on Mary giving Delta a belly rub.

She quickly stood up. "All's well?"

"As it can be," he replied. "It was nice to meet you, Mary."

Simon snapped his fingers and Delta scrambled to his feet and followed him past the doors to the sanctuary. He stopped for a moment and peered through the glass into the darkened room before continuing on.

———————————

"You're staring, Mary."

Mary jumped, startled at Ray's interruption. She had been watching through the front door of the church as Ray got into his truck and left.

"Sorry. I just…" She shook her head. "He seemed really hurt when he looked into the sanctuary just now."

"Everybody has a past. Scars and marks we try to hide."

Mary's gaze fell as she rubbed her sleeved arms.

"Is Beth in the nursing mother's room?" Ray asked.

Mary nodded. "She is. Want me to go get her?"

"Yes, please," Ray said. "No rush, though. Just let her know we're heading home soon."

———————————

When Simon drove back up to the Torrington residence, he noticed Eggsy's truck still in the driveway. The man himself leaned against it.

"What's the plan?" Eggsy asked.

"We're moving the Torringtons out today and tomorrow," Simon said as he rolled up and parked the truck. "Then we have to wait for Ryan's report for the insurance company. After that, we can start working on the rest of the demo."

"And if the insurance doesn't bite?"

Simon let out a slow breath and looked up at the small house. "Then I'll have to talk to the Torringtons about cutting some costs. For now Winston wants you at the Lechtemen place."

"You got it, Sye," Eggsy pushed off his truck. "Let me know when you need me."

Simon gave him a nod and watched him drive off.

"This is the last house I'm going to do, isn't it?" Simon mused to Delta. "Well, let's make it a good one."

TEN

SIMON ROLLED UP to his parents' ranch with the Torringtons close behind. He got out with Delta and guided the couple to the older barn near the house. He heaved open the main barn doors to reveal the clean interior and a large travel trailer, already hooked up to power and water.

The Torringtons pulled up and got out as Simon unlocked the trailer.

"Simon?" Bethany was cradling Annabelle in her arms. "Could you hold her while I help Ray bring our things in?"

Simon froze, everything inside him screaming for him to say no. "Oh, uh, I don't—"

She started to hand off the infant. "Don't worry, I'm the only one she bites."

He quickly moved his arms to catch the cradled child, his heart racing.

"Thank you," she said sweetly as she moved off to help Ray, leaving Simon to stand there with the slumbering infant in his arms.

He sat on the hitch bar of the trailer, Delta lying beside him on the floor, his body completely rigid as Annabelle slept in his arms. The seconds crawled by as he watched the pair move their things.

After a few moments, Annabelle began to stir. She opened her eyes and stared up at him, her dark brown gaze locking with his. He fought tooth and nail to keep the storm behind his eyes under control, desperate to prevent his own damage from spilling over, as if the simple act of holding her could corrupt her.

Eventually Ray stopped and glanced at Simon. "I can take her, if you like."

Simon stirred and cleared his throat. "Yeah."

He handed Annabelle off to Ray, and when she saw her father's face she started to coo and babble. Ray lightly bounced her.

"She didn't cry," Ray commented. "That means she likes you."

"I'm not so sure about that."

"It says a lot, coming from her." Ray smiled down at his daughter. "You like Uncle Simon?"

Bethany spoke up. "Ray, I think—" But the rest of her sentence was drowned out as Annabelle started to cry.

CHAPTER TEN

Delta's ears went flat at the assault on his hearing.

Ray sighed. "I can't help you with that, Annie. Guess you need your momma."

"Oh, I know what she wants," Bethany replied, taking the child into her arms. "Could you get the last of the luggage?"

"I got it." Simon went to their car, grabbed the last suitcase, and brought it back to the trailer. "The place has a few years under its belt, but it's in good condition."

"It's more than enough," Ray said as he opened the door.

All three stepped inside.

"Water, electrical, temperature control." Simon showed them around. "There are some dishes and cooking utensils in here too. The main bed is at the front, as I'm sure you saw." He looked down at the counter and found a pair of keys and a piece of paper. "Here are the keys to the trailer, and the paper has the phone numbers for the main house, the head cowboy Clyde, and the wi-fi password—"

"Simon, you didn't say they were already here."

They all looked back at the door to see Shelby climbing in.

"Hi, I'm Shelby Fletcher, Simon's mother." She held out her hand and Ray shook it. Shelby's eyes fell to Annabelle. "Oh, isn't she just precious. What's her name?"

"Annabelle," Bethany replied.

"What a lovely name." Shelby beamed. "Well, I'm sure you saw the main house on your way in. I'm usually home, so if you have any problems, or if you just want to hang out, feel free to swing on by. Our door's always open."

Ray nodded. "Thank you very much, Mrs. Fletcher."

"Shelby, please," she replied warmly. "My husband is Mark. He's around somewhere. I'm sure he'll introduce himself at some point."

Simon saw his chance to leave and decided to take it. "I've got to get back into town, so I'll leave you to it."

He turned and left before any of them could protest.

———————

Shelby's gaze lingered on the empty doorway of the trailer long after her son had disappeared through it. Worry was etched on her face.

"You've got a wonderful son," Bethany said.

Shelby brightened a bit as she turned to face the couple. "Yes, I think so. I can hold little Annie while you unpack. Then you three can come to the main house for lunch."

Ray cleared his throat. "We wouldn't want to impose—"

"Nonsense," Shelby said with a dismissive wave of her hand. "It'd be my pleasure."

Bethany looked at Ray, who nodded, and then handed Annabelle off. "Thank you."

"There's something so special about these early years," Shelby said as she accepted Annabelle and her bottle.

Ray and Bethany started to unpack.

"The trailer has some hefty memories attached to it, huh?" Ray asked as he noticed some of the damage and markings carved into less visible nooks and crannies.

"Yes, it does," Shelby said softly. "We used to do yearly trips, from the time Simon was Annabelle's age, right up until he was eighteen."

"That's quite something," Ray said with a smile. "Not many folks can say that."

Shelby nodded. "We've been very blessed. And now we can turn this blessing around for someone else."

"God's very generous."

"I'm sure my son would disagree with you." Shelby's gaze fell. "And some days, I'm afraid to say I would too."

Ray sat down. "He's lost a lot."

Shelby sniffed. "His leg is the least of it. That's what my intuition tells me anyway. Last week was the first time I'd seen him, let alone heard from him, in ten years."

"He hasn't spoken about anything?"

She shook her head. "I don't expect him to, but I feel so helpless. I can feel his pain and there's nothing I can do but pray." She let out a breath. "I'm afraid to say the internet knows my son better than I do at this point."

She watched Annabelle sleep in her arms, then smiled.

"But I shouldn't be bothering you with myself. How about we head inside for lunch? I'm sure there's plenty of brighter things to speak about."

ELEVEN

SIMON LOOKED UP at the concrete structure looming over him. It seemed to be halfway between a modern opera house and a bunker. Something in his heart raised arms against it, urging him to leave. He'd just turned to follow this internal advice when Eggsy's voice caught him.

"Hey Sye!"

Taking in a breath, Simon mustered a smile. "Hey."

"Glad you could make it, bruv. Come on. It's about to start."

Simon struggled to conceal the apprehension gripping his heart as he followed Eggsy inside. They found their way to their seats and Simon observed the people around them as they greeted one another and discussed their weeks. It all felt familiar, yet the air seemed wrong.

A woman's voice came over the speakers, drawing the attention of the people gathered.

"Good morning, everyone! Would you please make your way to your seats?" The sea of conversation died down, although a few continued. The woman laughed. "Rashid, come on. I can not only see you but hear you."

The conversation fell away, leaving an eerie silence in its wake. Simon turned his attention to the frail woman on stage, her weathered skin treated with a rub-on tan. A plastic smile clung to her lips as she lifted the mic.

"How are we all doing this morning?" she asked.

Simon shifted uncomfortably at the unanimous "Great" that came from the crowd. He noticed Eggsy paying keen attention.

"Now, most of y'all know me, but for those who are new, I'm Pastor Carey, and we welcome you to our humble church, First Light Centre."

Simon glanced at the massive crowd. *Humble?*

"Today we're going to discuss our great teachers and their stance on pacifism."

Teachers? Plural? Simon felt the unease in his chest grow. *I wish Delta were here...*

"Jesus taught that we are to turn the other cheek."

He also whipped people off the temple steps...

"And when one of his students cut off the ear of a man who'd come to arrest him, he healed the man's ear and admonished his student. Muhammad wrote that there is no greater sin than to take the life of an innocent."

Simon tried to keep a neutral expression. *What kind of a place is this?*

"Gandhi spoke on the evil that is anger and violence, and that if we're all going to coexist, we need to set them aside!"

He heard the affirmations of the crowd with each statement. *Gandhi had notorious anger issues...*

"Violence is never acceptable! There is always a peaceful solution to every problem, if we are only willing to sit down and talk. But the police? They gun people down in the streets. They don't care about you and me. They don't care about anything but their paycheque."

Simon's fingers curled into fists, his nails digging into his palms.

"And don't even get me started on the military. It's just a way for murderers to kill legally. We don't need these horrible institutions! We just need to stand together as one!"

Simon's rage boiled up inside him and his left leg began to ache below the knee.

Carey fell silent for a moment, letting her accusations hang in the air. But as she took in a breath to continue, her voice softened along with her expression. "We have all come from different walks of life. We all have things in our past we aren't proud of, things that bring us so much shame we don't know what to do with. Some of us were the aggressors, some the victims. But the Energy that flows through all of us doesn't care about our past. Jesus told us all that the one and only thing we need is love. We must love each other enough to stop hurting one another, To bring about peace amongst us all."

He felt his rage flicker.

"He spoke on behalf of the Energy, saying that whatsoever we do unto the least of us, we do to it." Carey took a moment to let that sink in. "We must not only love one another but love ourselves. Freely, without guilt or shame. Even those who disagree with us, and those who do things we know are wrong. Because we all do wrong, but the Energy accepts us. You can keep doing wrong until the day you die, and it will still welcome you in to be a part of it, to become one in a fullness that we can't even imagine." She smiled. "That's what we're going towards. That's what comes after this life, fellow seekers."

Carey stepped off the stage as the crowd erupted into applause. A young woman took her place to give the announcements.

Simon stood up and made for the exit, Eggsy quickly following.

"So what'd you think?"

Simon's thoughts and feelings were colliding like rogue waves. "I don't know... I really don't know."

"Like I said, I don't come here for the sermons. I come here for the community."

The word *liar* slammed through Simon's thoughts like a freight train, but he kept it from reaching his lips.

"Stay and talk with the people," said Eggsy. "You'll see what I mean. They're all really nice and supportive."

Simon furrowed his brow, weighing his options, but he finally acquiesced to his friend's request. "Sure."

Simon turned and followed Eggsy back towards the gathering. After some time of talking to a few different members of the congregation, he felt someone's eyes boring into him. Then he heard her voice. Both felt like unwanted fingers trailing up his spine.

"Eggsy! Aren't you going to introduce me to your friend?"

Simon turned to find Carey herself striding toward them. Her smile seemed less plasticky now than it had on the stage.

"This is Simon," said Eggsy.

The pastor extended her hand and Simon shook it. He kept from reacting to her grip, which was firmer than he expected.

"I haven't seen you here before," she said. "Is today your first time?"

"Yeah," replied Simon. "Eggsy invited me."

"That's wonderful, Eggsy." Carey smiled. "It's always a gift to see new people here."

"You bet," Eggsy said.

"Would you mind if I speak to your friend privately for a moment?"

Eggsy smirked. "Go right ahead. There's some other people I wanted to catch anyway."

"Thanks, dear."

Simon narrowed his eyes at the word but refocused as Carey started to speak.

"What did you think of the message today?" she asked.

He took in a breath and decided to be honest. "I disagree with the way you started... on a number of levels."

She smiled and nodded respectfully. "Of course. You've served yourself, haven't you?"

Simon nodded.

"When I mentioned the military and police, I wasn't speaking about the individual," she said. "I was talking about the organizations themselves and how they promote certain behaviours."

"*Permit* is different than *promote*," Simon said. "And yeah, the bad stuff sucks. It'd be wonderful if everyone just stopped hating each other, but they don't. What happens when some jihadist decides to blow up this church? Or any innocent person, for that matter? Or a murderer decides to go after someone? Your ideology can only exist in ordered societies like ours where there are police and military to deter those who might attack you."

"That's all very true. But what I teach isn't about how we as people are, but about how we should strive to be. None of us are perfect. We all fall flat in many, many ways. I myself fail in some way every day on my way to being a better person."

He tried to read her for signs of deception. *She's a true believer in this stuff,* he realized.

"But it's about striving to be the best we can in spite of that," she added.

He slowly nodded. "All right. Thanks for the talk. I've got to get going."

"I hope to see you next week, Simon."

He walked away, but something made him look back. She'd found Eggsy. Simon couldn't help but notice her finger lingering on his hand.

So that's why he pays such close attention.

Simon shook his head and left.

TWELVE

THE GENERAL HUM of conversation filled the main hall of First Light Centre and Simon stood in the middle of it with Eggsy and a few other members of the congregation. One, a slender man with light brown hair and a scraggly beard, took his turn to speak.

"You've been here a few weeks now," the man said. "What do you think of it?"

Simon considered his words for a moment. "I'm still figuring it out, but it feels good here. Comfortable."

"Glad to hear it," a woman called behind them.

Carey's voice nearly sent a chill up his spine from behind. He turned to face her.

"We try to make this as welcoming and comfortable an environment as we can. After all, we're here to seek that peace and comfort." She turned her gaze to Simon. "In any case, I'd like to have a chat with you, Simon."

Simon let the chill dissipate. "Am I in trouble?"

Carey laughed. "Should you be?"

He shrugged and glanced at Eggsy. "Not for anything I can remember."

"Then no, you're not in trouble." She beckoned him to follow as she started to walk away. "Come on. My office is just over here."

Eggsy gestured for him to go on with an enthusiastic smile plastered on his face.

Taking in a breath, Simon followed Carey to her office. *I hope she's loyal to Eggsy…*

When they reached her office, she indicated the seat. He glanced about the room and couldn't help but add up the prices for all the furniture, lights, and other items on display. He figured it must have cost about as much as a corporate executive's office.

She made herself a cup of coffee. "Want anything?"

"No thanks."

He watched her add an obscene amount of sugar before she took her seat behind the desk. "So you've been enjoying your time here?"

"Yeah. The community's pretty great."

"And the teaching?" She smiled when he fell silent. "I'm not going to kick you out for disagreeing with me. Give me your honest thoughts."

He sized up the value of her claim. "I both agree and disagree with most of what you say. The idealism is wonderful, but it falls apart when it meets the real world outside these walls."

"Hmm…" She watched him with a glint in her eye that reminded him of a cat eying a mouse. "I'm sure that first message you heard from me didn't help."

He held her gaze. "They've all been relatively similar in that way."

Carey finished stirring her coffee and tapped the spoon on the side of the mug. "How about this? Give me one of your real-life situations and let's see if I can take some of that idealism out of it and add some reality."

A frown took hold of him. "What?"

"It'd be like when we first spoke." She took a sip, then added another spoonful of sugar. "Like when you told me there are people who want to destroy things, and we need people like soldiers and police officers to keep them in check."

He considered her offer for a moment. "All right. Well, I broke up with my girlfriend about a week before I came here."

She lifted her mug to her lips. "Go on."

"We'd been trying to have a kid for roughly a year. She told me she wanted children and I doublechecked with her a few times over that period of time. When she finally got pregnant, she—"

He caught on it, the words gripping his throat.

"Take your time."

He slowly worked his airway open by taking short breaths. "She aborted the child and got a… I don't remember the word, but she sterilized herself. All with my money. And she tried to hide it from me."

She watched him from over the lip of her mug. "And you did… what?"

"I got my personal stuff out of the apartment, switched banks, and broke up with her."

She gave a slight nod, as if supporting the decision. "What was her explanation?"

"She got scared and said she hadn't realized the clinic would sterilize her."

"Hmm. And what part was it that made you break up with her? Specifically? The lying, the unsanctioned use of your money?"

Simon fidgeted for a moment. "She killed our child."

"That's her right."

He blinked a few times at her snappy yet casual response. "But Jesus said, 'Whatsoever we do unto the least of these you do unto me.' You quoted that!"

She sipped her coffee. "A fetus has no spirit."

His frown deepened. "You've said before there is no spirit, only energy. If there's enough energy for a child to have a heartbeat at two weeks, how is that child not alive?" He felt anger rising from his stomach. "Besides, why should anyone have the right to decide that a person isn't human? That's the same mentality that justifies slavery, racism, and all the other horrible things in the world you yourself have spoken against. Every single one of those things!"

CHAPTER TWELVE

"This is the world we live in, Simon. You have no right to that child in any way. Even within my views, whether you agree with them or not, it sounds like she regretted what she did. But she did nothing wrong."

His jaw tightened and he was about to speak when she continued, a ghost of a smirk skewing her thin lips.

"Besides, what about your service?" she asked.

He froze.

"Overseas, and back here. You've killed more children than she has, so you don't really have a leg to stand on, if you'll excuse the pun."

Simon stood up and made for the door.

Her ghostly smirk had turned into the smile of a predator that had just finished playing with her food. "I don't appreciate wolves in the midst of my flock, Simon. Don't come back."

Simon swiftly made his way to the exit.

"Hey, wait up!" Eggsy called.

Simon reached his truck by the time Eggsy had caught up. He grabbed Simon's arm, but Simon shrugged him off.

"What gives, bruv?"

The words snapped out of Simon's mouth like a whip. "What did you tell her?"

Eggsy frowned and looked back at the building for a moment. "Who? Carey?"

"Who the hell else?"

"Nothing, man. Just that you'd broken up with Sue, that's all. I thought she'd be able to help talk you through it a bit."

Simon's jaw tensed up, his grip tightening on the handle of his truck door. "Nothing else?"

Eggsy shook his head emphatically. "No, bruv."

"I'm pulling Carson off the Lechtemen house and putting him on the Torringtons. Get him up to date and ask him to get you up to date on the Lechtemens."

The shock and pain were clear in Eggsy's eyes. "I was just trying to help, Sye."

Simon kept his gaze locked on his truck, his tone low and sharp, like a father disciplining his child. "Do I need to repeat myself?"

Eggsy's gaze shifted away, but he nodded. "I got it."

Simon started his truck a few moments later. He gripped the steering wheel, turned the key in the ignition, and barely waited for the engine to roar to life before peeling out of the parking lot.

Left alone in front of the church, Eggsy clenched his fists and turned to go back inside. With purpose in his step, he located Carey across the room and hurried toward her. He grabbed her arm and started pulling her closer to the office.

"We need to talk."

She resisted his manhandling with nothing but a smile. "Of course, just one—"

"Now."

They stepped into a secluded hallway and looked at each other. The look in her eye was like a pawnbroker analyzing a piece prior to sale.

"What did you say to him?" he demanded.

She pursed her lips. "I'm afraid that's private, Eggsy."

He struggled to keep himself composed. He let go of her arm to keep from squeezing it. "You're messing with my job."

"And you messed with mine by bringing a predator into my house." She said it quick and casual, detached, as though describing something menial.

It was too much for him. Eggsy punched the wall.

"He is not a—" He let out a shaky breath, reining himself in. "He is a good man. One of the best men I know, which I'll admit may say more about me than him. But I trusted you, and you just burned one of my most important friendships."

"I didn't make you tell me anything," Carey said as she fiddled with his shirt, straightening it out. "You gave the information willingly. I didn't even have to sleep with you."

He twitched and stepped back from her touch. "Because I thought you'd help him."

"The people in this church are more important than a rabid stray." Her tone was dismissive. Her body language told him she was done with him. "If you've caught his mange, it may be best for you to leave as well."

He looked ready to say something, but just then the door to the office opened.

"Pastor?" said the secretary.

Carey turned to her. "Yes, Sherry?"

"I've got something I need to talk to you about, when you have time."

"I was just leaving," Eggsy grunted.

He walked swiftly away, then left the building and marched to his own truck. His chest heaved as his rage spilled over. With a growl of frustration, he punched the door.

THIRTEEN

THE SHRILL RINGING of tinnitus sliced through Simon's ears. His vision blurred like a poorly made mirror as he tried to grasp the world around him. He tried to move but found his body rebelling against his commands, opting to remain dormant.

Slowly the blur faded and he took in the hellscape around him. People littered the streets. Civilians. Some cried out, their voices filled with shattered desperation. Others simply sat amidst the wreckage in shock. Still others lay on the ground, their bodies as unresponsive as Simon's.

The thunderous cracks of gunshots pierced the ringing in his ear and hands groped and clawed at him. His body finally responded and he struggled weakly against his assailants. The sound of Arabic blasted in his ear and he felt a sudden and final crack against the back of his head—

Simon almost sprang forward, his skin slick with a cold sweat as he reached for the handgun beneath his pillow, but his fingers groped hopelessly in the dark. The sound of Delta's whine wafted up and he slowly became aware that he wasn't overseas.

The curtains were suddenly thrown back and Simon covered his eyes with a sharp intake of breath. He tried to blink away the early morning light and looked around the vaguely familiar room.

"Good morning, *hermano*."

Simon frowned. Suddenly, the hangover split his skull like an axe. "Aw, hell..."

"Here."

He cracked one eye open to see a mug with a dubious liquid being held out to him. "What...?"

"Trust me."

He looked up to see a stocky Hispanic man standing in front of him.

"Carson?" Simon asked. "What am I doing here?"

"Drink this first, *jefe*."

Simon sipped the drink, then coughed. "What the heck?"

"Columbian roast, loads of honey, and pure jalapeño juice. Used to get my *papi* right as rain after a bender."

Simon grimaced, then downed the rest of it in one go. He gagged and coughed. "Ugh… no offence, but your dad was insane."

"Is it working?"

He begrudgingly nodded. "It's bearable. What day is it?"

"Sunday."

"I remember Wednesday…"

"I'm sure it'll come back," Carson Sucre said as he sat on the couch beside him. "We went for some beers last night. Well, I had some, you had… more. Said something about not being allowed to come home drunk, so I brought you here."

Simon ran his hands down his face, his mind slowly catching up. "Where are we at with the Torringtons?"

"Demo and cleanups done. We're just waiting for Ryan to come by and give us the go-ahead. He's slated us in for Monday."

Simon took in a breath and tried to clear his mind. "That's good." He glanced at Carson, thinking back on all the times this man had been there for him. "I'm sorry about this, man."

"*Olvídalo, hermano*. We all get knocked on our *culo* sometimes, eh?"

He looked down as Delta sniffed his hands and rested his head on Simon's knee. "Yeah…"

"You should take a shower before the *familia* wakes up."

"Right. Thanks."

Simon stood and made his way to the shower. He let the frigid water course over his head as he leaned against the tile wall. The cold water cleared his mind.

He finally turned off the water, dried off, and got dressed. He came out of the bathroom and almost bumped into a short Hispanic woman. She just smiled up at him, a towel in hand.

"Oh, Simon. I was wondering who was in the shower."

"*Buenos dias*, Ula. Thanks for the use of your couch."

"Of course. *Nuestra casa es su casa*, Simon. You know that."

With a slight nod, he walked back into the living room. He sat heavily on the couch and scratched Delta behind his ears.

"Sorry, bud," he murmured. "This probably isn't what you were expecting when Don brought you back here, huh?" The dog rested his head on Simon's knee. "I'm guessing I didn't drive myself here—"

They heard a yelp from the bathroom. "*Dios mio!*"

Carson smirked and stifled a chuckle. "You left the water cold, huh?"

Simon's eyes widened.

CHAPTER THIRTEEN

"Eh, it'll perk her up for the day," Carson said. "And I didn't do it, so I don't have to deal with her wrath." He rested his elbows on his knees. "Your truck is at the bar. I can drop you off after mass. Why don't you join us?"

"I'm not really—" He paused. "Sorry, that was rude."

"You went to Eggsy's church."

Simon nodded.

"*Aunque la mona se vista de seda, mona se queda.*"

"Monkeys and silk?"

Carson nodded. "A monkey can wear silk, but it's still a monkey."

A frown touched Simon's lips. "Oh yeah…"

"I'm not saying you gotta even come inside, but it'll be easier on the gas tank if I don't have to come back here to pick you up."

Simon watched the man for a moment, then nodded. "All right."

He took out his phone and fired off a message to his mother, who responded within a minute. *You okay?*

Simon's expression dropped as he texted back: *I'm fine. I went out drinking and stayed at a friend's place for the night.*

He was about to put his phone away when it beeped at him again.

Okay sweetie. I'm just glad you're safe. Love you, and I look forward to seeing you when you get home.

There was a hug emoji at the end. Simon couldn't help the smile that tugged at the corners of his mouth.

FOURTEEN

SOON ENOUGH THE rest of the Sucre household had awoken, readied themselves, and headed off to the St. Patrick's Cathedral in Fort Worth. As the family entered, Simon looked up at the structure and opted to stay outside. He walked around the side of the building and entered the courtyard with Delta.

He looked up at a statue of Mary and the baby Jesus, her gaze almost accusing. Her arms kept her child away from anyone who might take him.

The bell tolled eight times.

"I love that sound," a man spoke.

Simon glanced back to see an old priest sitting on a nearby bench, his weathered skin hanging off him like a poorly sized shirt.

"Did you know that the bell has been here since the cathedral was first built?" the priest asked.

Simon's brow furrowed. "No, I didn't."

The priest patted the spot on the bench next to him and Simon decided to sit with Delta at his feet.

"My name's Thad." He held out a shaking hand.

"Simon," he replied as he shook it. "This is Delta."

Thad smiled at Delta and scratched behind his ears. "Of all the animals God created, dogs truly are made for man, aren't they?" Delta barked and the priest chuckled. "I always imagine that the dog was the first animal Adam chose to name, and it stayed by his side through everything."

The thought produced in Simon a spark of warmth as he watched Delta soak up Thad's affection.

"Forgive me, but shouldn't you be in there?" Simon asked.

Thad had a mischievous glint in his eye. "Should I?"

Simon blinked. "I'm sorry. Listen, I don't want to make any trouble for anybody."

"You won't get trouble from me, son. Only the ramblings of a priest long past his expiration date." His eyes narrowed. "Or perhaps near it. What brings you here today, Simon?"

"I'm just waiting for my friend. He's going to give me a ride back to my truck."

Thad nodded. "And how did you get separated from your truck?"

"A few too many beers," Simon said with a sigh.

"Once is an isolated incident. Twice is a coincidence. Three times is a pattern. So which is it now?"

"Coincidence." The word quietly slipped past Simon's lips, laden with guilt and shame.

"Ah… but you actually know it's a pattern, don't you?"

Simon nodded, his face covered in defeat.

"Hmm," Thad murmured, as if he knew Simon's struggles. He lightly tapped Simon's prosthetic with his toe. "I served too, you know. 'Nam. Last quarter of the war." He sighed. "The things we humans do to one another… it makes me question."

"You question if God is real?"

"While I was in that green hell, yes. Every waking minute of every day. I came to realize, however, that we have our own free will. For God to simply put a stop to everything, to force us to live in a particular way without giving us the option to live differently… well, that would trample our free will. Respecting our freedom to choose is the second greatest act of love he has shown us."

"And the first?"

Thad gestured to the statue. "The Sunday school answer, my boy."

"Then what do you question?"

"How?" Thad noticed the confusion in the younger man's voice. "How can he love us in spite of everything? We kill each other without hesitation. The very land we walk on cries out for the sake of the unborn lives senselessly thrown away because we'd rather worship sex than God. Because we believe that our own pleasure is more important than the modicum of self-control necessary to curate a life." He sighed as he looked up at the statue. "But who am I to say anything to anyone? I sin every day. I have more blood on my hands than most." He averted his gaze from the statue and turned it on Simon. "Some of the things I did… I don't think he could ever forgive me. I took this position thinking I could atone, but every day I only feel further away. Like I'm a fraud. Like I've wasted the last five decades in search of something that can't be found." He sighed and gave Simon an apologetic look. "Forgive an old man his crisis of faith?"

Simon nodded. "Yeah. We all have our peaks and valleys, right?"

"That we do." Thad let out a breath and slowly stood. "I'm going to head off. It was a pleasure to meet you, Simon."

"Likewise." Simon also rose to his feet. "And thank you for your service."

Thad blinked, then smiled weakly. "Thank you for yours."

Even after Thad had shuffled off, Simon stood in reflective silence. At last he turned back to the cathedral entrance and walked inside.

"Uh, sir, I'm afraid dogs aren't generally allowed."

Simon made eye contact with the greeter. "He's my support dog."

THE LONG ROAD BACK

"Oh, sorry. There are seats further up if you want to be near the front."

"I'll just stick back here for now," Simon said. "Thanks."

He found a seat, sat down gingerly, and listened as the priest at the front continued his sermon.

"...evil prevails when good men stand to the side and do nothing. Money is a tough subject, I know. There are even those among us here who struggle to feed themselves on a daily basis. Which is why we've set up programs you can access simply by asking for help. But even those in that position will find themselves across from someone worse off. There are many ways we can do good in the world. None of us here are likely to solve something like cancer or world hunger, not in our lifetime, but the soup kitchen can always use volunteers. The homeless, the hurting, and the lost can always use a helping hand. Sometimes we just need to sit there and listen, because nobody else does. Paul wrote that we are to give as the spirit leads, and that means to give freely of what we can when the opportunity arises. After all, it is by our works that the Lord knows who his believers are. Let us pray."

As the priest prayed, a thought nagged at the edge of his mind. He felt consumed by confusion and closed his eyes as tight as he could. He felt his heart strike at his ribs like a rabid animal.

He felt a force collide with his chest, forcing his eyes open. Delta had jumped up and placed his head on Simon's shoulder.

Simon relaxed and hugged the dog. "Thanks, buddy."

He let go and Delta dropped back to a sitting position as the priest closed his prayer.

When people started standing up to leave, Simon took a few breaths to finish settling himself.

"Hey *hermano*." He looked up at Carson. "Missed the air conditioning?"

Simon smiled. "Something like that."

"What'd you hear of the sermon?"

Simon cleared his throat. "Evil prevails when good men stand by and do nothing."

"Ah. If nothing else, that is something I try to live by." Carson looked up to the front. "And something I know you try to live by too."

"*Try* being the key word."

Carson shrugged and sat next to him, stretching out. "Nobody's perfect, *hermano*. Even me."

"You're the closest to being a saint of all the people I know!"

"I could say the same to you," Carson shot back.

They heard footsteps approach and both looked up to see a slender blond-haired, blue-eyed young woman approaching.

"Hey Carson," she said.

Carson smiled warmly. "Good morning, Viola."

Viola seemed to analyze Simon. "Who's your friend?"

Simon stood up and held out his hand. "Simon Fletcher."

She shook it with a smile. "Viola Sharp." She looked down at Delta and knelt to tousle his fur. "And this handsome fella?"

"Delta."

Delta held up a paw. Viola giggled and shook it, then scratched him behind his ears.

"I haven't seen you two around before," she remarked.

"First time here," Simon replied. "And I was just waiting on Carson. He's my ride back to my truck."

Viola turned her gaze to Carson. "I thought you were volunteering today?"

He ran a hand through his hair. "*Mierda*… you're right."

"I can give these two a lift," Viola said.

"Are you sure?" Carson asked.

She raised an eyebrow. "I'm pretty sure we were listening to the same sermon."

The man snorted. "Right. If that's all right with you, *hermano*?"

Simon nodded. "Sure."

"Thanks a million, Viola."

Viola gestured to the door. "Let's get outta here."

Simon followed her out to her small red hatchback, the trunk opening at the press of a button on her keys.

"Come on, Delta."

The dog looked up at Simon.

"Go ahead," he said.

The dog got in and Simon moved to the passenger door.

"So where're we headed?" Viola asked as they both climbed into the vehicle.

"Lou's Bar."

"Ah," she murmured as she pulled out of the parking lot. "So it was one of those kinds of nights, huh?"

"Yeah."

"Military?"

He nodded.

"I can't even imagine what you've been through," she said.

He frowned. "Everyone's got their own trials."

Empathy fixed itself in her eyes. "Some trials last longer than others. You're the one who helped bring the Sucres into the U.S., right?"

Simon glanced at her. "What do you know about that?"

"Ula's said that Carson's boss helped him bring the rest of his family stateside, that they gave him a job."

"I only helped sort out the paperwork," Simon said.

"Just paperwork or not, they wouldn't have survived living where they were much longer, according to Ula. Their kids call you their ángel *de la guarda*."

Simon smiled. "They call me Uncle Simon to my face." He cracked his neck. "How do you know the Sucres?"

"Choir. I help with the kids, and I'm part of the church choir with Ula."

"Ah."

They pulled into the bar parking lot and Simon reached for the door handle.

"Want to get some lunch?" she asked.

Simon blinked. He was about to turn her down, then thought better of it. "Sure."

Viola beamed. "Sweet. I know this great little place nearby. Follow me there?"

"Sure."

He opened the back hatch of her car and Delta jumped out. Before long they had gotten into the truck and started following Viola out of the parking lot.

FIFTEEN

SIMON LEANED AGAINST his truck under the midday sun, his phone against his ear while the sounds of work belted out from inside the Torrington residence. The scratchy hold music blasted painfully, but he didn't dare move the phone away.

The hold music abruptly switched off, and a woman's voice came through. "Hello, Mr. Fletcher. It has been determined that the claim you filed on behalf of the Torringtons is valid. Here is the amount the company is willing to give."

She rattled off a number and Simon thought for a moment.

"That doesn't cover all of the damages," he said.

"It is what the claims department has determined."

Simon narrowed his eyes but forced a smile. "Ma'am, I don't think your claims department has a grasp on the issue. You see, the amount they gave out last time is what led to the situation we're in today. I'm guessing it comes from the same clerk who handled the previous claim, because he or she has experience with the case. Correct?"

"I can't give out that information." It was a rehearsed line.

"Which is a yes. They're trying to cover their own butts for the mistake of costing the company more than double what was necessary. Now, I've taken the opportunity to speak with other local homeowners. Some of them have policies with your company, and guess what I found in their homes? More black mould. This is building up to what could be a class-action lawsuit, and all because your claims department decided to hire crackheads to do the work. I'm not saying that lightly, either. I found needles in the attic of a home of a lovely elderly couple who've lived in that house for well over a decade, and they regularly have their grandchildren over."

Simon let that hang in the air, his heart striking at his ribs despite his outward confidence.

"One moment, please."

He went back on hold and crossed his fingers.

The hold music stopped abruptly and a man's voice came on. "You win, Mr. Fletcher. As long as you don't go starting anything up."

"I will be telling my clients to get the mould issue fixed," Simon said. "It'd be unethical to leave it as it is."

"Mr. Fletcher—"

"If it's found out they develop medical issues—or heaven forbid, if anyone died—because of the black mould your company didn't properly remove, you'll have a whole different kind of court case on your hands. This protects you and them, and generates more work for my company. Everybody wins."

The man was silent for too long.

I pushed too far. I just screwed this whole thing up. Winston's going to have my head mounted on his desk.

There was a sigh on the other end. "All right. For the Torringtons, you have a blank cheque, but I'll be handling this one personally. If even a penny is spent that doesn't have to be, I will cut your final bill in half. I'll be looking into those other sites myself, and then we'll talk some more."

"I understand. Pleasure doing business with you."

Simon hung up and practically jumped into the air.

"Hell yeah!" He took in a breath, let it out, and then took out his phone again and dialled Winston. "Hey boss. Guess who just got us a conditional blank cheque?"

"Holy…"

"And we may have a slew of other jobs coming from the surrounding neighbourhood."

Winston went quiet for a moment. Too quiet. Too long of a moment. "Are you all right, Simon?"

Simon went rigid. "Yeah, I'm fine enough. Even started going out with someone new for the last two weeks. Why?"

"Don't push too hard, Simon. And I'm not just talking about work."

Simon cleared his throat and glanced at the Torrington house. "I'm not."

"Good," Winston said. "I trust you're leaving business cards with these other homeowners?"

"Of course. And I've got a few appointments scheduled to quote more work."

"All right. I'll send Daniel to get those figured out."

Simon's eye twitched. "You're the boss."

"Great work, Simon. Keep it up."

After hanging up, Simon let out the breath he'd been holding. "Still in limbo…"

Next he went into the house and looked around. Carson was busy installing fresh drywall. "*Jefe!*"

"What's up?" Simon asked.

"Did we get it?"

Simon gestured for the man to follow him outside. When they got to the truck, Simon gave the man a wary nod. "Conditionally."

"Pinching pennies, huh?" ·

"Little bit." Simon ran a hand through his hair. "Realistically what we're having to replace is the stuff where the price point won't shift too much, and the work we've done is efficient." He looked back at the house. "Don't tell any of the trades where the money's coming from. I don't need any of them trying to play games."

CHAPTER FIFTEEN

"You got it, *hermano*." Carson stretched. "So is Eggsy still in trouble?"

A frown took hold of Simon and he sighed as he leaned against his truck. "I'm still trying to decide if I believe him."

"'Bout what?"

"He said he only mentioned my breaking up with Sue, but she seemed to know more than that."

"Your service?"

He shook his head. "Anybody can search that up on the internet."

"Did she explicitly say anything?"

"No."

Carson shrugged. "Then she did the harm, not Eggsy. I get it. He shouldn't have said anything. At most, maybe, that you were having a rough time and could use a little help. But I think he's learned his lesson, *hermano*."

Simon stared off for a moment before letting out a breath. "You're right. I'll talk to him."

"That doesn't necessarily mean I want to switch sites again, though."

Simon smirked. "I'll keep that in mind, don't worry."

"*Bueno*." Carson led them on the walk back into the house. "Say, how are things going with Viola?"

"Pretty well, I think. I mean, we've been going out almost every other day, so I'm pretty sure that's a good sign. We're going out tomorrow actually."

"She's been glowing to Ula about you."

"Glad to hear it." Simon stepped into the kitchen and gazed at all the work underway. "Well, let's get done what we can."

———————————

Later that day, Simon pulled onto his parents' property and parked in front of the house. Delta came running out to meet him and he knelt to pet him.

"Hey boy!"

Delta jumped up on him and barked.

"Yeah, I know. Today wasn't a good day for you to be at work." He straightened and noticed both Ray's and Bethany's cars parked outside the barn. He was about to head in that direction when he heard the front door open.

"They're having dinner with us today," his mother called.

He turned to see Shelby in the doorway.

"Thanks for the heads up," Simon said as he entered the house. He went upstairs to shower, then came down to find Ray and Bethany sitting in the living room. Both were going over paperwork.

Ray looked up. "Simon! Welcome home."

"Thanks," Simon said as he joined them.

Ray set his paperwork down and took off his reading glasses. "What's the news?"

"The good news is the insurance company will pay for it."

"And the bad news?" Bethany asked.

"They won't pay for anything more than the damage related to black mould. That means any electrical work still has to come from you guys."

Ray stared at him. "That's the bad news?"

Simon nodded. "Yeah. I think I was already pushing it, so I figured we'd be screwed if I tried to get any more. So—"

"That's amazing," Ray said. Simon blinked a few times. "I was only hoping they'd cover part of the mould work, but they'll cover all of it? How in the world did you manage that?"

"I can be persuasive," Simon said. "As for where we're at, the drywall is being installed. Then it's the mudding. It'll be a few days for that to dry properly. After that we'll get it primed, then do the trim and floors, and finally finish painting. That'll all be covered by the insurance company. I sent them the original materials plan and they greenlit that. So we can't upgrade the floors now—that is, unless you want to pay the difference."

Ray shook his head. "No, there's no need to upgrade anything."

"Maybe add a chest freezer," Bethany said, lightly touching Ray's hand. "It'll mean we can hold onto things for the church."

Ray gave that some consideration. "Okay. Yeah. We can probably fit it into the laundry room."

"Then I'll add that to the list for appliances," Simon said as he stood up. "I'll leave you to it."

Simon's phone began to ring as he climbed the stairs. He deftly answered.

"Simon Fletcher." He paused. "Yes, I'd like to sell my condo..."

SIXTEEN

THE BARKING OF dogs and shouting of their owners filled the air of the dog park as Simon and Viola walked through, Delta running ahead as Simon threw a ball with a rope attached—far enough that Delta had to work for it, but not so far that he'd run into anybody.

"So we've had some fun," said Viola out of the blue.

Simon glanced at her.

She sighed and then finished. "Now I want some serious."

When Delta came back, Simon tried to snatch the rope. The dog jumped to the side, but his owner managed to catch the end of the rope and give it a strong pull.

"Some serious?" Simon asked.

She nodded. "I want to know where this is going."

"We've been going out two weeks."

"I know, but I need to know if you're dating for fun or with purpose."

He managed to get the ball from Delta, then hurled it again and watched him take off in dogged pursuit.

"I'm seeing where things lead," he said simply. "Maybe they'll go somewhere great. If they don't, then it is what it is."

She watched him for a moment. "Okay. What do you want from your future?"

"I've already got a good job, so at this point a family, I guess."

"That's it?"

He shrugged. "Yeah." He knelt as Delta came back. "What about you?"

"I want a family, and to become a famous singer."

"You've definitely got the voice for it," he said with a smile. "But fitting a family in with that… it won't be easy. Not to mention any Christian label would expect you to project a certain image. That could make things even more difficult."

She shook her head. "I want to explore more than what Christian record companies would allow."

He let go of the rope and Delta noticed his shift. The dog lay down.

Simon slowly nodded. "The music industry is pretty rough. It's hard for anyone to get anywhere."

"You said I have the voice for it."

"People rarely get popular because they have a wonderful voice. Just look at all the online videos out there. You see these random people on the subway or whatever who can sing better than just about anyone. If it was only about sounding good, record labels would be hunting them down."

"Then how does someone get popular?"

"Marketability," he said. "The label's job is to sell you, not your music. In order for them to be able to sell you, you've got to sell yourself."

She shifted. "What do you mean?"

"You have a lovely voice. Personally, I'd buy an album on that alone. If you've got great lyrics, I'd keep buying albums. Most people aren't like that. They'll buy your albums for no other reason than that it's yours, or because you're the right genre. Look at the boy bands, not to mention the women who sing about nothing but breakups. They're all the same, but they still sell like they were one of a kind. You don't want to make pop music." He paused. "You have two options. Here's the first. Build up your following over time by putting out online videos, collaborating with other musicians, and maybe working for a small record label. This'll take a lot more effort on your part, since you won't have an agent or anyone else to do all the work beyond singing and songwriting. And you'll have to work another job until it pays enough to live off of."

"And the second?"

"Shop your demos around for about a year. Then someone will pick it up and decide to bring you in. They'll keep you small, dangling your dream in front of you until you reach the point of being ready to give up. That's when someone in the company will make you an offer: the full package. Ad campaigns, working with the best musicians, everything."

"And the catch?"

"You'll have to cheat on your boyfriend with the agent, or producer, or whoever it is who's making this offer."

She stared at him.

"One of the guys who works for me, he and his sister both got taken on by a record label," Simon said. "The labels pulled the same scheme on both of them. She walked, and eventually he washed out. So what would you do?"

"I'd only have to do it one time?"

His shoulders dropped. "It's never only one time, but say it was."

She was quiet, then let out a breath. "I think I would." She looked at him. "What about you? Someone offers you your dream job, or a billion dollars, or a chance with your celebrity crush, or some equivalent... would you cheat on your girlfriend?"

He shook his head. "No, I wouldn't."

"Why not?"

"Because I would never betray someone I love like that."

"Everyone has a price," she said. "Say you had a gun to your head."

He tapped his prosthetic leg. "Been there. The stakes were different, though."

"What if the gun is to your girlfriend's head, and she asked you to do it?"

He went quiet. "That's a different question. Besides, we're not really talking about these life-and-death scenarios."

"You're avoiding the question."

He sighed. "Because it's a different conversation."

"Fine. So you'd give up your dreams just because it would cost a one-night stand?"

He shook his head. "Remember when Satan was tempting Jesus?"

"I thought you were still figuring out what you believed."

He narrowed his eyes. "The lesson holds true, no matter the faith. Satan offered Jesus the world, and all he had to do was worship him. Satan could have given Jesus everything. Jesus could have chosen not to die, to take a shortcut to his end goal of ruling over everything, like Revelation describes. It was his dream, and the cost of going the hard way..." Simon trailed off. "So, no, I wouldn't give up on my dreams. I'd be content taking the long way."

"It helps that you already make a bunch of money."

He raised an eyebrow. "I do well for myself, but it was a long road to get here."

She glanced at his prosthetic leg.

"I didn't take any shortcuts," he added. "I had opportunities and didn't take them. I paid for everything."

"So what if your girlfriend did it?"

"I'd understand," Simon said. "But I'd break up with her."

"What if your boss would fire you if your girlfriend didn't sleep with him?"

"Then I'd find another job. I wouldn't use her like that."

When she didn't seem to have a response to that, he rose to his feet.

"I'll give you a ride home," he said.

His phone rang as he drove Viola home, but he declined the call. After he dropped her off, though, he called Neil back as he drove away.

"Hey Neil. What's up?"

"I was thinking about you lately. Wanted to see if you could drop by today."

Simon thought about it for a moment. "Sure. My evening just freed up. See you in fifteen."

"See you soon, son."

Simon pulled up in front of Neil's small house and studied it, the same dread clawing at his heart as when he'd looked in on the sanctuary at Ray's church.

He let out a breath and got out. Delta followed him up to the porch and Simon knocked. He waited for a moment, then opened the door and went in.

Neil looked up from the couch. "Have you eaten?"

"Not yet," Simon said as he took a seat.

"Ah, well, Mary should be done making dinner in a few minutes."

Simon's eye twitched. "Mary?"

He nodded. "A young lady from my church. She helps out around the house on Thursdays. Sometimes, when I'm lucky, she's got time to make dinner too."

Mary's a common enough name, he thought.

"So how've things been, Sye?"

Simon was quiet for a moment, weighing the last few weeks. He told Neil about his visit to First Light Centre, then about Viola.

Neil listened intently before leaning back. "I'm sorry to hear that, Sye."

Simon shrugged. "It is what it is."

"What do you plan to do from here?"

Simon shook his head and leaned on his knees. "I think I'm just done. With church, with dating… all of that. It's just not worth the energy."

"Hmm. I wouldn't give in so quickly."

"You married your first girlfriend," Simon said. "Not all of us are so lucky."

Neil nodded. "I know. Perhaps the woman you're searching for has been right in front of you the whole time? Or at least you may have already met her."

Simon frowned.

"And with regards to church, that Last Light or whatever it's called isn't a Christian church. It's just a feel-good cult. That's why she kicked you out. Predators don't like when others horn in on their territory."

"So I am a predator?"

"I'd say you're more like your friend here." Neil snapped his fingers and Delta immediately looked up at him. "Come."

Delta turned to Simon first, for permission.

"Go," Simon affirmed.

Neil smiled as Delta sat in front of him. "Men are made with aggression, Simon. It enables us to protect our families and friends when their safety is threatened. It allows us to compete, build, and stand against what's wrong in the world. You're not some stray predator. You're a trained, capable guardian who puts his own life on the line for complete strangers. She saw that. She knew you weren't like her. You're better. You'd lead people away from her, and she'd lose her power. You terrified her."

Simon let out a breath. "You've been reading up on me, huh?"

"I've always kept up with you as best I could, son. I'm sorry for all the things you've had to do to protect others."

Simon could only offer a slight nod.

"Dinner's ready!"

Simon flinched at the sound of Mary's familiar voice, but Delta just stood up and trotted into the kitchen.

"Hey Delta," Mary said. "Long time no see. How you doing, boy?"

Simon began to fidget at the thought of Mary overhearing their conversation, but when she poked her head out of the kitchen he relaxed; she was taking out an earbud.

"Hey Simon!" she called to him. "I didn't know you knew Neil."

"Old friend," Simon said.

"Emphasis on old," Neil said with a cackle. He was suddenly struck with a coughing fit and Simon made a move to help. Instead the older man held up a finger and got it under control. "Just recovering from that bug that's been going around."

Mary came back out with a couple of bowls. "Here's dinner. Simon, I assume you're staying to eat."

"What about you?"

She beamed. "I'd love to, but I need to head off. You two enjoy. There's more in the kitchen. Simon, would you be willing to put the soup into the fridge once you're done?"

"Of course."

"Thank you very much," she said sweetly. "See you Sunday, Neil!"

Neil nodded to her. "See you, Mary, and thanks again. God bless."

"God bless."

As she walked out, Neil seemed to take note of the thoughtful expression on Simon's face. "You know Mary?" he asked.

"We've met."

"She's a sweet young lady. Biggest heart you'll ever see."

They ate in silence, and once they had finished Simon stood up and started pouring the leftover soup into containers.

"Why don't you come to my church this Sunday?" Neil suggested as Simon gathered the dirty dishes and loaded them into the dishwasher.

"Considering my current track record, I don't think that's a good idea."

"My pastor's a good man. You won't get kicked out unless you're trying to cause problems, and even then he'd try to work on it with you."

"I've met him."

Neil blinked. "Oh. That's how you know Mary. You're the one working on his house."

"Bingo," Simon said. "Professionally speaking, it's a bad idea."

"Simon, let me give you the best piece of advice you'll hear this week: your personal well-being is infinitely more important than your professional."

Simon let out a breath as he finished putting the containers into the fridge. "Thanks for listening, Neil."

Neil's gaze dropped at his dismissal. "Any time, Sye. You just come on over."

"Will do. Anything I can do before I go?"

"Nah. You should get home. It's getting late."

SEVENTEEN

SIMON FOUND HIMSELF back in his condo. A frown curled his lips downward as he took in the all too familiar surroundings. Questions slammed through his mind.

Then he heard it—a soft whimpering from the bathroom door, which was open a crack, the light slicing across the floor like a knife.

He felt his body move on his own, carrying him to the door. He peered through and saw Susan shaking a pregnancy test in her hand, as if it would change its result.

"No, no, no, no, no! I can't—! Not his. This can't be happening."

He glanced down at his hand and saw the pistol gripped in his fingers. His body moved again, opening the door.

No! Stop!

His screams were silent and left unanswered as his body moved forward.

Susan heard the gun cock and turned to face him, terror in her eyes. "No, Simon! Please!" She backed away. "Please don't kill our child! I didn't mean to!"

Stop! he screamed at himself.

She tripped back into the bathtub, her body slamming into the smooth fibreglass. She covered her womb with her arms in a vain, desperate attempt to protect the new life pulsing in her depths.

"Simon! Please!"

He raised his hand, pointed the firearm at her womb, and pulled the trigger.

———————

Simon sat up in bed, a silent scream rattling in his lungs but withheld from his throat. His whole body shook as he frantically looked around the pitch-black room until he heard a quiet bark. He went still and looked down to see the rough shape of Delta in the darkness.

He slowly relaxed and scratched Delta behind the ears. "Hey boy. Sorry for waking you."

The dog whined.

"Guess I really can't sleep alone anymore." He sighed and dropped his head back down to his pillow. "What a lousy excuse for a man."

Delta rested his head on Simon's chest and silently stared at him. Simon's gaze remained locked on the ceiling until the sun started to paint the sky.

During his morning run, with Delta trotting along at his side, he pushed himself hard in an effort to drown out the images that threatened to rip his mind apart. He was running past the working cowboys when his foot suddenly caught in a hole. He tumbled to the ground. His prosthetic unlatched and flew off.

"Dammit!"

Simon struck the ground, his fist hitting a rock. He grunted and pulled his hand back, then curled up on the ground. Delta barked, looked around, and then took off.

———————————

Neil woke up, his gaze on the familiar ceiling above him. He sat up, ran his hands down his face, and yawned. When he reached back, his hand found no immediate purchase and finally landed on the bed. A frown took hold of him. He grunted as he carefully knelt, a new medical bracelet clinking on his wrist.

"Good morning, God. Thank you again for another day. I now understand why you haven't taken me home yet. Please pass along my love to my girls, and tell them I can't wait to see them."

He struggled to his feet and made his way through his morning routine, frequently scowling at the medical bracelet as if it were mocking him with each and every inconvenience.

Eventually he got into his car and drove to church. When he got there, he grabbed his Bible from the glovebox and walked to the front door.

"Good morning, Neil!"

He smiled as Mary gave him a hug. "Good morning, Mary."

She pulled back and tilted her head. "Did the soup last till the end of the week this time, or did you and Simon eat it all on Thursday?"

He chuckled. "It lasted, thank you."

"Any time." Her gaze fell to the medical bracelet. "What's that about?"

"Just my cough," he said dismissively. "It's taking longer to clear up, so they want me to wear this blasted thing in case they need to rush me to the hospital."

They both looked up as worship began.

"Let's find you a seat" She linked arms with him, guided him to a seat, then swiftly made her way back to the entrance and repeated the process with some of the other more elderly members of the congregation.

Soon enough the first two songs had run their course and Ray walked up to the front.

"Good morning, Foundations!" A fair few echoes of greeting came back to him. "I'll have the deacons pass the offering bags around. In the meantime, I'd like to start with corporate prayer. Are there any prayer requests?"

Neil listened as some of the other churchgoers offered up requests. He finally raised his hand.

"Yes, Neil?"

"There is a young man I know. He recently lost his child. I'm trying to be there for him, but I'm fumbling quite a bit as I work through it myself. I pray for wisdom and the words to give this young man. Or for someone else to be able to step in where I can't."

Ray nodded along as Neil spoke, quickly making a note of it. "Can I get this young man's name?"

"Considering the situation, I don't think it would be appropriate."

Ray's eyebrows shot up. "All right. Is he a believer?"

"He walked the path before, but he's been lost for quite a while now."

"Thank you, Neil."

Neil gave a single nod, then looked back down to his worn-out hands.

Simon felt the pounding of hoofbeats before he heard them. He glanced up as a shadow crossed over him. Clyde was hovering over him from atop his horse, Daisy alongside him.

Clyde swiftly dismounted. "Geez, Simon, did you try riding one of the new stallions?"

"No," Simon managed as he sat up. "I tripped."

Clyde looked down at his stump, then looked around for the prosthetic. "Must've been quite a tumble there, son."

"Delta!" Simon grunted. The dog trotted up to him and started to lick his bleeding hand while Daisy circled him. "Hey, stop! Can you find my leg?"

Delta whined. Simon sighed and pushed the dog back and pointed to his stump. "The leg. Can you find it?"

Delta sniffed his stump, then started sniffing all around the area. He disappeared into the tall golden grass, Daisy close behind.

Clyde knelt next to Simon. "Lemme see that hand."

"It's fine."

"If that dog can't find your leg, you're riding back with me. And you aren't getting blood on me, my saddle, or my nag."

Simon squinted at the old cowboy but held out his hand. Clyde got a small first aid kit from his saddle. Simon winced as Clyde poured some disinfectant on it.

"What did that rock do to deserve this?" Clyde asked as he applied a bandage.

Simon looked off to the side. "I'm not sleeping."

"So you clocked a rock?"

"I... I killed my kid."

Clyde raised an eyebrow. "Didn't Sally do it, or whatever her name was?"

He nodded. "I mean… last night. In my dream. I… I shot—" He cleared his throat. "I've killed kids before. If I hadn't been with Susan, then—"

Clyde grunted. "Whoa there, Sye. She made her choice. Regardless of her reasons, she did that, not you. And I read up on your time as a cop. I can guess what happened in the military. You wouldn't kill someone unless they were trying to kill too. That's on them. You were protecting life, Simon. I know my words probably don't mean much, since I never served, and I ain't never killed nobody before neither. But I do know you, Simon. You're a good man, and it's because you're a good man that the world's putting you through the wringer."

He finished wrapping Simon's hand, and a few moments later Delta and Daisy showed up with the prosthetic. It was bent out of shape.

"The world wants to stamp out any light it can find, Simon. Don't let it snuff you out."

Simon glanced away, the pit in his chest left ever vacant. He mustered what cordiality he could. "Thanks, Clyde."

Clyde held out his hand and Simon took it. The cowboy then pulled him to his feet and helped him onto the horse.

"All right." Clyde picked up the prosthetic and tied it to the back of the saddle. "Let's get you home."

EIGHTEEN

SIMON SAT AT the kitchen table, a pair of old wooden crutches beside him. Shelby and Mark came through the door with Hailey, and the young girl was babbling about what she'd learned in Sunday school.

Delta lifted his head as they came in, then got up when Hailey called for him. The dog looked up at Simon before taking off.

"Go ahead."

Delta launched out of the kitchen, his tail smacking Shelby as he ran past.

"Delta! Walk!"

The sound of Delta's pawsteps slowed, followed by the front door opening and closing.

Shelby took in the sight of her son, her amusement devolving into terror. "Oh my! What happened?"

He took in a breath as she started to fuss. "Mom, I'm fine. I just tripped and broke my prosthetic. Clyde took me to town. It's going to be a bit before they can get me another one cause I'm going through a different manufacturer this time. They've got to work out the VA stuff. Hopefully the new one's more durable."

"You need to be more careful." She floundered as she tried to figure out how to make him comfortable. "I did some research. There are these athletic prosthetics that have a sort of bending metallic ski blade thing. They're great for running on uneven ground."

He frowned. "Really?"

She nodded and took out her phone. She typed away on it and then turned the screen to face him. "There."

He saw the price tag. "That's a bit much just for morning runs."

"It could be an early Christmas present."

"Mom, no. That's way too much."

"Honey—"

Mark put a stop to her pressuring as he entered the kitchen. "He said no, Shel. He's a man, not a child. Have some respect."

Shelby looked back at Mark, and then her gaze fell. "Okay."

CHAPTER EIGHTEEN

She turned back and started to putter around the kitchen as she prepared lunch.

Mark gestured for Simon to follow him. Simon grabbed his crutches, got up, and followed his father into the living room. Mark eased himself onto a couch and Simon did the same across from him.

"Make sure you thank her for the thought," Mark said.

"I know."

Mark grabbed a newspaper and opened it. Neither man spoke, until Simon noticed the date on the newspaper.

"Dad?"

"Yeah?"

"Why are you reading a six-year-old newspaper?"

Mark lowered it some and peered at Simon over the top of the yellowed paper. "This is the only way we get to know our son."

Simon's eyes widened and he looked away, guilt dragging down his features.

Mark sighed and set the paper off to the side. "I'm sorry."

"It's not your fault," Simon said, pushing himself into the cushions to make himself smaller.

"I'm talking about when you went to join the military."

Simon's jaw tensed up. "Oh."

"I was afraid." Mark mulled over his words, trying to pick them as carefully as he could. "I didn't have a problem with you joining the military, but I did want you to wait… because joining up right after Heather passed meant you wouldn't have the support of people who love you. I wanted you to be able to grieve with us. She was like a daughter to your mother and me." He sighed. "Back then, I fumbled my words. You inherited my aggression. A useful tool, but a dangerous master. I didn't handle you properly and I pushed you away. I'm sorry for not being a good enough father that day."

Simon stared at him, no words forming in his mind. He suddenly cleared his throat. "I'm sorry for pushing you. Was that how your back…?"

Mark shrugged. "Doctor said if it hadn't been that, it would've been one of the horses. I pushed myself too hard when I was younger."

"I still shouldn't have done that."

"Apology accepted."

Simon let out a breath he'd been holding for the last decade and the two men finally sat in a comfortable silence.

NINETEEN

SIMON LEANED AGAINST his truck outside the Torrington house while Carson walked out to meet him.

"Hey, Simon. I thought you'd be offsite till your new leg came in."

He patted the crutches next to him. "I'm fine. I just can't walk around in there. Where are things at?"

"Hernando's coming in to prime the place tomorrow. There were some last-minute things we had to do today. Otherwise things are right on track."

Simon withheld his frown. "Anything you need from me?"

"*Sí, hermano*," Carson said. "Rest up. Take it easy."

Simon's lips tightened to a thin line. "All right."

Carson gave him a single nod and turned.

"You haven't asked about Viola," Simon remarked.

Carson stopped. "*Escoge una persona que te mire como si quizás fueras magia.*"

"Person looking magical?"

"Find someone who looks at you as if you were magic, *hermano*." Carson smirked. "Viola is sweet, but she's no *magia*."

Simon's brow came together.

"You would say, 'If it is not meant to be, don't pursue it.' We meet people, and sometimes they stay, sometimes they go. It is easier to move on now than later, no?"

Simon sighed and nodded. "Yeah. You're right."

"You going to see Eggsy today?"

"Yep."

"*Buena suerte, hermano.*"

Simon grabbed his crutches. "*Gracias.*"

He got into his truck and started the engine. All the while, Delta watched him from the passenger seat.

"What's up?"

Delta tilted his head and whined.

"I'll get you some water at our next stop."

Delta barked.

"And some meat."

Delta panted, his tongue hanging out.

"No drooling in the truck, though, or you're only getting water."

Delta licked his chops and closed his mouth and Simon scratched between his ears.

"Good boy."

He pulled away from the house and took off down the street, heading to Vera's Diner. When he got there, he walked toward the front door with Delta at his side. The dog followed him in and sat under the booth.

The waitress came by. "What can I start you on?"

"A coffee for me, Yorkshire tea for my friend who'll be here soon, and a couple of sausages for my buddy here."

"You got it."

She came back just a minute later with a mug of coffee and cup of tea, already steeping.

"I'm Emma, by the way," she said.

"Simon."

She looked ready to say something more when she turned and noticed Eggsy walking towards them. "Well, I'll leave you to it."

Eggsy sat across from Simon, fidgeting. "Hey boss."

"Eggsy."

They sat in silence for a time, Eggsy continuing to shift in his seat until Simon let out a breath.

"I overreacted," Simon said. "I'm sorry about that."

"Nah, I'm sorry, Sye. I got Carey involved without talking to you first." He shook his head. "I honestly thought she'd help, not do whatever it is she did. And I only told her you'd recently broken up, too. I didn't give her any details, not that I had many to begin with."

Simon quietly stared down at his coffee. "I forgive you, Eggsy. Do you forgive me?"

"Are you a nutter, bruv? Of course I forgive you. I'm the one that let some twa—"

He stopped as Emma came back and set the plate of sausages in front of Delta.

"Here you are, handsome." She scratched the dog between his ears before she stood back up. "Is there anything else I can get the two of you?"

"This is fine for me," Simon said.

"I'm good, luv, thanks."

"All right. Want a top-up, Simon?"

He looked down at his coffee, then nodded. "Please."

She filled the mug.

"Thanks, Emma."

She smiled and walked off.

Delta looked up at Simon and whined, asking for permission to eat.

"Go ahead, boy," Simon said.

Eggsy raised an eyebrow. "First name basis with the bird, huh?"

"I come here often enough," Simon said dismissively.

"Well, I broke things off with Carey. I'm not going to her church or any of that. She actually kind of kicked me out."

"Sorry, man."

"Nah," Eggsy muttered. "I'm better off. All the blind yes-men and -women following an old bag like her? I don't even know how they snookered me in."

"Carey's tall, pretty, older, and the take-charge type. Exactly your type."

Eggsy sipped his tea. "That's my type?"

"Every woman you've been with since I've known you," Simon replied.

"I thought I was a little more of an anything-that-moves kind of bloke. Huh." Eggsy shrugged. "How's the Torrington place coming?"

"I got the insurance company to pay for a bunch of stuff they originally weren't going to pay for," Simon said. "And it's getting primed tomorrow."

"That's cracking, innit?"

"Yeah…" Simon took in a breath. "I can't switch you back."

"I know, bruv. I wasn't expecting anything. Just glad we're all squared up now."

Simon nodded. "How're the other sites going?"

"Well. And that's all that ol' Winston's letting me say."

"I see." Simon let out a breath. "Well, you should get back to it."

"You got it, bruv." Eggsy pulled out his wallet, but Simon shook his head.

"I got it, man."

"You're a right saint, you know that?"

Once Eggsy had walked out of the diner, Simon's gaze fell to his own half-full mug of lukewarm coffee.

"A saint, huh?" he asked himself.

He finished his coffee, left money on the table, and went back to the truck with Delta. He drove aimlessly for a while, frowning as he found himself nearing Foundations Church. He pulled into the lot, right next to Ray's car.

After a few minutes, he got out of the truck and walked up to the doors. They were locked.

"This is stupid…"

Just then, he turned to see Mary pulling in. She smiled and offered a wave before she shut off her car and got out.

"Hey Simon!"

"Hi."

She eyed the crutches. "Leg in for repairs?"

"Something like that."

Delta barked and she knelt to pet him. "Don't worry, I didn't forget about you!"

The dog sat down and soaked up the attention.

"Need to see Ray?" she asked.

Simon's lips formed a thin line. "Something like that," he said again.

"Well, come on in." She produced a set of keys and unlocked the door. "These doors lock themselves. We normally come through the back on weekdays."

He followed her in with Delta trotting alongside

"Ray was meeting with someone last I remember." She opened the door to the sanctuary. "You can wait in here, if you like. I've always found it peaceful when it's empty like this."

He looked into the room but hesitated. "No, I'll just wait out here."

"I'll get you a chair then."

"I'm good, thank you."

Mary raised an eyebrow, but her smile was ever-present. "I'll check in on Ray."

She walked off to the office, knocked, and poked her head into the pastor's office. After a moment, she came right back.

"It'll be a while," she said. "How about this? I'm prepping some food for the local soup kitchen and I could use some help peeling vegetables. Mind lending me a hand?"

"Sure."

"Come on."

He followed her around to a multipurpose room with an attached kitchen. He sat on a chair just as she handed him a peeler. He got to work, moving as swiftly as she did. It seemed she made short work of everything she set before herself.

"You make a lot of soup, huh?" he asked.

She laughed. "It's simple, healthy, and nearly infinitely reheatable. Well, as healthy as you make it. It's also easy to make en masse." She glanced at him. "I can cook more than soup, though. I even bake plenty."

"You a professional cook or something?"

"Nah, nothing like that. I just did a lot of cooking and baking growing up. My mother... couldn't. And my father had to work a lot in order to support us."

"Where are they now?"

Mary was quiet for a moment. "They passed a few years ago." She took in a breath and let it out, after which her smile returned. "But I found my calling in all that, and here I am. Making soups, cleaning houses, and just doing what I can."

"Must be a pretty crazy schedule."

"It's only as crazy as I make it. My dad had shares in some company, so I've got a passive income that covers the basics."

"No play money?"

She giggled. "This is my play, and I don't need a cent to do it."

They heard a knock on the doorframe and both looked backward to see Ray standing there, his eyes betraying his fatigue.

"Hey Simon," the pastor said. "Is something wrong at the house?"

"No, everything's good."

Ray blinked a few times. "A social visit? We already practically live together, Simon. You don't have to come into town to talk."

"I was already in town."

Ray slowly nodded.

Simon continued, "But if you're busy—"

"No. In fact, I could actually use your help."

"My help?"

"You're sharp and thorough," Ray said. "And you convinced an insurance company to pay out for something they didn't legally have to pay for. I have a young man in my office who could use a man like you."

Simon looked to Mary, who waved her hand at him. "Go on ahead, Simon. Thanks for the help!"

She looked down at Delta, who sat out of the way, but the dog's gaze switched between her and the meat on the counter.

"Ooh, you're just trouble with a capital T, aren't you?" Mary looked at Simon. "Does he have any diet problems?"

Simon thought for a moment. "If it's real food, he should be fine. Stay here, Delta."

Delta barked but held his gaze on the meat.

TWENTY

SIMON FOLLOWED RAY the short distance to his office, the rubber on the bottom of his crutches making that sound only rubber can make on linoleum. The noise was a constant reminder of his missing leg, each sound like a nail being driven into his skull.

He couldn't stop the sigh of relief that escaped his lips as he made it to the cheap, worn-out carpet in the office.

"Tyler, this is Simon."

A young man had been sitting in the chair in front of the desk, but he was already up on his feet and holding out his hand toward Simon.

"Shoot, sorry," Tyler said, noticing the crutches for the first time.

"Nothing to apologize for." Simon propped himself up and extended his hand.

Tyler hesitantly shook it, then stepped to the side.

"You can have the seat," Ray said.

Simon shook his head. "I'm good, but thanks."

Tyler hesitated but then retook the chair. Meanwhile, Simon leaned against the wall.

"So Ray says you could use my help with something?" Simon asked.

Tyler blinked a few times. "I–I don't know what…" He frowned, looking at Ray. "How can he help?" He quickly glanced to Simon, his eyes wide with worry. "No offence."

"None taken."

Ray's eyes would have sparkled with amusement at Tyler's floundering, but he kept his focus on the task at hand. "Simon here is quite intelligent, and he knows the Bible almost as well as I do."

Tyler's eyes widened and turned to the scarred man before him. "Really?"

Simon shifted. "I wouldn't go that far. What does my Bible knowledge have to do with anything, anyway?"

"Tyler's church just went through a merger of sorts." Ray let out a sigh. "The old lead pastor handed over the reins to a different church that's moved in. They're teaching some things that… well, they like the sound of specific verses while ignoring all the ones around them."

"Cherry pickers," Simon remarked. "What do you want me to do? Walk in on a sermon and start heckling?"

"No!" Tyler exclaimed. He cleared his throat and lowered his voice. "No. I don't want to cause trouble. I just… the problem we're having right now is about money."

"Too much or not enough?" Simon asked.

Tyler stared at him.

Simon sighed. "Most problems come back to either having not enough money or too much, in one way or another."

"I guess. But too much?"

"The new church leadership is part of a larger network of churches that have certain requirements," Ray interjected. "It includes a membership system in order to be involved in the church, and that membership requires a ten percent income donation."

"A paywall for spiritual service and growth?" Simon asked. "Reminds me a bit of scientology."

"They aren't scientologists," Tyler said quickly.

Simon shook his head, then took in a breath. "Okay, so they've got their little club. People can just go to a different church."

"It's not about that," Tyler said. "A lot of people already have."

"Then what's it about?"

"They're twisting the Bible. They're using verses to support their tithing, but none of the verses match up. I just don't know how to address it. Anybody who's tried has been shut down pretty quickly." He glanced to the side. "And my family and my girlfriend are kind of buying into it."

"What do you want from me?" Simon asked.

Ray spoke for the young man. "They have membership classes. You could attend, challenge them, and leave without much to lose. Should be a fun exercise of the old grey matter."

"What?" Tyler asked. "I mean, couldn't he just coach me or something?"

As Tyler and Ray kept conversing, Simon began to plan out ways in which to pull off this plan.

"Yes, but what happens if they push you out of the church?" Ray asked. "That's friction with your family, your girlfriend, and her family."

"Still, asking him to come in and just challenge them and make a scene wouldn't do anything."

"It would if he's prepared with the verses they're using," Ray shot back. "And the lesson plan."

Finally Simon broke in. "Sure."

The other two men looked toward him.

"I've gotten pretty good at getting kicked out of churches lately," Simon said.

Tyler cleared his throat. "Is that a good thing?"

Simon shrugged. "More of a what's-one-more kind of a thing. Like Ray said, it should be fun."

Tyler glanced at Ray before settling his gaze back on Simon. "You'll do it then?"

"Yep."

"Okay." Tyler reached into his pocket and pulled out a folded-up pamphlet. He passed it to Simon. "Um… here's the lesson plan and all that. The class is on Wednesday, at the church."

"All right," Simon told him. "See you then. Pretend you don't know me when we're there."

Tyler looked uncomfortable. "Isn't that deceitful?"

"I'm not telling you to lie if they ask about me. I'll just be there one night, and they'll never see me again. Besides, members of the church are supposed to be discerning and question what they're taught. Otherwise they don't actually believe. They just warm the benches."

Tyler stood up. "Okay. Thank you for helping out. See you Wednesday."

"See ya."

"Bye, Ray, and thanks for the help."

Ray smiled at the young man. "See you around, Tyler."

Simon waited for Tyler to leave, then took the recently vacated seat. "How'd you end up organizing inter-church warfare with this kid?"

"It isn't warfare." Ray paused. "Well, it is spiritual warfare, but you know what I mean."

"And Tyler?"

"He called the church asking for advice. Apparently he'd been calling around for a while and kept walking into walls he couldn't climb over."

"So you just gave him C4 to blast through those walls?" Simon asked as he opened the pamphlet and began to read through it.

Ray opened his mouth to say something, then changed his tack. "Anyway, what brought you here today, if it wasn't the house?"

"I just ended up here."

"Huh." Ray thought for a moment. "Do you know a man by the name of Neil?"

"Yeah, if you're talking about the one who attends this church."

"I see. You know him well?"

"We're reconnecting," Simon said hesitantly. "Did he say something?"

Ray shrugged. "Mary mentioned you'd met with him while she was there. Neil's a good man. Had a real rough go of it, though."

Simon continued to peruse the pamphlet as he spoke, his tone dismissive. "That's life, right? Some of us get hit with a breeze, others with a freight train."

"Were you hit with a freight train?"

"Ever heard of triage, Ray?"

Ray nodded. "Yes. Deciding which patients need immediate care, which can wait, and which won't make it. Why?"

Simon stopped flipping through the pamphlet. "It applies to more than just the medical context."

Ray leaned back in his chair and interlocked his fingers behind his head. "You came to me, Simon. Whether it was God or your subconscious at the wheel, something made you think you could get help here. And you can, if you let yourself."

Simon sat in silence for a moment, then grabbed his crutches. "See you later."

"See you, Simon. And thanks again for helping Tyler out."

Simon left the office and whistled for Delta, who came trotting out of the kitchen. Together they left the church.

The whole ride home, the covert mission for Ray and Tyler ran circles in Simon's mind. And he kept screaming internally that he couldn't do anything to help.

Upon arriving home, Simon sat in the living room with a cup of pens and a pad of paper. He pulled up multiple translations of the Bible on his phone and started making notes. Delta lay silent on the floor by his foot.

As Simon worked, cross-referencing scriptures he had read in the pamphlet, the hairs on the back of his neck suddenly stood on end. He gripped the pen a little tighter. His whole body tensed.

Sensing something, Delta's ears perked up and he rested his head on Simon's knee. Simon relaxed just in time for a pair of small hands to lightly push his back.

"Boo!"

Simon let out a shaky breath and glanced back at Hailey. "Hey."

"Aw…" She groaned as she rounded the couch and sat next to him. "How'd you know?"

"I just did. Can I ask you a favour?"

Her eyes sparkled at the prospect of helping him. "Sure."

"Please don't sneak up on me."

She blinked. "Did I actually scare you?"

He frowned down at the paperwork in front of him. "Not exactly. I spent a lot of time fighting bad people. It means that sometimes I react without meaning to when people sneak up on me, and I can end up hurting them. I don't want to accidentally hurt you."

Her eyes widened and she looked down at her hands and made herself small. "Sorry."

"You don't have to be sorry," Simon said gently. "You didn't do anything wrong, and now you know. This is to help keep you safe."

"Are there other games we can play?"

Simon paused. "You want to play with me?"

"Yeah. Auntie Shelby talks a lot about you, and I always wanted a big brother."

"Well…" He noticed that she already seemed to be accepting defeat. "I can't play any running games until I get my new leg. But I can play cards, puzzles, or other things like that."

Her gaze snapped up to him, her eyes sparkling again. "Really?"

"Sure, but right now I'm studying."

She looked down at the page. "You're at school too?"

He chuckled. "No. I'm helping someone out, so I've got to read up to make sure I can do my part."

"Can I draw with you?"

He ripped a page from the pad and took out another pen from the cup. "Here."

She dropped to her knees and started to draw, the paper pressed down onto the surface of the coffee table. "Thanks, Simon!"

"Mmhmm."

He looked back down at his notes.

They're using the shotgun strategy, he thought as he scanned the list of pamphlet verses he had looked up so far. *If you can't dazzle them with your brilliance, then blind them with your bull—*

He stopped the thought, then frowned.

Now I'm censoring myself in my own head. Jeez... well, what we say inside inevitably makes its way out. It'll be easier not to swear around her.

He sighed. How had he ended up here? Why had he offered to take on this bizarre task for some random kid he didn't even know?

He set down his pen. It didn't matter. He'd said he would do it, and he was a man of his word.

I'll just get it over with...

He glanced over at Hailey's drawing and had to repress a smirk. It was the stuff of nightmares! Although when he studied it a little closer, he realized what she'd done.

Oh, it's Delta. Now he let the smirk touch his lips. *I guess he is terrifying—if you're the enemy, that is.*

TWENTY-ONE

BULLETS SNAPPED PAST Simon and his team, the dirt road at their feet snatching each missed shot and puffing out dust. Many struck the large truck they had taken cover behind. The fatigues of two of his men were slowly changing colour from desert camo to grim crimson. One of them was his medic. He tried to manage the wounds while the few still standing returned fire. They were caught in the open.

"Hemmy, get that door open!"

Hemmy sprinted towards a building and kicked in the door. Before the man could even step through, his body jerked back and collapsed to the thunderous reports of more fire from within the building.

"Dammit! Teller, take over here!"

One of his men dropped to his knees and set to the wounds Simon had been tending to. Simon sprinted to the door and opened fire inside. Someone screamed in Arabic as he entered. He swiftly cleared the building, then dragged Hemmy's unresponsive body inside.

He grabbed his radio. "This is Viking 1-1. All Viking units move in to building Charlie 43."

Simon dashed out to help bring one of his injured squad members. He threw him over his shoulders and waited. As soon as his men opened fire again, he ran back to the building.

Soon enough they'd all made it inside and he looked around. "We missing anybody?"

The rear door suddenly blasted inwards and Simon raised his rifle and fired. He went pale as he saw the American uniform of the man he'd shot. He immediately discarded his rifle and raised his hands.

"Blue on blue! Friendlies!"

The rest of the Americans stormed in and Simon slowly walked forward. "I'm Sergeant Fletcher, Viking 1-1."

The man he'd shot groaned. "At least help me up, will ya."

As Simon approached, the other soldiers watched him warily. He grabbed the man's hand and pulled him to his feet.

Grunting, the sergeant looked down at the three bullets that had struck his front plate. "Nice shots." He took in a few breaths. "Sergeant Donald Relna, Bard 3-1."

CHAPTER TWENTY-ONE

One of Simon's men slammed the front door shut and leapt away from it. "RPG!"

An explosion blasted the wall inward, concrete striking everyone not behind cover.

The room in which Tyler's church held its membership meetings was fairly large, with low panelled ceilings and recessed lights. It reminded Simon of a schoolroom. A couple of windows let in the waning Texas sun, illuminating the thin layer of dust.

He sat in a chair opposite the open end of the U-shaped table, his arms crossed as other people filed in. Tyler and a young woman holding his hand were two of fifteen attendees. Simon's crossed arms tightened as he fought off the terrors of the night before that still clawed at the edges of his mind, slowly chipping away at his sanity.

It's been five years since I've had these, he thought. *Why do they have to hit so hard now?*

Delta leaned against Simon's leg and he instinctively reached down and scratched between the dog's ears.

"All right, everyone!"

Simon looked up to see a middle-aged man standing between the ends of the U-shaped collection of tables, his greying cul-de-sac of hair containing thin patches on top of his head.

"For those who don't know, my name's Randy. Now, just to be sure you're all in the right place, this is the entry-level class to becoming a member of Dutch Creek Church."

When nobody got up to leave, Randy smiled.

"Fantastic. So I'm going to start us off with a prayer, and then we'll get right into it." He closed his eyes. "Lord, we thank you for this day and the opportunity to reach out to more people. Please use me to speak to those here and help us all get closer to you. Amen."

He opened the book in front of him.

"All right," Randy said, finding his place. "To start, has everybody here been baptized?"

Most of the people raised their hands.

"For those who aren't, might I ask why?"

The rest were quiet, but Simon spoke up. "I think there's a lot of contention over baptism."

Randy raised an eyebrow. "Your name?"

"Simon," he said. "And I have been baptized."

"Well then, Simon, would you like to explain the importance of baptism?"

Simon shifted. "It's a statement of faith. Look at it like a marriage ceremony: you're making a declaration in front of people you know and love so they can celebrate with you and help keep you accountable. Beyond that, it has spiritual significance, since it represents one's union with God. A person shouldn't get baptized unless they accept the basis of the gospel and truly believe it. Not to mention it symbolizes a spiritual cleansing of sin."

"Perfect," Randy said. "It is a requirement for church membership, so if y'all are intent on being a member, you'll want to get in on the baptism class, where they'll go into this with a little more depth. Now, let's continue on to the basic gospel message. Jesus was fully man and fully

God, born of a virgin. He lived a perfect life, died on the cross, and rose again, paying for our sins, and he will come again. Anybody here not believe that?"

Still deciding, Simon thought.

"No? Good. Moving right along…"

Randy went through a few other items. Throughout the next half-hour, Simon was just about the only one to answer his questions.

"Well, Simon, you really know your stuff."

Simon smiled. "I just try to do my research. Which is why I've got some questions for you, Randy."

A spark of excitement lit up in Randy's eyes. "Hit me."

"Something I noticed from a fair number of sermons is that Pastor Greg talks about spiritual giftings as if it's something we can force the Holy Spirit into doing for us. Where is his biblical foundation for that?"

Randy blinked a few times. "Greg doesn't think we can force the Holy Spirit to do anything."

"But he said, and tell me if I'm misquoting here, that we ask the Spirit, and it will be given to us, whether it be a spiritual gift, healing, or anything else of the Holy Spirit. He continued on to insinuate that it's something we have a right to demand, without directly saying that. He also mentioned instances where he did certain things without asking God first. I know he's getting there by paraphrasing some Bible verses, but the context of those is that it must be within God's will. When Jesus said we could tell a mountain to throw itself into the sea, he wasn't saying that we should. He was saying that when we walk with God and act in his will, he will work with us and do great, impossible things to help us on that path within his plan. But Greg seems to have taken it to mean that we can tell God's creation to break the rules God has placed upon it on our own whims and for our own gratification. For example, he talked about prophesying. He seems to think he can force the issue, despite that never being in the Bible, at least not for anyone other than false prophets. The true prophets would pray for revelations, of course, but they wouldn't tell God to do it. In fact, most of them seemed to just wait for God to speak to them."

Randy stared at Simon, then cleared his throat. "Well, that is an excellent question, and perhaps one that is better suited for Greg himself to answer, as it's his words that seem to be causing the confusion."

Now that I've got everyone here seeing that he doesn't have all the answers…

"Fair enough," Simon said.

"So—"

"I have another question, if you don't mind."

Randy paused, then gestured for him to continue.

"Well, it's more than one, but they relate to one another a bit," Simon said. "People can't serve in the church without being a member, correct?"

"That is correct. As you'd be representing the church, we want to ensure that these people truly understand our beliefs and can convey them properly to anybody who comes through those doors."

"That's great," Simon said. "Makes a lot of sense. But it leads me into my next question. You require people to tithe in order to be members. If service is restricted by membership, then you've set up a paywall to spiritual service and growth. There are verses in your church's pamphlet that claim to support this: 2 Corinthians 9:6–7, Mark 12:41–44, Luke 6:38, Matthew 6:21 and 23:23, and Acts 20:35. There is one more, but that's another issue so I'll save it for after. Every single one of those verses talks about giving freely and with a joyful heart, and giving as the Spirit leads. It doesn't mention tithing at all. To require a specific number when none is given doesn't make any sense to me. Tithing was only ever a part of the law of Moses, which was intended for the Israelites when they came into the Promised Land. It was meant, by and large, to pay for the Levite priests to do their thing, since they didn't have time to work any other jobs to make money and support themselves, not to mention the social programs the temple ran. It was old covenant—or as we usually call it, Old Testament. However, Jesus fulfilled the old covenant by being the sacrifice. The new covenant, or New Testament, actually begins with Jesus's resurrection, as exemplified by the temple veil being torn in two. So my question is this: where does the concept of ten percent tithing come from? Because it's not in the new covenant."

Randy's jaw tightened. "The Bible does say to give the best of the firstborn, and the first of our crops."

"Of course. We ought to give our best to God. But what happens when someone gives their skills? Say, as a cook, or a tradesman, or an accountant? Or they give food, or maybe clothes? The verse is about quality, not quantity."

Simon noticed Randy's expression twist into contempt.

"You can look in Titus 3:9–11, 1 Timothy 4:1, Matthew 7:15–23, Matthew 24:24, and 2 Corinthians 11:13."

He really just pulled that? Simon thought to himself.

He noticed the unease of the other people around him. "Randy, those verses all have to do with sowing discord in the church. I'm not trying to cause problems. I'm just asking questions to try and understand why you're making the claims you are, because they make no sense to me and have no biblical support, yet you're claiming the Bible supports it."

Randy's face went red.

Let's bring it home.

"The last verse I wanted to talk about is Acts 5, the part about Ananias and his wife Sapphira. They sold excess property and hid a large portion of the earnings while giving a small portion. Keeping a portion, no matter how sizable, wasn't wrong. What was wrong was that they lied about how much they were giving to make themselves seem to be more righteous, after having seen how the disciples praised others who gave much from selling their excess. They lied directly to God, claiming a righteousness that wasn't theirs to claim, and they died as a result. This verse has nothing to do with giving set amounts, nor does it concern socialism, as your pastor said in the sermon he gave in August. It seems to me this passage was chosen specifically to scare people without giving any context for it at all."

"Get out."

"Why? I just want to understand and get some answers. You're acting like that Jehovah's Witness church that excommunicated a child for asking questions. Do you have any answers for me, or is everything just company policy, the truth in the Bible be damned?"

"How dare you!"

Poor word choice.

Simon raised an eyebrow and continued calmly. "I'm trying to understand how this is any different than the Pharisees and moneychangers on the steps of the temple who Jesus kicked out and rebuked." He looked around at the other people. "For those who don't know the context, the Pharisees would turn away offerings, then say that they could buy good ones from the moneychangers and those selling doves. You know, they probably had to pay rent to use the steps." He returned his gaze to Randy. "I wonder if rent was ten percent of their income."

"Get out of here, now!"

Simon smiled and gripped the edge of the table, slowly struggling to his feet. He grabbed his crutches as he spoke. "The Bible tells us there are many people who cast out demons and perform miracles in the name of Jesus, yet he doesn't know. We are supposed to be mindful of false prophets and false teachers, because they can lead us away from the Father. Something to take to heart."

Randy fumed but managed to keep his mouth shut as Simon left, Delta at his side.

TWENTY-TWO

SIMON PULLED UP to his parents' house and got out, his prosthetic leg now affixed. He grabbed the crutches from the back seat and Delta followed him in. He left the crutches by the front door, then walked in to find Ray sitting in the living room with Mark.

"How'd it go, Simon?" his dad asked.

Simon's gaze flicked to Mark, but he sat down. Delta lay at his foot. "I don't think I accomplished anything."

"Oh?" Ray's eyebrows shot up. "You did your research?"

Simon nodded. "Yeah. I was even ready for when he threw some verses about sowing discord in the church at me."

"But…?"

"He got pissed and threw me out."

"And the other people in the room?" Ray asked.

"Uncomfortable. I don't think any of them have seen debate over the Bible before or had their own faith challenged, which…" Simon sighed. "They'll probably just keep following their pastor without question."

Ray grunted.

"I may have also compared the instructor to that JW church that excommunicated a kid for asking questions," Simon added.

"Ah, yes," Ray murmured.

"I also may have worded a couple other things that didn't help."

"Like?"

Simon recounted the whole session.

Ray let out a breath. "Well. I can't say that's how I would've done it, but the points are still true."

"It's better than how I would've done it," Mark remarked. "Simon's always known the Bible way better than me." He turned to his son. "Whenever you had a question, you'd throw yourself into finding the answer. Your Bible got so worn out that it looked like my great-grandfather's."

Ray chuckled. "I wish I'd been that studious when I was younger."

"I didn't like not knowing," Simon said simply.

"Mark, mind if I talk to Simon for a minute?" Ray asked.

Mark nodded. "Sure. Just don't try to start any more wars. I think he's fighting on enough fronts as it is."

Ray smiled. "I'll do my best."

"We can use my room," Simon said. "That is, if the subject is that private."

"Sure," Ray said.

Mark spoke up. "Also, Simon?"

Simon looked at his father. "Yeah?"

"Fairly certain that dog of yours knocked up Daisy."

"Oh." Simon looked down at Delta.

"Not really a problem," Mark said. "We have a couple of dogs, and now I guess we'll have some more. Just thought you'd like to know. And of course you're welcome to some of the pups."

"Thanks," Simon replied. "I'll keep that in mind."

Simon and Ray went up to his room. When Simon closed the door, Ray took a moment to look around the space. "Quite clean."

"Military drills it into you," Simon remarked as he sat on the bed.

He gestured to a chair at the desk and Ray sat on it backwards.

"What did you learn?" Ray asked.

"I don't know what you mean."

"Hmm. Let me rephrase it: how did you feel while doing it?"

Simon thought for a moment. "It was fun, I guess. Exposing lies and deception. Felt good to know that I was standing up for Tyler."

Ray snapped his fingers. "Right there."

Simon raised an eyebrow. "What?"

"You're a protector. Like a shepherd dog."

"Sure."

"I heard from Carson that you once helped him out of a tight spot," Ray said. "And that you did the same for Eggsy, and another guy who works for you... Roman, I think he said."

Simon narrowed his eyes. "What all did he say?"

"He didn't get into details. Only that they owe you their lives."

"Yeah, well." Simon cleared his throat. "They got a rotten deal. I was just trying to make it a little less rotten."

"Exactly. You stood up for them. Helped them out of whatever it was they were facing, probably at a cost to yourself."

Simon let out a breath through his nose, his hands firmly planted on the bed. "What's this about, Ray?"

"Come to church this Sunday."

"I'm working on your house, not to mention hosting you. I don't think it's a good idea, considering my current track record."

CHAPTER TWENTY-TWO

"I think we can both be adults about it if you find it's not the place for you."

Simon looked down at his hands. "I don't think I can go to your church."

Ray tilted his head. "Why not?"

Simon was quiet, and then Ray noticed the picture frame next to the bed that was face-down.

He stood up and reached for it. "May I?"

Simon shrugged.

Ray picked up the photo and saw a younger, more whole Simon standing next to a lovely young woman.

Ray's gaze softened. "That's how you know Neil."

Simon could only nod and offer a one-word response. "Yeah."

Ray set the picture back down, upright this time. "Well, I understand your concerns. You should try to meet with Neil once a week at least, though. He could really use it."

Simon looked up at Ray for a moment, then nodded. "I'll try."

"Good man." Ray lightly gripped Simon's shoulder.

When Ray left the room, Simon took out his phone and pulled up Neil's contact. His thumb hovered over the call icon for a moment. He finally locked the screen and put it away.

Instead he grabbed one of his gun cases, took out a handgun, and started to go through the process of stripping it down on his desk, methodically examining and cleaning each piece.

———————————

The next afternoon, Simon drove into town. Anxiety ran its fingers along his heart, but he tried to dissuade the feeling as he focused on Neil's open invitation.

He eventually pulled up to Neil's home to find Mary's car already parked out front, reminding him of her weekly routine.

He got out of his truck with Delta and walked up to the door. When he knocked, Mary opened it with a bright smile on her face.

"Hey Simon!"

He couldn't match her enthusiasm. "Hey Mary."

She stepped to the side. "Come in."

Simon entered and saw Neil sitting in the living room, a newspaper in hand.

"I'm just about done for the day," Mary said as she walked towards the kitchen. "So I'll be out of your hair in just a bit."

"No need to rush." Simon sat on the couch.

"Welcome back, Sye." Neil set down his newspaper. "How's things?"

"Well enough, I guess,"

Mary started to putter around, tidying up the room.

Simon noticed the medical bracelet on Neil's wrist. "What's that about?"

"My new ball and chain," Neil said with a sigh. He cleared his throat, coughed, then cleared his throat again. "This cough has lasted a little longer than expected, so they want to have my information ready or something. Apparently I'm allergic to most meds that help with this."

"Huh."

"So what's new?"

Simon returned his gaze to Neil. "Just got kicked out of another church."

Neil took a sip of his coffee and raised an eyebrow. "Oh yeah?"

"It was partly the goal." Simon paused, then took in a breath. "Well, it was expected."

Neil maintained his expectant expression as Simon explained the situation.

"Ah," Neil remarked when Simon finished. "Yeah. Getting kicked out would be the expected outcome."

Mary piped up as she reached the stairs. "You know the Bible that well?"

Simon looked over at her. "I do my research."

"Hmm," Mary murmured as she walked upstairs.

"So what's the plan now?" Neil shifted to get more comfortable in his seat.

"What do you mean?" Simon asked.

Neil shrugged. "I mean, what are you going to do? You've been invited to a good church, with good people. You're already reading into the Bible again."

Simon glanced away. "I–I can't go."

Neil's gaze softened. "Sye, it's just a room."

Simon looked up sharply. "How...?"

"It's not a matter of what you believe. You can still go to church and try to figure it out. You've gone around to other churches, so it's not a problem with church. That just leaves the specific room."

Simon was quiet.

"And that's all it is, Simon. A room. One where I got the opportunity to give my final goodbyes to my wife and daughter. Where you got the opportunity to say goodbye to Heather."

Simon looked down at his hands.

Neil smiled. "Come to church this Sunday, Sye. You can even sit with me if it'll help."

Simon didn't respond at first. Just the thought of the Foundations Church's sanctuary gave fuel to the anxiety scratching at his heart.

"We'll see."

TWENTY-THREE

ALL SOUNDS OF work met a swift end at the Torrington site as Simon walked into the house. Most of the workers immediately walked out for their smoke break, passing him by without meeting his gaze. He withheld his vexation and took the opportunity to inspect their work.

"No Delta today, *hermano*?"

Simon glanced back at Carson. "Hailey had the day off. She's keeping him company."

The Mexican national watched Simon for a moment as he inspected the work. "You good, *hermano*?"

"No, I'm not. We're well behind schedule. And what the hell is this?"

Carson followed Simon's accusatory finger. "Are we seeing the same thing, *hermano*?"

Simon fought to keep a growl of frustration from rising in his throat. "This drywall seam is cracked. Wasn't this taped properly?"

"*Si*, it was taped properly. That isn't a seam, though, *hermano*. The seams are above and way to the side of that. One of the guys tripped and fell into it. We're lucky it isn't a hole."

"What happened?" Simon snapped.

Carson shrugged. "Someone left their tools on the floor."

Rage built up deep within Simon. "Who?"

"You did."

Simon's whole being ground to a halt and he stared at Carson as if he'd been slapped. "What's going on, *hermano*?"

After a moment, Simon looked down at his hands. "Who all knows about this?"

"Everyone onsite."

Simon's shoulders dropped. "Damn."

"You've been on edge since you got your leg back last week. What's going on?"

Simon couldn't meet his gaze. "Nothing."

"If you don't want to tell me, that's fine. But don't lie to me, huh?"

Simon kept his gaze away from Carson.

"You look like you haven't slept in forever. If you need to take some time, I've got this handled."

Panic dug its claws into Simon's heart. "No."

"Simon…"

Simon barely managed to meet Carson's gaze.

"Your job is to manage. You helping onsite is extra, and we all respect you for it since you usually know what you're doing, but right now it'd be good to take a step back. Reset. You've lit the candle at both ends and in the middle."

"I can't step back."

"Why?"

"Winston's managing me out."

Carson blinked. "What makes you say that? You're better at this than his sons."

"He restricted me to this site, sent his sons to get started on all the other sites I brought in, and keeps telling me not to push myself. What else am I supposed to think?"

"That he knows you're dealing with some heavy *mierda* and he wants you to take it easy. The only reason he isn't forcing time off is because he knows you'd go *loco*."

Simon shook his head. "Did he tell you that?"

"No," Carson replied. "But I've known both you and Winston for a few years now. It's the kind of man he is, and the kind of man you are."

Simon's frown only deepened.

Carson sighed. "Whether you believe it or not, that's what I think. Also, if he is managing you out, there is nothing you can do to change it. So you might as well enjoy the pay and new-found free time. You only need to check in once a day here. Otherwise I'll call you if we need anything else, *comprende*?"

"All right. Where'd my tools end up?"

"In the front closet. Was most out of the way."

"Thanks."

"Of course, *hermano*."

Simon went to the closet, grabbed his toolbelt, and walked outside. He tossed the toolbelt in the backseat before getting in his truck and driving off.

As he drove through town, the honks, roaring engines, and noxious fumes of automobiles only served to give him a headache instead of the peace he sought. He eventually came to a red stoplight and drummed his fingers on the steering wheel.

A school bell rang in the distance. For most, it meant lunch. For Simon, something snapped inside him. His heart raged in his ears. Chest tightening, stomach twisting, his eyes darted about, searching for everything and finding nothing. His breath was quick—

—and got knocked from his lungs at the sound of a car horn. He veered into a parking lot and came to a lurching stop.

The honker pulled alongside him. A man got out, shouting. Simon stared at the white man, but the language he heard was Arabic. Simon clutched at his ears and curled over. His ears rang as the man continued to scream.

CHAPTER TWENTY-THREE

"Leave him alone!" a woman shouted from somewhere just outside Simon's perception.

The man turned on her. "He almost—"

"Sir, take a second and actually *see* him."

The man went quiet as he focused on Simon. He just snorted and left.

A hand lightly touched Simon's shoulder through the truck's window and he recoiled.

"Simon?" Her hand settled on his shoulder, her touch gentle. "It's Mary…"

When he didn't respond, she stepped up on the runner and reached for his keys. She turned off the truck.

"I'll bring my car around," she said. "Just wait right here. I'm taking your keys. Okay?"

He didn't respond.

Soon enough she came back in her car. She got out and realized that Simon remained in exactly the same condition as when she'd left. Tears streamed down his cheeks and he'd started to shake.

"Come on," Mary coaxed. "Let's go to Neil's."

Again, he didn't acknowledge her. She watched him helplessly for a moment, then leaned in and gave him a hug. He weakly struggled against her, but she didn't let go.

"What do you need, Simon?"

His tremors didn't subside.

She gently stroked his hair. "Simon, you're safe. What can I do for you?"

"Can't. Breathe." He barely choked out the words.

"Focus on my breathing, okay? Can you do that for me?" She took in slow breaths and let them out. "Focus on my breathing, Simon. Nothing else."

His breathing slowed to match hers.

"Good job, Simon. I'm proud of you. Think you can move?"

He nodded and she took a step back.

"Come on," she said. "I'll take you someplace quiet."

As Simon hesitantly got out of his truck, she grabbed his phone and rolled up the windows of the truck. Then she locked the doors.

"It's okay, Simon," she said as she opened her passenger door. "You're safe."

He stared at the seat, voices screaming in his ears. He fought against them. The sounds of vehicles and horns lashed out at him as he became aware of them once more.

Simon got inside her car, practically jumping to get it over with.

She closed the door and got in the driver's seat. "Are you hot or cold, Simon?"

"C–cold."

She turned up the heat and drove slowly through traffic.

TWENTY-FOUR

SIMON FOUND HIMSELF in the hallway of a middle school, clearing rooms. A gunshot rang out and Simon ran towards it. He stopped outside the library, took in a breath, and burst through the door with his sidearm. He saw a gun.

"Drop it!"

Simon's gaze was so focused on the gun as it turned on him that only after he had squeezed his own trigger did he see the child behind it—

———————————

Simon shot up in bed, breathing heavily. Darkness crushed in on him and sweat soaked through his clothes, making them cling to his skin. He fought to bring his breathing under control, but panic overwhelmed him.

"Hey Simon."

His head whipped to the left, but he couldn't make anyone out in the darkness.

"It's Mary."

She turned the lights on low and his eyes slowly adjusted. She sat on the edge of his bed as he continued to hyperventilate.

"Focus on my breathing, Simon." She breathed slow and loud, and Simon managed to get his breathing under control. She smiled and touched his arm. "Good job, Simon. Do you remember yesterday?"

He shook his head.

"You had a panic attack while driving. I happened to see you and brought you here to ride it out somewhere quiet."

"Where's here?" His voice didn't sound like his own.

"My house," she said. "It was closer than anywhere else I could think of."

He looked down at his hands, then searched his pockets.

"I've got your keys. Your phone's here too." She handed him his phone. "Your mom called. She was a little panicked when I answered, but I explained the situation to her."

CHAPTER TWENTY-FOUR

"You…?"

"No details," she said gently. "Just that it was better for you to rest than keep driving."

He stared down at the darkened screen of the phone. When he spoke softly, his voice almost broke. "Thanks."

"Of course," she said as she stood up. "I'm going to make some breakfast. Come out when you're ready."

He silently nodded.

"Also, you'll want to put your leg back on."

He looked down at his stump, watching as she picked up the prosthetic from the floor and laid it next to him on the bed.

"You were tossing and turning so much, I didn't want you hurting yourself with it."

After she left the room, he sat in silence for a while, his mind racing. Eventually he affixed the prosthetic and stood up.

Opening the door, he was forced to shield his eyes from the light. He blinked away the brightness and then slowly made his way down the hallway. There were no pictures on the walls, but the smell of food drew him forward.

He stepped into a great room and stopped as his eyes settled on the massive kitchen. He acclimated himself as the sound of Mary's soft singing wafted over to him mixed with the smell of breakfast.

She glanced over her shoulder. "Feel free to sit where you like, island or table."

He hesitantly sat on a stool at the island. She resumed her singing, then finished making their breakfast and soon set a plate before him.

"Lord, thank you for today, and for the people around us," she began, cracking her eye open to peer at him. "Please guide us where we need to be and help us see your love in all its forms, as it's easy to get lost in the world around us. Bless this food to our bodies. Amen."

"Amen," he echoed.

She got a plate of her own food and began to eat when his phone went off. He took it out and frowned at the number on the display.

"Aw crap," he murmured as he lifted the phone to his ear. "Hey Winston. Yeah. Sorry about that." He was quiet. "No, I–I'm fine. I'll be—"

Mary eyed him, seeing his expression darken. She snatched the phone.

"Mary—!"

"Hi Winston," she said warmly. "I'm Mary. I help Ray out a lot at the church. I need to borrow Simon today, is that okay? Can Carson handle it? Thank you so much. Have a wonderful day, Winston. God bless."

Simon stared at her as she handed the phone back.

"He's worried about you," she said.

"He's trying to make me quit."

Mary tilted her head. "That's not what it sounded like to me."

"He cut me down to a single site," Simon said. "He wouldn't be doing that if he meant to keep me around."

"He would if he was worried about you and wanted to ease your load a bit so you can work through things."

His gaze snapped up to her.

She smiled as she leaned against the island. "He doesn't want to fire you, and he doesn't want you to quit. He wants you to be happy and healthy, so you can work again. And because you're his friend."

"How do you know?"

"Because I do," she said simply. "And it's not because I only ever see the best in people. I'm not that naïve."

His jaw tensed up.

"Now, because you're clearly a workaholic, I'm going to keep you busy today."

"I'm not a workaholic."

Her eyebrows shot up. "Really? Either way, you've got the day off now, and I'm sure you wouldn't want to sit on your hands."

He held her gaze, then sighed. "Doing what?"

"Helping me help people. We'll be doing some cleaning and cooking. You can cook, right?"

"Yeah."

"Good. Do you have a change of clothes in your truck?"

"No."

"Then you can have a shower and borrow some of my dad's clothes."

He was quiet and still as she finished her meal.

"Eat up, Simon. It's going to be a long day if you don't have fuel in the tank."

He set to his food as she walked off and put her dish in the dishwasher. With that, she left the kitchen, disappearing down the hall.

When she came back, she was dressed for the day.

"My parents' room is the third one on the right," she remarked.

Simon nodded and went into the bedroom she had indicated. He glanced about the clean room and frowned to himself.

Even after they've passed, she still keeps this room clean? he asked himself.

He opened the walk-in closet and started looking through the clothes on the man's side. If they were going to be cleaning and cooking, then jeans and a T-shirt would be best…

Once he found what he was looking for, he dressed and went into the ensuite to fix his bedhead. That's when he noticed the makeup supplies on the counter. He picked up a container of foundation and noticed that it had been bought recently. The container was running low.

Does she use her parents' room now? Why not just call it hers?

Simon shook his head. It wasn't his business.

He went back into the bedroom and noticed the wedding picture of a man and woman on the bedside table. The woman's face was concealed by a veil, but the man shared some of Mary's features.

He walked back out to join her.

"Ready to go?" she asked.

"As I'll ever be."

"Good."

TWENTY-FIVE

THE SMALL-TOWN scenery passed like a blur to Simon, despite Mary's cautious driving.

"The first stop is Mrs. Knox," Mary explained. "She absolutely adores people, and for the most part she just needs someone to talk to since she's not as mobile as she used to be. I often just clean up or do some other busy work when she isn't baking."

Mary parked her car in front of a modest one-story house. The lawn had been recently mowed and the small garden immaculately kept. Its red stone bricks had long ago faded and the once-white shutters had cracked and peeled in places to reveal the sun-bleached wood underneath.

Mary got out of her car. "Keep her company while I do my rounds and take care of things she shouldn't be doing. She lives for meeting new people." She smirked. "You'll love her."

Simon hesitantly followed Mary up to the front door, where she took out a key and opened it. She knocked on the door as she entered.

"Mrs. Knox? It's Mary!"

Simon glanced about the entry and living room, noting the dated furniture and photos of a middle-aged man and woman along with a young man in an army uniform. The smell of fresh-baked goods permeated the air.

A woman reminiscent of the one in the pictures came out of another room and stared at them for a moment.

Suddenly her eyes lit up. "Mary! Is it Friday already?"

"It is," said Mary warmly.

Mrs. Knox raised a shaky hand to her chin. "I could've sworn you were here just yesterday—"

"Then you get to have me two days in a row." Mary teased. "And I brought someone."

Mrs. Knox's eyes flicked up to Simon. "You finally found yourself a boyfriend! C'mere, lemme look at you!"

Simon glanced at Mary, wondering if she would set the record straight. In the meantime, he approached the older woman.

"He's just a friend, Mrs. Knox," Mary said with a smile. "He's got the day off, so he's helping me out. His name is Simon."

"A handsome young man like him doesn't go around to old people's homes to help a beautiful young woman if he doesn't like her."

"I don't know what to tell you, Mrs. Knox." Mary shrugged. "Is there anything that needs doing since I was last here?"

Mrs. Knox looked like she wanted to continue her line of thought, but she stopped herself. "Yes, now that you mention it. I may have used up the last of my flour. Would you be a dear and get me a new bag?"

"Of course," Mary said.

Mrs. Knox turned. "Let me just get my purse."

Simon turned to the door.

"Where do you think you're going?" Mary asked him.

"To help with the flour."

"I'm not that helpless." She flashed a playful smile. "Like I said, keep her company."

Simon swallowed, then nodded. "All right."

Mrs. Knox came back with a twenty in her hand. "Here you are, dear." She looked at Simon. "And you can help me out in the kitchen."

"Play nice," Mary said as she turned to the door.

"I'm too old to play any other way," Mrs. Knox shot back with a chuckle. "Come on, Simon."

Once Mary had left, Simon took in a breath and followed their host into the kitchen.

"So, Simon, how do you know Mary?"

"I'm in charge of a home reno for her pastor."

"You're the one doing that? I've heard only good things."

"You go to Foundations?"

Mrs. Knox nodded as she gripped the handle of the oven door and leaned down to peer through the glass. "My whole life. If we had our own cemetery, I'd be on the list to get buried in it."

Simon shifted uncomfortably.

She straightened as she looked back at him. "Oh come now, Simon. You're allowed to laugh and smile. I'm fairly certain on where I'm headed, so it's something I look forward to. Now, I need a taste-tester." She walked over to the fridge and took out a few bins, then set them on the table. "The church Thanksgiving sale is coming up and I need to make sure I've still got it."

Simon looked over the cookies, brownies, pie, and buns that had been laid out. "Uh…"

"It won't kill you," she said with a chuckle. "But I'll pray over it first, just to be safe."

Mrs. Knox closed her eyes and bowed her head.

"Dear Lord, thank you for this new day to share with the people around me, and for letting me meet young Simon here." She cracked an eye open. "Please make sure my baking doesn't kill him, even though you know it's the best baking in the best state. Amen."

Simon couldn't help but smirk as she handed him a cookie.

"This is really good," he said with his mouth full.

"Is it?"

He nodded. "Yeah. Reminds me of some cookies I made last year for the guys at Christmas. Though these are better. You added cinnamon and paprika, right?"

She raised an eyebrow. "You bake?"

"And cook and clean. I'll make a great housewife someday."

Mrs. Knox laughed. "I'm sure you will, Simon. So you and Mary…?"

"No. I've gone through as many relationships in my life as I have churches in the past month, so I'm not looking, and I don't think she is either."

"Pity," she murmured. "You won't stay young forever."

"Youth doesn't amount to much when you're less than whole," Simon replied as he reached for a brownie.

She glanced at his leg. "Did you serve?"

"Marines. After getting pulled out of Afghanistan, I was assigned to the embassy in Jerusalem."

"My son was in the army," Mrs. Knox said. "A medic."

"Where is he now?"

"With the Lord."

Simon lowered the brownie. "I'm sorry for your loss."

"Thank you," she said. "He saved his squad, they told me. I didn't want the details. I knew they would be bad. But they did tell me that." Tears touched her eyes. "My boy did me proud." She sniffed. "Thank you for your service, Simon."

Simon's gaze dropped and he shifted his weight off his prosthetic. "You're welcome."

"Now try that brownie before I eat these all myself."

He smiled as he set to the task of taste-testing each of the baked goods on display.

"Ray told me that people didn't like him much at the start," he remarked after several minutes had passed.

"Oh yeah," Mrs. Knox said. "Well, I'm sure you can understand our trepidation."

Simon raised an eyebrow.

"He's from California," she explained. "And the church he came from was… less than biblical. Some left right away, without even hearing what he had to preach. More left when he started changing up the structure of the church a bit too much."

"I heard him mention deacons."

"Oh, that's just a title for a helper," Mrs. Knox said dismissively. "Assistant pastors or what have you, but we had those before. He actually considered renaming the position, but he chose not to in the end."

They heard the front door open.

"In any case, I'm very happy with Ray and the changes he made. We're properly going through the Bible with him instead of just doing the same circuit of lessons every year."

A moment later, Mary waltzed into the kitchen carrying a bag of flour. She opened a tall drawer and stashed the bag inside.

"Is there anything else?" Mary asked.

CHAPTER TWENTY-FIVE

"Not at all, dear. Simon here has already done everything I need."

"You sure?"

Mrs. Knox nodded. "Completely. See you Sunday, Mary." She turned her gaze to Simon. "I hope to see you there too."

"We'll see," he said.

A smile touched Mrs. Knox's thin lips. "Thanks again, both of you. Have a blessed day."

It wasn't long before Simon and Mary had stepped back out through the front door and aimed themselves at the car in the driveway.

"She's nice," Simon mentioned as they got into the car.

Mary smiled. "She is. Now we're off to Neil's. I missed him yesterday."

"Sorry."

"There's nothing to be sorry for." Mary started the engine and pulled out onto the street. "And it's not like he's helpless."

"Are all the people you help like these people?"

"What do you mean?" she asked.

"Lost their spouse and kids?"

Mary shrugged. "Some. One way or another, they're alone. Speaking of, where's Delta?"

"He got one of the farm dogs pregnant, so I thought I'd let him spend some time at home today."

"Congratulations to him," Mary said. "But since they're domesticated, there isn't much for him to do. Also, isn't he sort of a support dog for you?"

Simon frowned. "I don't—"

A sudden burst of lights and the scream of a siren blared out behind them, cutting him off midsentence.

Mary pulled over to the side of the road. "I was within the speed limit…"

Simon glanced back and narrowed his eyes at the two cops who were climbing out of the cruiser. He studied their body language as they approached.

"Do everything slow," he advised. "Don't give them more information than you need to. When they ask why they pulled you over, say that you don't know. Give your licence and registration when asked, and then ask for permission to reach into the glovebox. Otherwise don't say anything for any reason."

"Simon? What's going on?"

"I don't know, but they're on edge. Just remain calm. And as soon as you can, ask to leave." He hesitated a moment. "If they take me away, just continue on to Neil's. Everything will be just fine."

At last the cops reached the car and Mary lowered her window.

"Ma'am, please keep your hands on the steering wheel," the first cop said.

Mary blinked. "Okay…?"

Simon bristled as the second cop appeared right next to his door. "Sir, please step out of the vehicle and move towards mine."

Simon frowned but complied.

Before Mary knew what was going on, she looked through the rearview mirror and saw the cop placing Simon in handcuffs. Shocked but forcing herself to remain calm, she turned to the cop on her side of the car.

"Why are you arresting him?" she asked.

"Ma'am, did he force you to do anything?"

"What? No."

"He hasn't hurt you or threatened you in any way?"

"No!" Mary exclaimed. "What's this all about?"

"I'm sorry, ma'am, but for now we can't say. Why were you travelling with him?"

She opened her mouth to speak but then remembered Simon's instructions. "Do I need a lawyer?"

The cop raised an eyebrow. "Ma'am, you are not being detained."

"Then I'm free to go?"

"We'd appreciate it if you came down to the station for a statement. But yes, you are free to go."

She looked back as Simon was put into the back of the police car. "Fine. I'll come to the police station."

TWENTY-SIX

THE INTERROGATION ROOM was quiet, save for the soft tapping of the cop's fingers on his phone. Simon sat there, calm and collected, waiting.

"Need anything?" the cop asked.

Not a word slipped past Simon's lips.

"Water?"

Still, silence held his tongue. The cop shrugged and continued tapping on his phone.

Suddenly the door opened and a middle-aged man entered wearing a simple suit with a navy blue tie.

"I need a minute with my client," the man said.

The cop glanced at the lawyer, who produced a card.

After examining the card, the cop nodded. "Of course."

The cop got up with a soft grunt and left the room.

The lawyer sat down beside Simon. "Did they question you?" Simon warily watched the lawyer, who stared back. "Who are you?"

The lawyer took out his credentials and showed them to Simon. "Lionel Avery. Mary called me. Have they said what you're being charged with?"

"Rape."

Lionel slowly nodded. "Did they give a date of the incident, witness reports, who the victim even is…?"

Simon shook his head. "No. They asked me about my ex-girlfriend and when I last saw her, so she's probably involved in some way."

He explained what had happened to Lionel.

"I see," Lionel said. "Is there any proof of your last conversation with her?"

"I recorded it. The device it's recorded on is at home. If you call my dad, he'll be able to bring it here. I also changed banks and listed the condo. The investigators can check those records to get more context, if you think it'd help."

Lionel took out his phone and Simon gave him the number to his parents' place. Lionel then stepped outside the room and made the call.

The lawyer returned about an hour later, after having an opportunity to ask some questions of the cops.

"This whole case is shaky at best," Lionel said. "And to protect you, I would say we don't want this going to court. It could ruin your life even if you're exonerated, and you'd have no recourse against Susan."

"So she did call this in?"

"No, it was a man who wished to be anonymous. The whole thing is ridiculous. They shouldn't have been able to arrest you on something so flimsy. Do you have any enemies in the police department?"

Simon frowned. "I can only think of one, but he's in Austin right now."

"Name?"

"Sam Bulk."

Lionel blinked. "Captain Sam Bulk?"

"Yeah. I may have hit him a few years ago. He was preventing me from handling an active shooter situation in an elementary school."

Lionel sighed. "One of your arresting officers is a man named Luke Bulk."

"Hmm. His brother, I think. So the whole thing is fabricated?"

"No," Lionel said. "Well, maybe. I listened to the recording of the call. The caller mentioned Susan Quinlan by name. Either way, you're walking out of here today."

Simon nodded, his gaze on the table.

"But Simon, I do need to ask—"

"No, I didn't do it."

"All right."

The door suddenly opened and the cops came back into the interview room.

"I immediately request that Officer Bulk be removed from this case," Lionel said. "He has a personal vendetta against my client for an incident that happened some time ago between my client and his brother."

The one cop looked at the other. "You know this guy?"

Luke scowled. "Unlike your client, I'm a good cop. I don't let my personal feelings get in the way of my job."

"That statement in and of itself proves his prejudice," Lionel said. "My client has been compliant up until this point. Now, once Officer Bulk has been removed, I'd ask that Mr. Fletcher Sr. be brought in with the recording device in question."

Luke was about to speak, but the other cop turned to him. "Just go. Let's get this done so we can return to work."

Another scowl from Luke, but eventually he left with clipped steps.

The other cop went to the door and waited there for Simon to follow. "Mr. Fletcher? Over here."

It wasn't more than a few minutes later that Mark showed up at the door and saw Simon. "You good, son?"

CHAPTER TWENTY-SIX

Simon shrugged. "We'll see."

Lionel stood up and held out his hand. "The recording device, please."

Mark handed it over.

"I'd like to give this a listen with my client first," Lionel said to the cop.

"Just play it," Simon said. "It'll be fine."

Lionel looked back at him. "I would recommend—"

"I know what's said on it. I was there."

Lionel looked down at the recording device and then set it on the table. "All right."

The lawyer pressed the play button, and for the next couple of minutes they all listened to the final conversation at the condo between Simon and Susan.

When it was finished, the cop let out a sigh. "I see…"

"This, and the financial records my client so cooperatively made available to you, should set this whole matter right. Not to mention, my client was not read his rights. I'm also overlooking the personal connection that Luke Bulk has to my client, which clouded his judgment, and the fact that Mr. Fletcher has been entirely cooperative."

The cop nodded. "Yeah, I get it, Mr. Avery." He turned his gaze to Simon. "You're free to go, Mr. Fletcher. Sorry for the inconvenience."

Simon stood up. "Thank you."

He walked out of the interview room with Mark and Lionel in tow. Once they'd walked down a hallway and emerged into the building's foyer, Simon laid eyes on Mary. She was pacing around the waiting area.

"Oh, thank God." She fell into step beside them as they walked outside. "And thank you so much for showing up, Lionel."

"No problem," Lionel replied. "But I've got a mountain of paperwork to get back to, so I'll see you Sunday."

"See you Sunday," Mary echoed.

The lawyer gave a single nod to Simon and Mark, then hurried towards the parking lot.

Simon, Mark, and Mary approached Mark's waiting truck.

"So?" Mark said before any of them got in.

Simon's expression was hard. "Nothing else could have been done, Dad. Even if this went to court. I'd be in trouble. You know the court is biased against men."

Mark sighed. "I know. I'm just trying to think of a way to end this conflict with your ex once and for all. I'm just sick of this witch trying to hurt you."

"We don't even know for sure it was her. The caller was anonymous. And one of those cops had a personal problem with me."

"But she kills my grandchild, tries to ruin my son…" Mark trailed off, his eyes clouding over.

"Mr. Fletcher?"

Mark blinked and turned to look at Mary as though for the first time. "Oh? Right. You are the one who called that lawyer."

Mary smiled. "Yes. Lionel goes to my church. I'm Mary."

"Mark," he replied. "Simon's dad."

"Pleasure to meet you," she said. "I just need to know whether Simon's going with you or me."

They both looked at Simon, who took in an indecisive breath. "Let's finish the day together, Mary."

"You sure?" she asked.

He flinched as a police siren flipped on nearby. He turned to look just as the offending cruiser screeched out of the parking lot.

Simon nodded. "Yeah."

"All right." Mary returned her gaze to Mark. "It was great getting to meet you, Mr. Fletcher."

"You too, Mary." Mark gave Simon a stiff hug, then quickly let go and cleared his throat. "See you at home, son."

Simon nodded rigidly. "See you."

They watched as Mark climbed into his truck. A moment later, he had started the engine and drove off.

"He cares a lot about you," Mary remarked.

Simon didn't look at her. "Yeah."

"Well, we've got to get to Neil," she continued. "Let's hit the road."

TWENTY-SEVEN

SCREAMS RIPPED THROUGH Simon's ears. He knew they came from within rather than without, but they tore at his soul nonetheless. He stared down at his hands, his gaze tracing the faded scars in a half-hearted effort to ignore the harrowing echoes of souls long since passed.

He jumped as a hand touched his shoulder, and his own hand darted up to grip the offending wrist. He went rigid as he saw his mother's wedding ring on one of the fingers. His eyes followed up the arm to his mother's pale face.

Shelby stood completely still, like a deer in headlights.

He quickly let go and cast his gaze away from her. "Sorry, Mom."

She watched him for a moment, then sat on the bed beside him. "It's okay, sweetie." She put her arm around his waist and gave him a side hug. "Is there a better way to get your attention when you're lost?"

"The safest option is throwing something at me."

She blinked a few times. "Throw something?"

"A ball of paper, a bunched-up rag, or a shirt. That sort of thing. It's how I wake up Delta when he's having a nightmare."

"Huh," she murmured. "I'll make sure I keep a cloth on me then."

They sat in silence for a time, until Delta suddenly ran into the room. He jumped up on Simon and licked his face.

"Hey, stop!" he protested.

Shelby laughed as Simon tried to bring Delta under control. "He missed you."

"I see that." Simon managed to wrestle Delta into a hug. "I missed you too, Delta."

The dog whined and Simon gently pushed him to the ground.

"Have you been good for everyone?" Delta barked and Simon petted him. "Mom, you wanted to know what's been going on?"

She rested her head on his shoulder. "It's not about knowing what's going on, Simon. It's about knowing my son and being here to support him. If telling me helps with that, I'm more than happy to listen."

Delta stared up at Simon, panting, and Simon held the German shepherd's gaze.

He took in a breath. "In the military, I shot a kid."

Shelby didn't move.

"She'd grabbed her father's rifle and shot me in the chest. She would've killed more people. So I protected my squad, and any civilians behind us."

Shelby lightly rubbed Simon's back.

"When I came back stateside, I became a police officer," he continued. "That ended because I decked my supervising officer. He physically restrained me from handling an active shooter situation in a school. We had all the people we needed, but he was a coward. And when I got to the school's library, I realized the shooter was another kid…"

He felt Shelby's hand move to his shoulder as she gently pulled him into a hug.

"The day before I came home, my ex-girlfriend, she… well, Susan and I had been trying to get pregnant for a year. She said she wanted kids. But then she used my own money to sterilize herself and get an…"

He let out a shaky breath and Shelby pulled him close. Delta rested his head on Simon's knee as he started to break down.

"She killed our child." Tears broke free from his eyes. "You deserve to know. You lost your grandchild too."

Shelby nodded as her own tears struck her cheeks. "I'm so sorry, sweetie. I can't even…"

Any other words she could have summoned died in her throat. Simon held onto her as she held him.

A voice interrupted them. "Simon, I—"

They looked up to see Ray standing in the doorway. He cleared his throat.

"It can wait," Ray quickly added.

Simon shook his head and straightened. "Nah, it's all right. What's up?"

Ray looked from Simon to Shelby. Before he could explain himself, Shelby stood up and wiped away a stray tear.

She patted Simon's shoulder. "Thank you for letting me grieve with you, sweetie."

Simon quietly nodded as his mom left the room.

Ray hesitantly took a step in. "Sorry for interrupting."

"No worries. Is—" Simon sniffed. "Is it something about the house?"

"No." Ray put a hand on the desk chair and Simon gestured for him to take a seat. "I've got some news of my own."

Simon raised an eyebrow. "What news is that?"

"Jillian was very happy with your visit," Ray said. "She called me up as soon as you left to say that she hopes to see you again."

"Jillian?" Simon asked in momentary confusion. Then a smirk tugged at the corners of his mouth. "Oh… Mrs. Knox. She's a lovely lady."

Ray laughed. "And one of my greatest sceptics early on. Also, Tyler called me back. He and his girlfriend have decided to leave that church."

"And their families?"

CHAPTER TWENTY-SEVEN

"Split on the issues," Ray said. "But they're talking about it."

Simon swallowed. "Good for them."

"Mary also had something to say about yesterday."

Simon froze up. Had she said something to her pastor about the arrest? About what had happened at the precinct?

"She hopes she'll get to snag you to help out again sometime," Ray said.

Simon fought to keep his sigh of relief inside. Besides, Lionel wouldn't share the details of the case with Mary or anyone else. Client confidentiality. That would keep him safe, at least for the time being.

Ray tilted his head. "What's going on, Simon?"

Simon's gaze flicked up and he remembered that Ray was a client of his, not his pastor. He couldn't help but feel that his relationship to that church was getting a little too close.

But Ray is a good man, he reminded himself.

Simon took in a breath. "I've got a hypothetical for you."

Ray leaned forward, the excitement clear in his eyes. "Hit me."

"Say you had a person come into your church. He didn't mean to cause trouble, but it always seemed to follow him somehow. What would you do with such a person?"

"What kind of trouble are we talking?" Ray asked. "Gangs, dealers…?"

"Nothing criminal, just interpersonal. Like, arguments… or doing something stupid that causes an overreaction. Or maybe someone from his past is looking to cause problems."

Ray smiled. "I'd try my best to mentor him, or perhaps I'd have one of the deacons mentor him, if they were better suited. I'd mediate any issues. In any conflict, if one person is unwilling to forgive and move on, I'd strongly recommend the other person leave. That kind of person doesn't belong in the church."

"What if the person who couldn't move on was already a church member?"

"I phrased it the way I did for a reason, Simon. I don't care how long someone attends my church. If they can't forgive and move on, they're not a believer. They're just a churchgoer. But this only applies to squabbles between people, no matter how legitimate they seem. Once we get to the level of a crime? Well, that leads to far more complicated issues."

A frown dragged down Simon's lips.

Ray continued. "But if this hypothetical man were to come to my church and find it wasn't the place for him, or if he realized he had a problem with me he hadn't realized before, then I wouldn't treat him any different. I wouldn't call his boss over it. I wouldn't cause him any problems. We all have enough on our plates. I want my best for others, even for people I can't stand…" He studied Simon contemplatively. "Though I have a feeling I would get along with this hypothetical man quite well. And if he happened to have a well-trained hypothetical dog, that dog would be more than welcome to come to church as well."

Simon smirked.

Ray stood up and clasped his shoulder. "I hope to see this hypothetical man on Sunday."

TWENTY-EIGHT

SIMON PULLED UP in front of Foundations Church on Sunday, Delta looking excitedly out the window. Simon stared at the building for a moment, the morning's nightmare still running through his mind.

At last he got out of his truck. The dog trotted after him.

Where is everyone? he wondered as he approached the front door. *Am I early for the service? Ray only left a few minutes ahead of me...*

He went inside and heard the worship team already beginning their warmup. He peered into the sanctuary, the usual dread clawing at him.

Delta looked up at him, then quietly whined and pawed at his master's leg. Simon blinked and looked down before reaching for the door handle. He couldn't turn it.

"Simon?"

Simon turned to see Neil walking up. The older gentleman's eyes were filled with confusion and disbelief, but the expression turned to relief.

"It's good to see you here," Neil added.

Simon rubbed the back of his neck. "Yeah, well... I thought I'd see what all the fuss is about."

"I see. Well, come on then. Help me find a seat."

Neil opened the door and Simon walked with him to a spot near the front. Neil eased himself down and Simon sat next to him. Delta lay next to Simon's foot, staring up at his master.

"Now I know what Mary meant," Neil remarked.

"Mary knew I was coming today?"

"She didn't say. Only that I should be early." Neil relaxed into his chair. "I'm glad I did. Somebody else might have snagged ya."

Simon frowned. "Snagged me?"

The worship team stopped for a break. During the interlude, one of the members approached them.

"Good morning, Neil," said the man who had been playing bass guitar. He shook Neil's hand. "How'd your week go?"

CHAPTER TWENTY-EIGHT

"Well, overall. Still creaking about as much as my house, though."

The man chuckled. "You aren't a spring chicken anymore, huh?"

Neil cackled. "I look forward to seeing you at my age, Aiden."

"I don't." Aiden turned his gaze to Simon and extended his hand. "Aiden Holland."

Simon shook his hand. "Simon Fletcher."

Aiden's eyes widened. "I knew you looked familiar."

"Have we met?" Simon took back his hand. "Have we met?"

"No, but you used to be a cop in Austin, right?"

"Yeah."

"I have nothing but respect for you. I wish I had ba—" Aiden paused. "Well, I wish I was more like you."

Simon frowned. "It, uh… wasn't a situation I'd wish on anyone."

Aiden's gaze dropped a bit. "I haven't answered any calls like that yet, but people are really messed up."

Simon nodded. "Yeah."

"Aiden!"

The bass player's head snapped towards the stage, where the worship leader was calling him.

"One sec." Aiden returned his gaze to Simon. "It was a pleasure to meet you."

"You too, Aiden."

Once Aiden had gone back up onto the stage, the band resumed their warmup.

Simon sat there quietly, his chest tightening. *They're all going to find out about that shooting. They're going to know I… well, nobody's going to want me here. They'll kick me out, even if Ray doesn't have a problem with me.* His chest tightened even further until his throat started to close up. *This was a bad idea. I shouldn't be here. I should leave—*

Delta put his head on Simon's lap, shutting down the self-destructive thoughts. Simon's throat loosened and his chest started to free itself, though a bit of tightness remained. He brought his breathing under control and then noticed that Neil was talking to another member of the congregation.

"Good morning, Simon," said Mrs. Knox. "Glad you could make it!"

Simon managed a smile. "Thanks, and good morning to you too."

The middle-aged woman nodded, then turned to go back to her own seat. In fact, Simon realized, the entire sanctuary had filled up by now. Where had the time gone?

The worship leader made a few announcements, then got right into the first song. After it ended, Ray went up to the front.

"Good morning, everyone!" he greeted them warmly. "We'll start with a prayer and then get into some more worship."

The pastor bowed his head.

"God, thank you for another day and for all that you provide for us. Please continue to guide us and help us come to better understand you. Please let your words be on my lips as we all try to come closer to you. Amen." Ray opened his eyes. "We'll do corporate prayer now. The offering bags will be passed around while I take requests. If you're new, don't feel any pressure at all to give. Now, are there any requests?"

Simon sat quietly and listened as prayer requests were offered up, Ray jotting them down and either nodding his head or asking questions. He prayed at the end of the process and then worship continued.

For the sermon, Ray read straight from the Bible and closed with two more songs.

Once the service had ended, people milled about, greeting one another. Many approached Simon to introduce themselves. He felt his chest tighten again as people surrounded him.

He felt a hand on his shoulder and turned to see Mary.

"Sorry guys," she said. "I need to borrow Simon for a bit."

Simon bid farewell to the people, including Neil, and swiftly followed Mary. She disappeared into the kitchen and started working.

"What did you need me for?" he asked.

"I thought you might need a breather."

"Thanks." He took a few breaths. "Can I help?"

"Mmhmm. That pot in the sink. I need it three-quarters full and then placed on the stovetop."

Simon started to fill the pot just as a middle-aged woman came into the kitchen and put on an apron.

"Already roping the new guy into helping out, huh?" the woman said.

Mary looked up. "Hey Isla."

"I offered," Simon said quickly.

Isla took a handful of vegetables out of the fridge and laid them on a cutting board. "You two know each other?"

"He's the one working on Ray and Beth's house," Mary said.

"Is that so?" Isla glanced at Simon. "Do you have a business card?"

Simon blinked. "Uh… in my truck."

"I'd happily take one," Isla said. "The basement of our house was never finished. No drywall, flooring, or any of that."

"I'll get a card for you before I leave."

"Wonderful."

As Isla began cutting the vegetables, she and Mary fell into a comfortable rhythm. They chatted for several minutes. Simon relaxed as he carried the pot of water to the stove.

"Anything else, Mary?" he asked.

"Nah, I'm good. Thank you, Simon."

"Then I'll go get that business card."

Simon walked to the front door, Delta at his side. His hand was on the handle when he heard Ray's voice calling after him.

"Leaving already?"

"Just getting a business card for Isla," Simon replied. "But after that, I don't know."

"How about we sit and have a chat?" Ray asked. "I'd love to hear your take on the sermon."

Simon thought for a moment, then nodded. "All right."

After grabbing a business card and bringing it back to Isla in the kitchen, he made his way to Ray's office. But Ray wasn't there and he was quickly met by another pack of church members. He'd barely gotten the chance to introduce himself when he sighed in relief to see Ray approaching.

"How is everyone?" Ray said. "Mind if I borrow Simon for a bit?"

When the congregants had dispersed, Ray gestured to his office and Simon followed him in. Delta settled onto the floor.

"Looking a little green there, Simon."

Simon averted his gaze. "Lots of new people all at once. Just a bit much."

"I always took you for an extrovert."

"It is what it is."

"So," Ray began. "The sermon?"

Simon shrugged. "You read some verses and explained them."

Ray raised an eyebrow.

"Most churches have their favourite lessons they repeat every year," Simon said. "Instead of teaching from the Bible, they just rip whatever they can from it to support their lesson, even if those verses mean something completely different when put back in context." Simon sniffed. "So I like what you did. But I didn't learn anything new."

Ray slowly nodded. "Fair enough. We do have Bible study on Tuesday night. We go into greater depth there."

"I might drop by."

"Glad to hear it." Ray smiled as he stood back up. "Well, I've got some more things to take care of. See you later, Simon."

"See you."

When Simon walked back out, it seemed that most of the people had gone home. He and Delta made their way to the door.

Mary came out of the kitchen and met them before they could leave. "Hey Simon. Wanna grab lunch?"

Simon went still. "Oh. Uh… I don't think that's a good idea."

She frowned, but then her eyes lit up. "Oh, no! I don't mean like a date. Just friends."

His hand froze on the handle as he thought about the invitation. He finally nodded. "Sure."

"Sweet. Just give me ten minutes to finish up here, okay?"

TWENTY-NINE

SIMON SAT ACROSS from Mary at Vera's, Delta at their feet. The waitress approached and eyed Mary for a moment before offering Simon a smile.

"What can I get for the two of you?"

"Beef dip and an iced tea," Simon said. "And a few extra slices of beef for Delta. Please and thank you, Emma."

"You got it, Simon. And you, miss?"

Mary glanced about. "Is there a menu?"

"There is," Emma said, but she didn't move.

"Special of the day is a chicken Caesar wrap, it looks like," Simon said.

"I'll have that, and an iced tea," Mary said warmly.

"All right. I'll be right back with your drinks." With that, Emma walked away.

Mary turned her gaze to Simon. "She likes you."

"I'm not catching that tiger's tail," Simon muttered.

Mary raised an eyebrow as Emma came back with their drinks and a small plate with beef on it to set under the table in front of Delta.

"I'm not on the market," Simon assured her when they were alone again.

"I figured. I'd be lying if I said I didn't overhear your conversation with Neil that first time."

Simon went quiet.

"You should also know Neil added you to our corporate prayer," Mary added. "He kept your name out of it, but…"

Simon sighed. "What did he say?"

"Just that a young man he knows lost his child."

"That's it?"

Mary nodded. "Yeah. I'm sorry."

He shrugged. "Not like you're responsible."

"Don't close up."

He blinked. "What?"

"The response you just gave… you're deflecting. It's a way to close up and defend yourself."

He stared at her and then chuckled. She frowned, not knowing what to make of that.

"I was finally able to tell my mother a couple days ago," he said after a moment. "And thank you."

Her face went red and she hooked some of her hair behind her ear. "Is that what the other day was about?"

Simon went quiet. He opened his mouth to speak, but suddenly Emma came by with their food.

"Here you are," the waitress said as she set the plates before them. "Is there anything else you need?"

"I'm all good," Simon said.

"Same," Mary added.

"Enjoy."

Mary redirected her gaze to Simon. "You were about to say something?"

She can't understand. That thought circled in his head like a murder of crows over a corpse.

"I can share first, if that'd help?" she said.

He cleared his throat and nodded. "Sure."

"My mother had panic attacks on a daily basis. They even turned into psychotic breaks near the end of her life. She became paranoid, even thinking that I was trying to steal my father away from her. Dad had to work a lot to pay for the medicine and doctor visits, so I basically homeschooled myself from Grade Nine on and took care of Mom and the house. Technically, I haven't graduated high school. In any case, I learnt how to manage her." Mary shifted. "Then, one day, my dad took two weeks off and paid for me to leave town for a vacation. A few days after that, while I was away, I got a call from the cops. Turned out my mother had shot my father, and she was in turn shot by the cops when she didn't surrender."

Simon stared at her, not knowing what to say.

"It's why I said that today's just about having lunch as friends," she said. "And everything else? Also just friends. Everything I've researched says my mom's condition is hereditary. So I do what I can to help who I can where I can… until I can't."

"Wow."

She tilted her head. "I've never gotten a 'wow' before."

"I don't mean… it's just…" He trailed off. "How do you stay so happy?"

Mary picked up her wrap. "It's about finding purpose."

"Where does God fit into all that?"

"How does he not? People messed up the world, so we have all the messed-up stuff. We just have to make the best with what we have and try to follow him."

He frowned and looked down at his food.

She lightly tapped his foot with her own. "It'll be a long day without fuel in the tank."

"Planning on putting me to work again?"

"No, why?"

"You said the same thing the morning before we went to see Mrs. Knox."

She blinked and then broke into a giggle. "It's something my dad always said when I wasn't eating."

They continued eating for a few minutes. Eventually he looked her straight in the eye and decided to explain what was going on with him. If she was being vulnerable, he may as well return the favour.

"Coming home has brought up a lot," he began. "I'm not sleeping well anymore. It's probably why I've been having panic attacks lately."

"Like, triggers from your time in the military?"

He nodded. "Yes, that. But not just that."

"You mean Heather?"

His shoulders dropped. "Yeah, Heather's one of the things."

"You two were...?"

"Dating. Since we were fifteen. Friends even before that."

Mary looked down at her now empty plate. "Sometimes it can be hard to see anything beyond what we've lost."

Don't tell her about what happened overseas, he thought, having to stop himself from coming clean about the rest of his story. *And don't mention the school shooting. Keep it to yourself. She doesn't need to know.*

But she understands loss, another part of him insisted. *She could understand—*

No. It doesn't matter. She's your first new friend in a long time, and she knows how to help during panic attacks. If you tell her you're a child killer, she may change her mind and stop helping you. She may think you're weak...

He took in a breath to stop his raging thoughts. "I'm still trying to figure out the reason behind everything that's happened. I can't see one."

Mary raised an eyebrow. "The reason?"

"You know, God has a plan, everything happens for a reason, all that. It just doesn't make sense to me."

"God does have a plan. But apart from that, it's a load of crap."

"What?"

"God didn't plan to make my mom crazy and kill my dad," she said. "He knew it would happen and planned around it."

Simon stared at her.

"God knows everything, right?" she said.

He nodded.

"Then his plans are based around everything he knows in advance. If everything happens for a reason, it's not because God forces it. It's just cause and effect. My mother's genetics caused her brain to degrade. The effect was that she went crazy. God's saddened by all this as much as we are, if not more. But if he just steps in and fixes everything, what choice do we have? If Jesus himself came down into this diner right this second, all glowing and spewing fire like Revelation describes, would you believe in him? Would you be able to doubt?"

Simon looked off to the side.

"That's what he's about: choice," she continued. "Most people misunderstand hell. Is it a punishment? Sure. There has to be a place for people who keep messing up unapologetically and flip him off. But it's really about giving people a choice. If someone wants nothing to do with God, then heaven would be hell for them, especially if heaven is how the Bible describes it. They'd be stuck being around God at all times. He made hell suck because he wants us to choose him, and because being without him…? Well, look at how bad the world has got with him removed from it. Imagine how much worse it'd be without him at all. That's hell."

Without saying anything, Simon picked up his fork and finished eating.

THIRTY

NEIL WOKE UP in the middle of the night, a coughing fit ripping through his lungs. He tried to get it under control, but it wouldn't stop. He fought through the episode until his lungs felt raw. Wheezing, he let out a rattling breath and wiped his mouth.

He leaned forward and switched on the lamp next to his bed. In the dim light, he looked down and saw his palm covered in phlegm.

"Please God," he rasped. "I'm not ready just yet."

He stood up and went into the bathroom to wash his hands and face. After looking at his reflection in the mirror, he drank some water and went back to bed.

Simon was just leaving the Torringtons' house with Delta when his phone rang. He looked down at the screen to see how it was, then brought it up to his ear.

"Hey Neil, what's up?"

"You have some time to drop by today?" the man asked.

Simon instinctively glanced at his phone schedule, then frowned as he remembered how clear it was.

"Yeah," he said. "I can be there pretty quick. See you in a few."

Simon made his way to Neil's to find an unfamiliar sedan parked out front. When he got inside, he heard Lionel's voice. The lawyer was seated with Neil in the living room, paperwork laid out on the coffee table in front of them.

Neil looked up. "Ah, Simon. You got here a little earlier than I expected. This is—"

"Lionel Avery," Simon said. "We've met."

Neil blinked a few times. "Right. Must've met him at church. In any case, this'll all be ready in a few minutes. Go ahead and get something to drink from the fridge, and something for Delta."

Simon went into the kitchen. He poured himself a glass of water, then filled a bowl for Delta. He returned to the living room and sat in an unoccupied chair.

CHAPTER THIRTY

"And then just sign here, Neil," Lionel was explaining.

Neil signed the paper in front of them and looked up at Simon. "Now it's your turn."

"My turn?" Simon asked.

"I've had Lionel help me get my will in order."

"Are you all right?"

"I'm well past the age where I should've done this, Sye." Neil took in a slow breath. "I just need to get things in order. One less worry."

Simon nodded. "All right. What am I signing?"

"Right now I'm adding your name to the deed of the house, and turning my bank account into a joint account. With you."

"That's not long-term thinking. That's short-term." Simon sighed. "You're looking to avoid the government's taxes."

"It's all just in case." Lionel set a fresh pair of papers in front of Simon. "All we need from you is to sign the deed, then sign into the joint account and transfer a thousand dollars in. Neil has already provided the cash here so you don't have to use your own money to do it. He's also named you as the beneficiary of any assets he has."

"And I don't have any debt," Neil added.

Simon stared down at the papers. "Why me?"

Neil leaned forward and patted Simon's hand. "You're the only family I have left, Simon. I want you to have it."

Simon met his gaze and held it. "All right. Where am I signing?"

Lionel led him through the paperwork, after which Neil took out a bundled roll of bills.

"And here's the thousand to put in."

Simon accepted the cash. "Got it. Now I've got to go to the bank?"

"That's right," Neil said. "I'll go with you. Just let me—"

When he was struck by another coughing fit, Lionel's expression turned grim. He patiently waited for Neil to finish coughing.

"All right, let's go." Neil stood up. "Thank you very much for your help with all this, Lionel. How much do I owe you?"

"Two hundred," Lionel said.

Neil's eyebrows shot up. "That seems a little cheap."

"Friends and family discount."

Neil slowly nodded. "All right. Come with us to the bank and I'll get us settled."

It didn't take more than an hour to get to the bank and complete the process, after which they bid farewell to Lionel. Neil then invited Simon to join him for lunch at a nearby restaurant.

"What kind of law does Lionel typically practice?" Simon asked as he took a seat in the booth.

"He was a divorce lawyer. When he found it didn't fulfill him, he changed direction. This is around the same time he started coming to church. Now he kind of just does a lot of different things."

"Huh."

"So I saw you heading out with Mary on Sunday."

Simon's gaze flicked up. "We're just friends."

"I'm aware," Neil said. "She's a good friend to have is all. Just glad you're surrounding yourself with good people. They can be hard to come by."

Simon frowned as the waiter set their food in front of them. Simon cut off a piece of his steak and gave it to Delta. "Yeah."

They ate in silence for a while, then paid for their food and left.

"Got anything else planned for the day?" Neil asked as they walked towards Simon's truck.

Simon shook his head. "No. I'm pretty much on vacation these days. I'm sitting on my hands to keep them from shaking."

"Ah. Well—"

Simon's phone went off and he swiftly answered it. "Hey Winston." He frowned. "How long? Got it. I'll check in on him."

Simon hung up with a sigh.

"Got plans now?" Neil asked.

"Yeah. I'll drop you off at home."

"Much obliged."

After bringing Neil back to the house, Simon drove to a nearby apartment complex. He saw Eggsy's truck in the parking lot as he made his way in through the front door, Delta at his side like usual.

He got up to Eggsy's door and knocked on it, but there was no answer.

He knocked again. "Eggsy?"

Simon looked up and down the hallway, then lifted the floor mat and was happy to see the key there. He unlocked the door and stepped in…

…only to find the entire apartment an absolute mess. Days-old dirty dishes sat in the sink and garbage lay cluttered on the floor. He stepped carefully over the debris and pushed open the bedroom door. Nobody there.

Delta's ears perked up and he barked. Simon looked at the dog and saw him sitting patiently in front of the bathroom door.

Simon tried the doorknob and found it locked.

"Hey Eggsy?" He knocked. "It's Simon. You all right in there?"

Hearing a soft groan come from inside, Simon knocked again.

"C'mon, Eggsy. I need you to answer me or I'm breaking down the door."

When he still got no response, he took a deep breath and kicked in the door.

THIRTY-ONE

SIMON KNELT NEXT to Eggsy's prone body, collapsed on the floor, and pulled the needle from his friend's arm.

"C'mon, Eggsy…" He lightly slapped Eggsy's face. "Wake up. Stay with me, buddy."

Eggsy's eyes fluttered open, but his gaze rolled all over. "Rena? What…? Rena, I told you…"

"It's Simon," he said as he glanced into the trash to find plenty more discarded needles. "All right, you aren't OD'ing at least. Let's get you to your feet."

"No… No! I don't… don't wanna…" Eggsy weakly fought against him. "L–leave me here!"

"Can't do that," Simon insisted as he pulled Eggsy to his feet. "Now come on. I'm taking you home."

"Home? No, no, no, no, no… Mom and Dad, they'll kill me!"

"My home. Your mom and dad won't be there. You'll be safe."

Eggsy tried to focus on Simon, but his vision blurred.

"C'mon, this way." He guided Eggsy to the couch in the living room. "I'll pack some of your clothes for you." He looked backwards for his dog. "Delta. Guard."

Delta walked closer and sat in front of Eggsy, staring at the drug-addled man.

"Stop staring at me, bruv," Eggsy remarked as Simon went into the bedroom. "I can feel you judging me. Stop it!"

Delta barked and Eggsy recoiled. The dog whined and rested his head on Eggsy's knee, which was trembling.

Simon came back out with a duffel bag over his shoulder. He grabbed Eggsy by the biceps. "All right, buddy. Up we go."

He pulled Eggsy to his feet and guided him out of the apartment. He locked the door behind them.

"He's judging me," Eggsy whispered.

"No, he's not," Simon assured him. "Nobody's judging you. You're perfectly fine."

"He thinks I'm worthless, just like my dad."

"He's a dog. He doesn't have thoughts that complex. And your dad is wrong."

They walked outside and Simon guided him to his truck. He opened the passenger door. "Come on, get in."

"No. No deathtraps!"

"I'll be driving," Simon said. "You'll be safe."

Eggsy looked towards Simon, though his eyes still couldn't focus. When Delta barked, the man jumped up onto the seat.

"Good man." Simon fastened Eggsy's seatbelt, closed the door, and let Delta up into the backseat.

A minute later, they were driving away. Simon placed a call to Clyde, but it went straight to voicemail.

Simon sighed and then placed the next call.

I didn't want to get Dad involved in this...

"Hey Simon," Mark said when he picked up. "What's up?"

"Who's there?" Eggsy demanded.

Mark went silent.

"Eggsy, I'm on the phone," Simon said to his friend before refocusing. "Dad, could you tell Clyde I need his detox expertise please?"

Mark cleared his throat. "What's he coming off of?"

"Liquid cocaine, I think."

"All right. I'll pass it along."

"Thanks."

Simon hung up and they drove the rest of the way to the Fletcher farm.

"Where are we?" Eggsy asked as they pulled up to a farmhouse he didn't recognize. "I've never been here."

"This is where my parents live. Where I grew up. I've got someone I want to introduce you to."

Simon looked up just as Clyde rode up on his horse.

"Simon, this your friend?" the man asked.

"His name's Eggsy," Simon replied.

Clyde dismounted his horse and walked up to Eggsy. He took hold of the man's hand to shake it. "Hello Eggsy. My name's Clyde. We're going to be good friends."

Eggsy tried to move away, but the old cowboy's grip was like iron.

"I've got a nice bunk here with your name on it. Come on."

"Sye, don't go!" Eggsy begged.

"Simon won't be going anywhere," Clyde said gently. "He'll just be in that house over there. You'll be bunking with me and the boys. Come along now."

Delta barked and Eggsy flinched. "All right, all right..."

"Thanks, Clyde," Simon said.

Clyde tipped his hat, then led Eggsy away to the bunkhouse.

As Simon watched them go, he heard gravel crunch under a pair of boots. He turned around and saw Mark approaching.

"Hey Dad. Thanks for helping out."

"No problem," Mark replied. "Think he'll be good to return to the civilized world once he's clean?"

"I don't know. He was clean for five years before now, but with the number of needles I saw in his trash bin…" Simon ran his hands down his face. "It's bad. Thankfully I caught him when he was coming down, otherwise I'd have had to knock him out. He's going to be messed up for the next while. I don't know if I'll be able to convince Winston to keep him after this."

Mark hooked his thumbs through his beltloops. "Well, you can cross that bridge when you get to it. For now, he's got a roof over his head and food in his belly."

"All right. Thanks again, Dad."

Mark gave a dismissive wave of his hand. "Don't worry about it, son."

Simon's phone started to ring, but he didn't answer it. "Now I need to figure out what to tell Winston…"

"Does he know about Eggsy's past?" Mark asked.

Simon shook his head. "Only that he has one."

"Then you can just say it caught up with him."

Simon let out a breath and finally answered the phone. "Hey Winston. Yeah, I found him. He's in pretty bad shape. No, he… uh, his past caught up with him. I've brought him back to my parents' place to get him sorted out. We'll see what we can do. It'll be a bit before he's back at work." Simon put a hand on his hip and shook his head. "It's a little early to say. Can we put him on his two-week vacation? He hasn't used it yet this year. And yes, I've considered that. I'll keep him away from those guys, don't worry. Okay. Thanks, Winston. I'll keep you updated. Bye."

He hung up and stared at his phone for a few long moments.

"What's wrong, son?" Mark asked.

"I…" He sighed. "You'll just tell me the same thing everybody else does."

"Won't know unless you try."

Simon thought for a moment, then leaned against his truck. "I think Winston's trying to manage me out. This situation is only going to make that easier for him."

"Huh. What makes you say all that?"

Simon told his father about his sites getting cut down. He went on to explain that all the other jobs he'd brought in were getting shuffled to Winston's sons.

"I thought I might be winning back some favour, but Eggsy is one of my guys. I brought him in myself, and I promised Winston he wouldn't be a problem." Simon's fingers curled into a fist. "I got him clean last time, and I kept him clean."

"Are you just worried about how Winston will take this?"

"No," Simon said sharply. "I'm worried about how Eggsy's going to handle this. He was suicidal when I first found him. I don't even want to imagine how he's going to be now that he's slipped up."

"Ah," Mark murmured. "So you're avoiding all that by focusing on Winston."

Simon blinked a few times, then cast his gaze off towards the horizon. "Yeah. I guess I am."

"Well, he might be managing you out. Or you might be his best worker and he wants to make sure you're doing your best work with what's going on in your life. Or you're his friend and he's just trying to help." Mark ran a hand through his hair. "I can't speak for him, and it doesn't really matter what he says, because you won't believe a word of it until he puts you back on your old workload. But what I can tell you, son, is that you should take advantage of this opportunity. Grieve. Help people. Work on personal projects. Even if he is managing you out, you've got a home and a job here. All of this is yours, after all."

Simon blinked a few times. "What?"

"The farm. It's yours."

"Dad, I... I can't—"

"Sell it then. I'd like the place to stay in the family for a few more generations, but it'd be yours. After your mother and I have passed, of course."

"It's not that, Dad," Simon said. "It's... I mean, after..."

Mark watched his son try to stammer through his thoughts, then clasped his shoulder. "You never stopped being our son, Simon. We never stopped loving you and praying you'd come home."

"And Hailey?"

Mark shrugged. "Take care of her, but she has an inheritance of her own coming her way once she's eighteen."

Simon took in a shaky breath. "I'll think about it."

"All right." Mark looked down at his wristwatch. "Speaking of Hailey, would you mind picking her up a little later? I can kick you some gas money."

"The last time I was near a school..."

Mark blinked. "Ah. I see... well, why don't you and Delta come with me then?"

"Dad—"

"Do you want kids?"

"I–I don't know anymore."

"Simon," Mark began gently. "The nightmares won't stop until you face them."

Simon went still. "You...?"

"Do you think I haven't heard you waking up? Or see just how tired you've been?"

Simon swallowed.

"Come on, son," Mark said, prompting him.

"Dad, I—"

"Do you want to end up like your friend?" Mark crossed his arms. "That's why you've spent so many nights out, right? You've been getting hammered?"

CHAPTER THIRTY-ONE

Simon looked off to the side.

"It won't help. You're just trading tomorrow's happiness for a little bit today." Mark fished his keys out of his pocket. "If you want freedom, though, you've got to fight for it. And you aren't alone in that fight, son."

Simon couldn't meet Mark's gaze.

THIRTY-TWO

SIMON'S CHEST ONLY tightened more the closer they got to Hailey's school. Delta sat between his feet, head resting on Simon's knee, but his presence didn't halt the steady march of panic. Simon kept petting the dog, hoping for some semblance of calm and strength.

The dog emitted a whine as they pulled up to the front of the school. Simon looked out at the building, panic's march turning into a charge. He felt shots ring out as the bell rang. His throat closed up and his ribs threatened to cave in.

Delta jumped up on him and he desperately clung to his canine companion. Eventually, slowly, air slipped through his throat once more.

Mark quietly gauged his son's reaction, then reached for the door handle. "I'll get her."

"Wait."

The father stopped and glanced back at the son. Simon took a few breaths, watching as kids started trickling out of the school.

"I–I'm okay."

Simon guided Delta back down to a sitting position. He looked out the window, took in a breath, and opened the door. He stepped outside, Delta following him, and stared at the building with dread.

I'm here. This is real. This is safe. Just focus on your breathing. That's what Mary had me do before.

Delta leaned against Simon's leg.

You need to face this. You can't keep being a coward.

"Simon!"

He looked up in time to see Hailey running at him. He managed a smile and she practically collided with him in an embrace.

She looked up at him. "You came to pick me up?"

"I came with my dad, yeah. My day was pretty open."

She let go of him and petted Delta. "Hey Delta!"

The dog didn't move from Simon's side, but he did soak up the attention.

"Ready to go?" Simon asked.

CHAPTER THIRTY-TWO

"Uh-huh."

Simon opened the door for her and she got in the back. He then got in himself, Delta still at his feet.

"How was school?" Mark asked as he started to drive away.

Hailey stared absently out the window. "Good, I guess."

"Learn anything new?"

She just shrugged.

Mark frowned, deciding to try again. "How about your friends? Cindy and Dalia?"

"They're fine."

This time, he let it go.

When they got home, Simon got out first.

"Can I play with Delta?" Hailey asked.

Simon looked back at her. "Sure. Go for it."

Her eyes lit up. "Thanks! Come on, Delta!"

The dog looked up at Simon.

"Go," he said.

Delta trotted off with Hailey and Simon watched them go.

"Can't even go near a school without having a panic attack," he muttered to himself. "Pretty pathetic, isn't it?"

"No." Mark joined him on that side of the truck. "I'm proud of you, son."

Simon tensed, his tone of voice revealing his inner thoughts. "How?"

"Something terrified you, but you faced it anyway." His dad leaned against the truck beside him. "What's there not to be proud of?"

Simon felt his eyes burn, but he cleared his throat. "I'm going to see how Eggsy's doing."

"I'll be praying for him."

"Thanks."

A minute later, Simon stepped into the bunkhouse and found Eggsy on a bunk, shivering. Simon reached out and felt his friend's forehead. He was burning up.

Simon spotted the door to the bathroom slightly ajar and went in search of a towel. He found one hanging from the side of the vanity and poured some water onto it.

"Geez, man," he said when he draped the damp rag over Eggsy's forehead. "Why didn't you talk to me?"

Eggsy was in no condition to answer, so Simon just allowed a few minutes of silence to pass. At last, his shoulders dropped and he answered his own question.

"Because I took away that option. This is my fault." Simon closed his eyes and whispered a prayer. "God, if you're there, please stop letting others pay for my mistakes. I'll take whatever punishments you give me, just stop letting me hurt them."

He stood in place, as though waiting for a divine response. None came.

"Yeah right," he murmured, shaking his head. "Like that's going to change anything."

Simon spotted a lone wooden chair by the small round table and dragged it over. He sat heavily and watched over his friend. Every once in a while, Eggsy whimpered softly, cracked an eye open, and looked around the bunkhouse only to retreat within himself once more.

After a while, Simon stood up again and knelt next to Daisy, who was lying on her dog bed in the corner. There was no sign of Clyde. The man must have gone back to work but left his dog behind.

Daisy looked up at him, her tail starting to wag. Simon saw that her bowls were empty, then searched through the bunkhouse for some food and water.

He gently petted her as she drank. "Delta did a number on you, huh?"

She looked up at him at the mention of Delta. She barked once and watched him expectantly.

Simon shook his head. "He's out."

She whined, licked his hand, then lay back down.

She misses him, he realized. *He probably misses her too.*

Simon sighed and left the bunkhouse. He missed Delta as well and didn't like being apart from his constant companion.

He decided that he would arrange for Delta and Daisy to spend more time together, especially now that she was expecting. He couldn't keep relying on Delta anyway. And it wasn't like he was all that helpful with Simon's nightmares.

I need to be able to face things alone, he told himself. *I didn't face my fears today. Delta faced them for me.* His fingers curled into fists. *I'm weak. Completely worthless.*

His eyes clouded over as he picked up speed on his way back to the house. What a sorry excuse he was for a man. He should have brought Eggsy to a detox centre, not here. What had he been thinking?

The sound of tires crunching on gravel made him look up. Ray was just pulling in from the driveway.

And I should've gotten the insurance company to cover a hotel for Ray and Beth. Dammit! It doesn't matter what I do, I just keep screwing up.

He took in a breath and let it out.

Keep calm, Sye. You can handle this. You've been through worse. His time overseas flashed through his mind and his expression darkened. *Much, much worse.*

THIRTY-THREE

SIMON LURCHED FORWARD in bed, his ribs gripping his chest like a vice. He raged against the terror that had ripped him from his sleep and slowly, painfully, forced air back into his lungs. Glancing at the clock, he let out a sigh and stood up.

During his Sunday morning run, he tried to focus on the familiar scenery, but tortuous screams and visceral images brewed in his mind, blinding him to anything but the past. He eventually returned home and showered. Despite the cleansing water on his skin, the red stains on his hands only seemed to darken.

After his shower, Simon exited his room and almost collided with his father.

"Shoot, I—"

Mark patted Simon's shoulder. "Take a breath."

He couldn't meet his father's gaze for a moment, glancing down and to the side. "Morning, Dad."

Mark offered a nod. "Good morning. I've got something to tell you… and ask you."

Simon met his father's eyes. "Yeah?"

"We've got a conference coming up that's out of town. We'll be gone Friday and should be back Monday."

"All right." Simon started to walk past.

The sound of Mark's voice stopped him. "Would you be able to watch Hailey?"

"You want me to watch…"

"The two of you've been getting along and it'd be a good opportunity to get to know her better." Mark listened to Simon's silence, then glanced to the side. "If you can't, we'll call around and see what we can arrange."

"I can do it." Simon cleared his throat. "Friday to Monday. So I've got to take her to school and pick her up those days. Anything else I should know?"

"Nope."

Simon took in a breath. "All right."

His thoughts clawed their way into the forefront of his mind. *You haven't slept a single night on your own, you idiot! How are you going to go to the school?*

I'll figure it out, he answered himself. *I'll bring Delta with me. That was the plan anyway, to take him with me into town.*

So you'll just let a dog face all your fears for you? Coward.

Simon's jaw tensed up as he left the house and approached his truck.

I know I'm a coward! I know I'm weak. But I can't lift a hundred-pound weight properly without building up to it.

Delta ran up to Simon and leaned against him, giving a single bark.

Scowling, he opened the door and Delta jumped in.

He drove into town and made his way to Foundations Church. Upon arriving, he realized that he had arrived for the service before even Ray.

He looked at his phone and confirmed that he was actually only a little bit early. Besides, Mary's car was already here.

Simon got out and went into the church through the back door, Delta following along in his wake. He heard Mary singing to herself and he followed the sound to the kitchen.

"Good morning."

She practically jumped and spun to face him. She pressed a hand over her heart and finally managed a smile. "Good morning!"

"Sorry. I didn't mean to surprise you."

She shook her head. "Don't worry about it. I'm just not used to other people showing up so early." She returned to the task of putting groceries away in the fridge and freezer. "So what brings you here?"

He didn't respond at first and she seemed to notice the lingering fatigue in his eyes.

"Not sleeping?" she prompted.

He shook his head and started helping with the groceries. "I fall asleep. It's the staying asleep that's the hard part."

"I'm sorry to hear that," she replied. "Anything I can do to help?"

"Not unless you don't mind hitting me with a baseball bat every time I wake up."

"Medication?"

"No."

She blinked a few times at how sharp his tone had become.

He cleared his throat and his voice softened a bit. "No. Can't do that stuff."

"Okay," she said. "Then I'll pray for you."

He felt her hand on his shoulder. When he looked up, he saw that her eyes were closed.

"God, please help Simon," Mary prayed. "He's really struggling, and it's keeping him from sleeping. Please grant him your peace and help him find rest. Amen."

She opened her eyes, held his gaze for a moment, then blushed ever so slightly. Without another word, she went back to putting groceries away.

"Thanks," he murmured after a few moments.

"Of course." She hooked a strand of hair behind her ear. "I already added you to my list."

He raised an eyebrow. "Your list?"

CHAPTER THIRTY-THREE

"People I pray for every night." She finished organizing a row of groceries on the counter. "If I know a person with something specific going on, I pray for them every night."

If she didn't have her mother's mental issue hanging over her head, she'd make a Christian man very happy.

"I usually pray when I can't sleep too," she added. "Whenever I start to worry about how much time I have left."

"Does it get you to sleep?" There was a trace of hope in his voice.

"Sometimes. Other times I get to spend the night talking to God. I'm usually so busy running around during the day that I don't, so it's a good opportunity."

"Does he talk to you?"

She shrugged. "Depends on your definition. If you mean, do I hear an audible voice? Then no."

"Why do you believe?"

"There isn't really one answer to that. Different people have different reasons."

A frown tugged at his lips.

"Like, some people think God has already chosen who's going to get saved and that these people have no choice but to believe," she said. "Kinda contradicts the idea of free will. But that's like when we talked about God's plan. He knows who's going to come to him, but that doesn't mean he forces them to. He calls to everybody, so each person can make the choice. It's like Jesus's parable about sowing the seeds. He knows that most won't answer His call. I mean, Revelation talks about how people will oppose Jesus even when he's here on the earth, so it's not about just believing that God's real or not. It's about following him."

"Did you grow up Christian?"

She shook her head. "No. My parents weren't, nor were their parents. I became one when I was fifteen. I needed someone who'd actually listen to me, and God was the only one. I found a lot of peace in that and ended up at this church because a girl at school recommended it to me. My faith grew from there, and I've held on. At this point, I can't even imagine not believing. I checked out other religions and philosophies, but none of them felt right." She looked at him. "What's keeping you from following?"

"You assume I believe."

"A part of you must, otherwise you wouldn't keep coming back here. There are plenty of support groups out there."

He fell silent and was about to answer when the sound of Ray's voice through the speakers cut him off. Church was about to start.

"I don't need the answer," she said gently. "But you do. Whether you end up with us or not, you should at least know the answer. Now let's head in there."

After the service, Simon got up and exited the sanctuary. He would have left the building right away were it not for Mary tracking him down again.

"Hey Simon?" she said.

Delta's ears perked up at the sound of her voice.

"Yeah?"

"We doing our usual lunch?"

He nodded. "Sure."

"Sweet. Let me just finish up what I need to do here."

Simon looked back into the sanctuary and noticed some of the church members glancing in his direction, but none of them approached.

He felt someone walking up behind him and glanced over to see Ray.

"Morning, Simon."

"Good morning."

"You got here even before I did."

"Guess I wasn't watching the time."

"Huh," Ray murmured. "How's the house coming?"

"Good. Some of the materials are taking a bit longer to arrive than expected, though."

Ray nodded knowingly. "I remember when my parents renovated their house. What was supposed to be three months turned into six."

"These delays shouldn't add *that* much time," Simon said quickly.

Ray chuckled. "I hope not, else I'm spending more than just Thanksgiving at your place."

"Right. That's coming up."

Simon frowned. *Is that why Dad's having me look after Hailey? They won't take her with them to Israel this year?*

"What's wrong?" Ray asked.

Simon blinked. "Oh, uh…"

Ray gestured to his office. "If you want."

Simon looked at the door, then nodded, and he and Delta followed him in.

THIRTY-FOUR

"MY PARENTS ARE going to some conference thing this coming weekend. They're leaving Hailey with me."

Ray nodded as he took a seat.

"Hailey's a wonderful kid," the pastor said, analyzing Simon for a moment. "But you're worried."

"Yeah."

Ray leaned back in his chair, his gaze resting on Simon. "Does it have to do with your time as a cop?"

Simon went rigid. "Aiden said something?"

"No." Ray interlocked his fingers behind his head. "I looked you up."

"When?"

"The day you set us up in the trailer."

Simon's mind raced until it hit a brick wall. He slumped. "And you still invited me here?"

"Should I not have?"

Simon's gaze dropped to the floor and he shrugged.

"Simon, you're not evil for what you did," Ray said. "You were protecting others. Anybody with half a brain could see that. I'm sure it doesn't make it any easier to live with, but it's the truth."

Simon's gaze stayed locked on the floor. "It wasn't the first time."

"Overseas?" Ray asked.

Simon nodded.

"Similar situation?"

"Does it matter?"

"It does," Ray said. "To you."

Simon took in a breath and recounted what he'd gone through while in Afghanistan.

"You're right. It is very similar." Ray paused. "But as much as these experiences get to you, there's something more recent hitting you too."

"Neil said something."

"He made a prayer request. No details. He wanted to keep your privacy as best he could."

Simon let out a breath. "Seems to be happening a fair bit lately."

Ray tilted his head, his eyes narrowing. "What is?"

"Doesn't really matter."

"So you don't trust yourself with Hailey?"

Simon's gaze snapped up to Ray. "What?"

"It'd make sense, with everything you've been through."

"Yeah."

"Well, Beth and I will be here," Ray said.

"You'll watch her?"

Ray shook his head. "No. I'm saying we're here if you need advice. Well, I'm sure we can watch her in case of an emergency, but you need to do this."

Simon's jaw muscles tensed up. "Need to?"

"It'd be good for you. You're a good man—and capable, according to everyone who knows you. It may just help you see in yourself the same man they see. Not to mention the fact that if you want to have a family of your own down the road, this'll be a good opportunity to understand better what that looks like."

"I don't know if I can do it."

Ray raised an eyebrow. "This'll help you find out."

"It's not just…" Everything inside him screamed not to continue. "I had a panic attack just from hearing the school bell."

Ray shifted. "Oh?"

"Mary happened to find me and helped me through. That's why I was helping her out that Thursday."

"Has it happened again?"

"They keep coming, but Delta helps them from going too far."

Delta perked up at his name and sat up. He rested his head on Simon's knee and Simon scratched him between his ears.

"My dad convinced me to go with him to pick up Hailey. To do that, I needed Delta." Simon let out a breath. "And even then…"

"You don't think you can be there for her when she needs you?"

He was quiet for a while before he sniffed. "And I thought I could have a kid of my own one day. How naïve is that?" He punctuated his question with a mirthless chuckle.

A frown took hold of Ray and his brow came together. "It was hopeful, Simon."

Simon shook his head. "It was selfish."

"How so?"

Simon looked off to the side.

"There's no judgment here, Simon."

"I thought that by having a kid, it'd maybe prove I'm not just some… death machine."

"That's a lot of pressure to put on a child," Ray said.

CHAPTER THIRTY-FOUR

Simon shrugged. "Then things are probably better this way." He froze at the words that had just come out of his mouth. He started to feel sick. "I didn't mean—"

Ray let Simon sputter for a moment, then gently interrupted. "Don't worry, Simon. Everything you're feeling is natural. You should be feeling what you do. And as long as you can identify those feelings, you can work with them."

Simon struggled to keep his chest from getting tighter. "You sound like a therapist."

"I may have gotten some education before I found myself on a different path." Ray smirked. "But let's get back to you. You didn't mean that it was better the child died."

"My child," he said quietly.

"Your child." Ray smiled and sat forward. "Now I've got an assignment for you."

Simon glanced up.

"Call it a mission, if that helps," Ray said. "During the week, spend more time with Hailey. Treat her as you would your own daughter. Go with your dad to drop her off and pick her up from school each day. That way, the days when it's just you and her will get easier. It *will* happen. I can't promise you'll never feel how you feel now when you're around a school, but it can be better than it is." The pastor glanced at the door. "For today, though, I believe you've got plans with someone."

Simon remained seated. "Could I stay here another minute or two?"

"Absolutely," Ray said as he stood up. "Take your time. Mary has keys to lock up the church."

Ray left the office to find Mary waiting in the hallway near the church entrance. Ray closed the door and approached her. "Give him a couple minutes."

"Is he having…"

"Probably the start of one," Ray said.

"He told you?"

Ray nodded. "Yeah."

Mary walked towards the office door, but he moved himself to block the way.

"Ray, I can help him," she insisted.

"I know you can. But right now, it won't do any good. He needs to be able to handle this on his own. He's not always going to have you around."

She tensed up.

"When it's a full attack, out of control, then by all means," Ray added. "But for now, he needs to know he's not weak."

"Weak? I know he's not weak."

"I know that. You know that. But he's a man of action, and there's nothing to fight. There's no enemy to shoot, no one to pull to safety. If you were in a situation where your greatest strength couldn't help you, wouldn't you feel weak too?"

Her gaze dropped and she nodded.

Ray sighed. "Sometimes the hardest thing is to do nothing, but he's not a tool that can be fixed. He needs to heal and grow."

Mary sniffed. "I know. Isn't there something I can do?"

"The best thing right now is to remind him he's reliable and appreciated." He lightly touched her arm. "I hope you two have a good lunch."

THIRTY-FIVE

SIMON STARED DOWN at the table before him in the diner, his eyes seeming to see through it. He stirred as he felt something poke his leg and he looked up to Mary, whose head was tilted to the side.

"What?" he asked.

"Just wondering where you were."

He cleared his throat. "Sorry. I'm just really tired. I was thinking a bit on our conversation before."

"Oh yeah?"

"Neil had said that if I walked away, it meant I didn't believe in the first place."

Mary raised her coffee mug to her lips. "He and I've had that conversation before. He abbreviates his thoughts. Sort of boils down the larger ideas. What he means is that if the worldly stuff can lead you away from God, your faith was in the stuff, not God." She took another sip, then set her coffee back down and added some sugar. "As you know, people will always disappoint. So will the world."

"And how does God not disappoint?"

"He's upfront about who he is," she said. "The only way you end up disappointed with him is if you don't know him. But he gave us the Bible so we can know him."

Simon frowned. "Why follow him if he doesn't do anything?"

"It's not about getting something out of this life, Simon. It's about what comes after. About being with him, because he loves us and wants us there with him for eternity. I can't even imagine how amazing it'll be."

He fell silent.

"But the start of that is believing he's even real." She lightly tapped the side of her mug with her fingernails. "And there's no halfway. You either do or you don't."

"I think I do."

She raised an eyebrow. "You don't sound so sure."

He straightened and met her gaze. "I can only say what I think I know. I think I believe."

"Then what's eating at you?"

Don't tell her. She'll hate you.

His jaw muscles tensed up and he fought to form words. Eventually, he gave up and muttered, "Whatsoever you do unto the least of these, you do unto me."

Her gaze softened. "It was Susan who did that, not you."

He let out a breath through his nose, then took out his phone. She watched him scroll, but then he slid it over to her. His chest tightened as she started to read the news article he'd pulled up.

"I think I remember hearing about this a while back. A kid went and shot up the school, and an officer had to shoot them…" She trailed off as she saw the picture of Simon striking his superior officer. Chills went through her. "Oh."

He conjured up all the horrible responses he expected her to have. His breathing turned shallow and short.

"That's horrible," she remarked.

He squeezed his eyes shut and his breathing stopped. He flinched when he felt her hand take hold of his.

"I'm so sorry you went through that."

He blinked a few times, then looked up at her.

"It must still hurt," she added.

Something inside him seemed to snap. His breath came back and his chest loosened. The voices left and he simply stared at her.

"Simon?"

His gaze dropped back to the table as he felt his eyes burn. All the pain, guilt, and rage had stopped crashing in from all sides. The terror had let go of his heart. Instead it all welled up from some unknown depths, threatening to burst out.

Mary watched his shifting expression and a hint of panic flashed in her eyes. "You're a good man, Simon."

The wellspring stopped.

Mary fought to keep a frown from taking hold of her. "You put your life on the line to save others."

He closed his eyes as it all started to crush in again. Delta whined and pawed at Simon's leg, forcing him to let go of her hand and reach down and pet the dog.

"Yeah. So everyone keeps telling me." He finally let out a breath and relaxed a bit. "So what do you talk to God about when you can't sleep?"

Her gaze dropped to her coffee. "Everything. How my day went. Things I'm worried about. I pray for people who need it, and for complete strangers. I tell him about all the things I'm excited about. And the one that helps me most is all the things I'm thankful for. I always try to find at least one thing."

"So it's just a conversation?"

She nodded. "Yeah. I mean, that's part of having a personal relationship with someone, which is what he wants with us. I don't just pray at night, either."

CHAPTER THIRTY-FIVE

He mulled over her words. "I'll keep that in mind. You said a girl from your school intro-duced you to Foundations, but didn't you homeschool?"

"Yeah, but not in middle school. That's when I bumped into her one day while we were both out shopping."

"Is she still at Foundations?"

"No," Mary said, an undercurrent of pain in her voice. "Simon, I recognized you the first time we met."

He frowned. "What does that have to do with anything? Did you and I know each other at some point?"

She shook her head. "No, but you knew the girl. I recognized you because we both went to her funeral."

Simon went still. "Heather?"

Mary tried to make herself smaller as she gripped the mug. "Yeah."

Simon was silent for too long.

"I'm sorry, Simon. I should have said something sooner, but... I mean, it just never seemed like the right time to say anything, with everything you're dealing with."

"I see."

"I was going to say something," she said. "Eventually."

He nodded. "So you two were friends?"

"I don't know. We talked at church, but that was about it. She was the only person apart from God who listened, though. She let me vent and helped me walk through things." She sniffed as her eyes burned. "I had no idea about the hell she was going through."

"She was really good at hiding things," Simon said quietly. "You could always trust her to keep secrets, and conceal the fact that she had her own."

"She never opened up to you?"

He shook his head. "No, she didn't. It didn't matter what I said or did, she never trusted me enough to let me in." An expression of deep pain took hold of him. "I guess I just wasn't good enough."

"She loved you."

He glanced at her. "More intuition?"

"No," she said. "You were one of the few things she'd talk about. A lot. A lot of good things. She was worried about you and your father."

"Yeah..." Simon trailed off. "We, uh... we were similar in all the wrong ways."

Is that why she never opened up to me? Because she thought I was dealing with too much already?

He glanced at Mary. "Did she say anything specific?"

"She said plenty," Mary said with a smile. "Honestly, I felt like I knew you myself. Of course, it's been ten years, so I don't know how much of it still applies. So far a good portion of it does."

That's why she's been reaching out to me so much, he thought. *It's why she even brought me to her place.*

"I really wanted to talk to you at the funeral," Mary said. "But I ended up talking myself out of it."

"Why?"

She shrugged and looked off to the side. "I was awkward and shy." She took in a breath and met his gaze. "I really am sorry about Heather."

He sniffed. "Me too."

They spent the rest of their lunch in silence.

THIRTY-SIX

SIMON WALKED INTO his bedroom alongside Delta. The dog sat at the foot of the bed and looked up at him expectantly.

He reached into the bedside table and took out an old flip phone. He opened it, but the screen didn't light up. A part of him was relieved. He still grabbed the charging cord in the drawer and plugged the device in.

He was about to flip it open when he stopped himself. He stared down at the phone and it seemed to mock him.

He set it down and instead left the room, Delta padding just ahead of him as he walked right out through the front door and aimed for the bunkhouse.

When they walked in, Delta swiftly left him to lay next to Daisy.

Eggsy looked up from the table, his skin pale and eyes haunted.

"How are you doing, Eggsy?"

Eggsy stared at Simon as he sat across from him, until recognition finally passed through his eyes. "Simon! I'm so sorry!"

Simon leaned forward. "What happened?"

Tears broke free from Eggsy's eyes and he tried to get rid of them. "I messed up! I can't control myself."

Simon let Eggsy break down. He stayed there with him, quietly waiting for Eggsy's sobs to subside.

"Yeah, you did mess up."

Another sob struck Eggsy.

"And it's great that you can say that, Eggsy. Do you remember the second step?"

"I don't have—" He choked on another sob. "Faith in anything. Just you."

"I'm not perfect, Eggsy," Simon said calmly. "I'm going to mess up and fail you. You need something bigger than me."

"What Carey said was a bunch of bollocks—"

"It was." He paused. "Give me a minute. I'll be right back."

Simon left for the house, returning to his bedroom and grabbing a worn-out book from a drawer in his desk. There were sticky notes with shorthand stuck to almost every page. He stared down at the book for a moment, then opened it and moved the bookmark to John 3:16.

He went back to the bunkhouse but stopped before going inside. He closed his eyes.

"I get that I'm not exactly… whatever… but please help Eggsy," he prayed. "He needs something, or he's going to keep falling back."

Simon opened his eyes and went in. Eggsy looked up as Simon sat and slid the book over to him. Eggsy hesitantly cracked it open and read the first line where the bookmark was.

"Do you believe in this?"

Simon was quiet for a moment. "Yeah, I believe in it."

Eggsy's gaze dropped back down to the book, but his eyes were unfocused. His frustration seemed to be building.

"You don't have to read it right this second," Simon said. "You should get some more rest."

Eggsy stared at the page for a moment longer, then closed the book. "Okay."

Eggsy started to slide it back to him, but Simon shook his head. "Hold onto it. Don't worry about all the notes. Just read the main words. I'll check in on you again later, okay?"

With a nod, Eggsy stood up and went back to his bunk.

As Simon left the bunkhouse, he let out a long sigh.

Gotta keep Eggsy away from Ray and Beth, he thought to himself. *Finding out that one of my guys is going through rehab? Could hurt the company. Winston would have my butt in a sling… not to mention the fact that they've got a newborn. Just another tightrope to walk…*

Just then, Clyde rode up and reined in his horse.

"How's our patient doing?" Clyde asked.

"Guilty," Simon said heavily. "And accepting step one. I'm starting him on step two."

Clyde grunted as he leaned forward on his saddle. "It's only been a couple days."

"He's got some experience going through this." Simon glanced back at the bunkhouse. "But this'll give him a head start."

The two men stood in silence for a moment.

Clyde flicked his gaze to Simon. "This is his second relapse, isn't it?"

Simon nodded.

"You know he may not be able to go back to the city, right?"

Simon ran a hand through his hair. "I know."

Clyde sucked on his teeth. "Well, that only really leaves one option, Sye."

"Yeah. I'll talk to my dad. I'm just…"

"Just what?"

"I've used up my favours with my dad, and I also need to keep Eggsy away from the Torringtons."

"I don't think your dad much cares for tracking favours," Clyde said. "And regarding Mr. and Mrs. Torrington, I'd agree that it would be best, for now. I'm guessing they met him onsite when the renos were starting?"

CHAPTER THIRTY-SIX

Simon shrugged. "Not directly, but I don't want to chance it."

Clyde clicked his tongue. "Can he ride?"

"Yeah. He rode as a kid back in England."

"Then I'll take him for some rides during the day to clear his head."

Simon fell silent.

"Simon, I know you feel responsible, being his sponsor way back and all, but he did choose to do what he did." Clyde smiled. "And you're stepping up and being there for him now. It's all you can do, Sye."

Simon's jaw tensed up and he felt his heart twist in his chest. "I know, I know. Thanks for helping, Clyde."

Clyde tipped his hat. "Anytime, boss."

Simon walked off towards the house, went inside, and took the stairs two at a time. He entered his bedroom and stopped as his eyes fell on the old flip phone. He stared at it for a moment, then shook his head and went for a shower.

THIRTY-SEVEN

SIMON SAT IN his truck outside of Hailey's school, Delta in the passenger seat. He gripped the steering wheel tight enough that his knuckles had gone white.

The bell suddenly rang, sending a bolt of terror through him. He fought against it, desperate to keep from just driving off.

Delta whined and nuzzled Simon's hand, his eyes staring up at Simon. Simon managed to take a few breaths as he petted Delta.

"Thanks, boy."

He got out of the truck, Delta at his side, and watched the children flood out of the school. He kept a wary eye on them as they went to their parents. All the while, he scanned the sea of little people for Hailey, but he didn't see her.

Where…?

"Hi Delta!"

He glanced down and realized that Hailey had managed to reach them. She was petting Delta as she looked up at Simon with the brightest smile.

"Hi Simon! Where's Mark?" she asked.

"My mom and dad fell behind with packing, so I came alone."

She looked at his truck, her eyes wide. "So I get to ride in your truck?"

Simon opened the passenger door for her. "You do."

She clambered up onto the seat and he buckled her in. Delta climbed in and sat at her feet. Simon tried not to rush to get into the driver's seat.

"So you're going to be driving me to and from school from now on?" she asked once they were on the road.

Simon cleared his throat. "Tomorrow and Monday, yeah."

"What'll we be doing Saturday and Sunday?"

"I… I don't know," Simon replied. "Sunday I've got church in the morning."

"Can I come to your church?"

Simon noticed the excitement in her eyes. "That was the plan."

"Cool!" Hailey looked down at Delta. "Is he coming to church too?"

"He usually does. But Daisy's getting pretty close to giving birth, so I'm trying to let Delta stay home as much as I can."

Delta looked up at Simon when he mentioned Daisy's name.

Simon cleared his throat. "Wanna stop for ice cream on the way back?"

Her eyes went wide as a full moon. "Really? Before dinner?"

"There's still time between now and dinner."

"Then yes!"

Simon smiled and drove towards an ice cream parlour. When he pulled up, she practically vibrated with excitement at the giant ice cream cone on the store sign.

He helped her down from the truck and they went inside with Delta.

"Sir, dogs aren't allowed," the clerk said, coming around the counter to stop them from entering.

Simon smiled at the clerk. "He's my support dog, and he's better trained than most. He won't be a problem."

The clerk eyed Delta. "If he's a support dog, where's his jacket?"

"He doesn't wear clothes. He's a dog. You can test him, if you like." Simon took out a treat from his pocket and held it out to the clerk. "Try giving this to him."

The clerk thought for a moment, then walked around to the front and held out the treat to Delta. The dog immediately looked up at Simon expectantly.

"Satisfied?" Simon asked.

"Sure."

Simon nodded to the dog. "Go ahead, Delta."

Delta ate the treat.

"Good boy. So, Hailey, what do you want?"

She excitedly rattled off her order, and soon enough they were both seated at a table. He'd gotten himself a waffle bowl with mango ice cream. She had a fairly diverse range of flavours and toppings in her waffle bowl.

He finished his bowl relatively quick and quietly waited for her to finish hers.

When his phone started to vibrate, he looked down at the screen and frowned.

"Hey Winston," he said. "Sorry I haven't gotten back to you yet. Eggsy is recovering."

Simon's gaze fell and Hailey noticed his expression change as she continued eating her dessert.

"Yeah, I know. I recommend shifting Roman into the position. He's proven himself a few times over and I think we should give him the chance." There was a pause. "Yeah. The Torrington site is progressing well overall. We've got the usual setbacks, but that's because some of the subcontractors are spread thin. I think it's about time we started getting some in-house trades." Simon fell completely silent, his gaze falling. "Yeah, I'm good. Ready to get back to it whenever you need me." He closed his eyes. "All right. Bye."

Simon hung up and let out a breath.

"You look sad," the girl said.

Simon opened his eyes and mustered a smile. "I'm fine."

"That's what my mom always said when she was sad."

Simon smiled a little wider and shook his head. "It's a little complicated. I'll try to explain it some time, but not right now."

"Okay." As Hailey finished her ice cream, her face lit up. "I'm done! Can we go home now?"

Hailey grabbed his hand and he led her out of the shop.

Fifteen minutes later, they were parking in front of the house. Hailey ran off towards the bunkhouse with Delta in tow while Simon stepped into the house.

"Dad?" he called.

Not hearing an answer, he walked to his parents' bedroom and knocked on the door.

A moment later, he heard his dad answer. "Come in!"

Simon opened the door just as his dad was coming out of the ensuite. A half-packed suitcase lay open on the bed.

"How'd it go?" Mark asked.

"Well. I was able to pick her up. Then I took her for some ice cream."

Mark chuckled as he started tossing clothes into the suitcase. "I bet she loved that. Sounds like you should be good to handle her yourself for a while."

"Yeah." Simon took a step into the room. "So, about Eggsy..."

"What about him?"

"Going back to the city may not be an option for him."

Mark straightened. "If you want something, you gotta ask, son."

Simon took in a breath. "If Eggsy wants it, could he have a job here? He knows how to ride, at the very least, and he's a quick learner."

"We could always use an extra pair of hands around here."

Simon blinked a few times. "Really?"

Mark shrugged. "He'd have a job, a roof over his head, and he'd be away from the city. He'd also have a bunkhouse of guys to keep him accountable, many of whom have similar pasts. I don't see any reason not to."

Simon let out a sigh of relief. "Thanks, Dad."

"You're welcome."

————————

"Wanna see Daisy?" Hailey said to Delta as they stepped up to the door to the bunkhouse.

Delta barked and Hailey creaked the door open. Delta bolted inside and ran to the dog bed where a very pregnant Daisy looked up expectantly.

Hearing movement, Hailey turned just in time to see Eggsy sit up in his bunk. The two stared at each other for a moment.

Hailey smiled. "Hi! I'm Hailey. Are you a new cowboy?"

Eggsy cleared his throat. "Not exactly. I'm a friend of Simon's. He's helping me out by letting me stay here."

"Did you lose your home?" she asked, genuine concern in her voice.

"No. I did some stupid stuff I really shouldn't have. Being here will help me get better."

"Oh, I'm sorry. Are you okay?"

Eggsy looked down at his hands. "No. I'm really not. But that's why I'm here."

Hailey walked up to him. "Can I give you a hug?"

Eggsy felt tears pull at the back of his eyes and felt a crushing weight on his shoulders. He was about to say no, that he shouldn't, but a small part of the truth managed to slip through.

"That'd be nice," he admitted.

Hailey gave him a hug, which he hesitantly returned. After a few seconds, Eggsy relaxed and let go of the embrace.

The girl took a step back and smiled up at him. "I hope you feel better. I'll pray for you. See you later!"

She turned and skipped out of the bunkhouse.

THIRTY-EIGHT

SIMON LOOKED UP at the teacher at the front of the class and rubbed his tired eyes. At the same moment, he felt his phone vibrate and pulled it out of his pocket.

He looked down at the flip phone screen and read the text from Heather: *I love you to death, babe.*

Simon smiled, then texted back: *I love you.*

He refocused on the teacher, but he couldn't ignore a strange feeling in the pit of his stomach that weighed him down. He frowned, checked his phone again, and sent off a quick text.

Babe?

No response.

The strange, ominous feeling grew stronger and soon he felt nauseous. He left the classroom and quickly made his way to his old beater truck.

He fired off another text: *Babe, is everything okay?*

Simon sped to Heather's place, ignoring lights, signs, and speed limits. He arrived to find the front door open. He didn't even turn off his truck as he threw the door open; his seatbelt choked him as he tried to bolt out.

He sprinted into the house and heard water running upstairs.

"Babe, you in there?" he called when he got to the locked bathroom door.

Knocking got him no response.

Simon slammed himself into the door, throwing his full weight forward, but it wouldn't budge. He tried again. Letting out a shout, he kicked the door handle this time. The door broke inwards, pieces of the frame shattering across the tiles.

His blood ran cold as he saw Heather in the bathtub, blood pouring from her wrists. He rushed to her side and tried to prop her up as he called 911.

"I need an ambulance at…" He blanked, then rattled off the address. "Now! She's lost a lot of blood!"

Heather's eyes rolled, unable to focus. At least she wasn't gone yet.

"C'mon, babe, stay with me!"

CHAPTER THIRTY-EIGHT

Simon cried as he held her, then grabbed a towel and wrapped it around her wrists as tightly as he could.

"Please babe, don't leave me!" His voice cracked. "God, please! Don't let her die! Please! I'll do anything… just save her, God!"

When the ambulance and police car arrived,

He heard the distant wailing of ambulance and police sirens. They were getting closer, louder, piercing Simon's sobs as he held her. The blood and water soaked into his clothes and coated his hands.

Bootsteps pounded up the stairwell as the EMTs rushed up the stairs with a stretcher and swiftly tended to Heather. Simon backed away, only able to watch as they tried to stem her bleeding. He followed behind as they rushed outside with her.

The cop turned off Simon's truck and gave him the keys as Simon climbed into the back of the ambulance. Everything after that was a blur as they sped to the hospital. The back of the ambulance looked like a murder scene as the paramedics tried to stop the bleeding.

When they reached the hospital, she was ushered away for surgery, leaving Simon in the waiting room, looking down at his blood-soaked clothes. Streaks of red covered his arms.

He fell to his knees and desperately prayed. He didn't know how much time passed before a doctor approached.

"Simon Fletcher?"

Simon quickly stood up, hope in his eyes until he saw the doctor's expression.

"I'm sorry for your loss."

His knees buckled and he dropped to the floor. He didn't hear anything else the doctor tried to say. Simon found himself unable to move or think as his world was ripped from him.

After a while he felt a hand on his shoulder and looked up at Neil. He saw the man's lips move, but no words reached his ears. His wife Veronica was behind him, listening to the doctor and breaking down. Neil turned and held her…

───────────────

Simon sat up in bed, sobbing in the dark. His chest tightened as his heart twisted. He gasped for air but none made it past his throat. His whole body shook like a leaf. He managed to strike his chest and a whisper of air made it through to his lungs. Slowly, with each rasping breath, more air made it through, until he could breathe again. Tears streamed down his cheeks and he pulled his knees up to his chest. He sat in the dark for a while before he heard a soft knock on his door.

Simon wiped away his tears and cleared his throat. "It's open."

Hailey opened the door, the soft light from the hallway spilling in and caressing the room. She walked up to the bed, tears glistening on her cheeks.

"I had a nightmare," she said.

Simon took in a breath and patted the spot on the bed next to him. Hailey climbed up and sat beside him, leaning against his side as she pulled her knees to her chest.

"I dreamed the accident." Her voice was soft. "I miss my mom and dad." She held herself tighter and started to cry. "It was so scary. I still get scared in cars."

Simon put an arm around her shoulders and held her.

"I don't wanna be scared!" she cried, her voice breaking as she got louder. "I don't wanna hurt! I wanna be happy, but I feel sad all the time!" She sobbed into his shoulder as he held her. "Everyone needs me to be happy! I can't! I can't! I can't!"

She gripped his shirt and held on tight.

Simon's heart broke. He felt lost as he tried to find words, and eventually they came to him.

"You don't have to be happy for me." Simon's voice was gentle. "It's okay to be scared, and to hurt. And it's definitely okay to miss your mom and dad."

Hailey's sobs continued.

"It's hard, and it hurts. You feel alone, like you have to be fake. You don't have to be fake with me, though, and you're not alone. Just let it all out. I'm here for you."

He held her a little tighter, resting his head atop hers in an attempt to engulf her in a comforting embrace. Her tears soaked through his shirt, and eventually she cried herself to sleep.

Simon gently rocked her and he felt his own tears renew.

"God," he whispered. "Hailey needs you. Please enter her dreams and show her your love. Bring her the peace only you can offer. Above all else, help her grieve. Work and speak through me for her."

Simon fell quiet for a good long while. When his lips parted to speak next, his voice cracked as a sob of his own struck his chest.

"And God? Please bring someone who can do the same for me. Amen."

THIRTY-NINE

SIMON WOKE UP with Hailey in his arms. He nudged her awake and she yawned, looking around.

She hugged him. "Thank you."

Simon returned the hug. "No problem, kiddo. Now go and get some clothes on. We've got some shopping to do."

Hailey had confusion written across her face. "But Shelby said she did the shopping yesterday."

"For regular food, yeah. But she didn't get the good stuff," Simon said as he stretched. "I'll make breakfast."

Confusion still followed Hailey as she left Simon's room.

He got dressed, then made his way downstairs to prepare some bacon, eggs, and hash-browns for breakfast.

She soon came down and sat at the table. "Simon?"

"Hmm?"

Hailey fidgeted. "Do you miss your baby?"

Simon went completely still. "W–what do you know about that?"

"I accidentally heard you and Shelby talking about it. I'm sorry."

"No, it's…" He took in a breath. "It's all right. I do miss them."

"Was it a boy or girl?"

He shook his head. "I don't know. They weren't far enough along."

"Oh." Hailey's voice was small and quiet. "I'm sorry. It must hurt."

Simon nodded. "Yeah, it does."

Hailey hopped off her chair and walked up to Simon.

"What's up?" he asked.

She hugged him and he smiled while returning the embrace with one arm while he kept cooking.

"All right, breakfast's ready."

Hailey gave him one last squeeze and retook her seat. Simon loaded up her plate and sat down to eat his own breakfast.

Soon enough, they got Delta into the truck and drove into town. They pulled up in front of a small drugstore.

"This place has some pretty cool chips and candies you won't find anywhere else," he told her.

Simon got out and opened her door.

Together they went inside with Delta, who sniffed the air and began to wander off.

"Delta?" Simon called.

The German shepherd looked back at Simon and whined. Simon frowned and went after Delta, Hailey in tow. Delta suddenly turned down the makeup aisle and barked.

A woman in that part of the store yelped and dropped what she had been holding.

"Delta! No barking."

The dog looked back at Simon and whined softly as Simon and Hailey rounded the corner.

"Sorry, ma'am, he usually…" Simon trailed off as he realized it was Mary. She looked back at him with horror clear on her face. She wasn't wearing any makeup, and it revealed a birthmark that took up a little less than half her face.

Simon smiled warmly and knelt to pick up the dropped makeup containers.

"Hey Mary. How's it going?"

Still frozen, her gaze flicked to Hailey, who smiled up at her. "I'm, uh… I'm well enough. Just ran out of…"

Simon stood back up and handed her the makeup she'd dropped.

"Thanks," she said quietly.

"No problem. This is Hailey. My parents adopted her."

Hailey beamed up at her and held out her hand.

Mary hesitantly shook it. "I'm Mary, one of Simon's friends."

"Pleased to meet you," Hailey said sweetly. "Are you okay?"

Mary looked down at her and nodded as she pulled back her hand and held herself. "Y–yeah."

"Does it hurt?"

Mary blushed and looked away. "No. It's not…"

"It's a birthmark," Simon explained quietly. "Birthmarks are things we all have, see?" He turned up his wrist to reveal his own small brown mark. "Some are small, and nobody ever sees them. Some aren't. Some people like them. Some people don't. But they're all really cool and beautiful in their own unique way. They're like a signature from God."

Hailey looked at the mark on Simon's wrist, then looked up at Mary. "You shouldn't hide God's signature. Everything he makes is beautiful, and you are too."

Mary's heart nearly stopped at this.

Simon straightened. "Well, we've got some junk food to pick up. It was good seeing you. I hope to see you tomorrow at church too."

CHAPTER THIRTY-NINE

Mary's heart fluttered and she nodded. "Yeah. See you."

Simon took Hailey's hand and they walked off towards the junk food section. As they departed, Mary peered around the corner and subtly watched them. She couldn't help but smile as Simon picked Hailey up so she could grab a bag of chips.

Mary quickly took her purchases to the checkout and paid for her makeup.

"Is Mary your girlfriend?" Hailey asked as she spotted the woman leaving the store.

Simon glanced down at her. "No. Just a friend."

"But she really likes you. And Delta likes her."

Delta looked up at the sound of his name.

"We're just friends." Simon grabbed a few more things.

"Do you not like her?"

"I do," Simon admitted. "But there are some very good reasons for us not to be together."

"Like what?" Hailey asked.

Simon cleared his throat. "I can't talk about her reasons, because it's not my place to say."

"What's your reasons?"

"I…" Simon went quiet for a bit. "I don't know how to explain them."

Hailey frowned. "Being an adult sounds complicated."

A chuckle rose up in Simon's throat and he smirked. "Yeah. It definitely can be. Now let's get this stuff paid for and head out."

"Okay," Hailey replied. "Are we gonna see Mary at church tomorrow?"

"Yeah. But she may be covering up her birthmark with makeup. If she does, don't say anything about it to anyone, okay?"

"Why?"

Simon thought for a moment, then knelt in front of her. "She's trusted me with a lot of very big things, but she never told me about the birthmark before. So it's something she has a hard time with. She's probably got a lot of pain from it. Please promise me you won't talk to anyone about it, okay? Not even Mark or Shelby."

Hailey stared at him for a moment, then nodded. "I promise."

Simon smiled and hugged her. "Thank you. It means a lot to me."

She smiled and hugged him back.

"Now let's get out of here."

FORTY

AT CHURCH, HAILEY was the centre of attention, but she stayed by Simon's side. Delta kept near her too, trying to offer support.

When Simon noticed Mary, she had indeed covered up her birthmark. His heart sank, but he waved her over.

"Would you mind taking Hailey to the kitchen?" he whispered. "She's getting a little over-whelmed."

Mary nodded and took Hailey's hand and led her away while Simon distracted the nearby church members. Delta leaned against Simon's leg for support.

"Wanna help me out?" Mary asked the girl when they reached the kitchen.

"With what?"

"I could use some help peeling some onions."

"Okay!"

Mary set the onions and a trash bin before her and Hailey started peeling. As for Mary, she got busy cutting vegetables.

Mary broke the silence. "About yesterday at the store…"

Hailey smiled. "I won't talk about it."

Mary let out a sigh of relief.

"Simon made me promise."

"He did?" Mary asked.

"Uh-huh." Hailey set aside one peeled onion and started on the next one. "He also said you don't want to date him."

Mary sputtered. "It's not that I don't… I mean…" She sighed. "What were his exact words?"

"That you both have really good reasons not to date, but he didn't think it was okay to talk about what those reasons are. But if two people want to be together, can't they just be together?"

Mary glanced away. "It's not always that simple. Simon and I can't be together."

"May I ask why?"

CHAPTER FORTY

Silence held Mary's tongue for a while. When she finally found her voice, she spoke softly. "I'm sick, and there's no cure. It'll make me stop being myself. I could end up hurting people, especially those closest to me."

Hailey stared up at her with misting eyes. She dropped the onion on the counter and hugged Mary, holding on tight. "That sounds really scary. I'm so sorry."

Mary felt her voice catch in her throat. She knelt and returned Hailey's hug, trying to hold back tears of her own. "It is."

They stayed like that for a bit, until Mary finally cleared her throat and stood up.

"I would love to date, Simon. But I just can't."

Hailey nodded and went back to peeling onions. "I understand. You don't have to worry about him being alone, though."

Mary smiled. "Yeah, he's got you."

Hailey giggled and shook her head. "I can't be his girlfriend. He's too old. Yanah's coming."

Mary frowned. "Yanah?"

"Uh-huh." Hailey froze and looked up at her. "That's a secret. Don't tell Simon. It's a surprise."

"Okay… I won't say anything. Who's Yanah?"

"She's special." Hailey continued to peel her onion. "She's known Simon forever, and…" Hailey leaned forward and lowered her voice. "She loves Simon a lot. Normally Mark and Shelby go out to visit Yanah's family every Thanksgiving, and they take me too since they adopted me. But she's coming out here just for him."

"From where?"

"Jerusalem."

Just then, Delta came into the kitchen and sat beside Hailey. Soon other members of the congregation joined them. All started to pitch in.

"I'm gonna find Simon." Hailey hopped off her chair and gave Mary a quick hug before leading Delta away.

"She's such a little cutie," one of the women said. "How come she's never come here with Simon before?"

"She's technically his adopted sister," Mary explained. "I imagine she goes to church with Simon's parents."

"They seem like father and daughter," another woman remarked, her tone not as warm as the others.

The first woman shifted uncomfortably and Mary stopped what she was doing.

"Is there something you want to say, Gertie?" Mary demanded.

"Oh, nothing at all."

Mary narrowed her eyes. "No, come on. Let's hear it. Say exactly what you mean."

The woman's sour face only became more pinched. "Simon has clearly led a life of… well, we've all seen him. This girl is probably the result of that life."

"Well, she isn't." Mary's tone was sharp. "You know literally nothing about Simon or what he's gone through. And what you just tried to do is start a rumour against a member of this church. You know, for someone so righteous, I'd think you'd remember the Bible mentioning that gossips destroy churches. That if they can't be convinced to stop, they should be treated like false teachers and kicked out." Mary's fiery gaze held Gertie's. "And you've been gossiping for a while. Maybe I should bring it up with Pastor Ray and Beth? I'm sure you remember what he did with the last person who tried to sow division in the church."

Gertie narrowed her eyes as Mary let those words sink in.

"If you want to know the truth about Simon and what he's dealing with, ask him for his testimony. But don't spread rumours. It's filthy and evil. Now get out of my kitchen. Enjoy the rest of your day."

Gertie kept her gaze on Mary for a moment longer, then left.

Mary watched her go before letting out a sigh. She summoned up a smile and looked to the other ladies who had joined her.

"Let's get this soup made quick. I'm sure you've all got things to do this afternoon."

FORTY-ONE

MARY WAS LOCKING up the church when she decided to call Ray. She frowned as she heard the pastor's cell phone ring from Ray's office. She looked in to find Ray's phone resting on the desk.

She texted Bethany about it and soon got the whole story: Ray had forgotten it there and already gone home. Bethany gave Mary an address and instructions to drop it off.

Mary locked up the church and followed her GPS. Before long she found herself on a large ranch. The name *Fletcher* was printed on the archway above the gate.

"Right…" she murmured as she drove up.

She pulled up to the main house and knocked on the door.

Shelby answered. "Hello. Can I help you?"

"I'm Mary," she said. "I'm Simon's friend, and I'm involved at Ray's church. He forgot his phone there, so I brought it over."

"Simon or Ray's phone?" Shelby asked.

"Ray's."

"They're staying in a trailer inside the barn just over there," Shelby said warmly. "Oh, and where are my manners? I'm Shelby, Simon's mom."

"I thought you and Mr. Fletcher were gone for the weekend?"

Shelby chuckled. "We were supposed to be, but we drove all the way out to the conference to discover it had to be cancelled since the lead speaker got sick and they couldn't get a backup in time. So we're back."

"Well, it was nice to meet you, Shelby."

"You too. You're welcome to stay for lunch, if you like."

"I wouldn't want to intrude."

"It'd be no trouble at all," Shelby said. "It's always good to meet more of Simon's friends."

Mary thought for a moment. "I'll get back to you after I get Ray's phone to him."

Shelby turned to go back inside, then paused. "You sound really familiar."

"We spoke once before. On Simon's phone."

Shelby's eyes lit up. "Right! Thank you so much for helping him."

Mary nodded silently and looked off. "Of course. He's a good friend. See you, Mrs. Fletcher."

As Shelby went back inside, Mary walked towards the barn. She was about to enter when she heard Simon and Ray speaking just around the corner. She hesitated before stepping closer, leaning against the rough, sun-bleached wood of the barn to listen in.

———————————

Simon let out a breath as he and Ray sat just on the other side of the barn on lawn chairs, looking out over the fields.

"I don't think I can be in a relationship again," Simon was saying.

"Why's that?" Ray asked.

Simon relayed the details of his situation first with Susan, and then Viola.

"I had a few flings before Susan. Seems to me that women all hide what's important. They seem to care more about their own dreams than their partner. I get that it's not every one, but… well, I just don't have it in me to keep going through this."

Ray watched him for a moment. "And before all those flings… was Heather."

Simon fidgeted. "Yeah."

"It's been a difficult road, huh?"

Simon's expression finally broke and his hands went still on Delta's fur. The dog glanced up at him.

"It has," he said simply.

"Do you know what you were searching for?"

Simon was silent for a while, trying to process the answer. "Paul said it's better for man to be single so he can focus on God, and marriage is a means of attaining sexual purity."

Ray nodded and leaned back in his chair. "Yes, but you've already shown that sex is a driving factor for yourself."

"It wasn't about the sex," Simon said.

Ray raised an eyebrow. "Are you craving intimacy?"

"On some level, sure. But I can't sleep alone."

"Why not?"

"Everything comes back. When I shared a bed with Susan, I didn't have a single nightmare. As soon as we ended…"

Ray sighed. "I'm sure it was compounded by the abortion."

"I feel the same way I felt before. It's why I didn't care that Susan didn't contribute in any other way to the household. She made me able to bear living."

Ray was quiet.

"But I guess this is my punishment, right?" Simon said. "I lived by the sword and haven't died by it, so I've got to suffer in some way."

"That's not what that verse means, Simon," Ray said as he leaned forward and plucked a long blade of grass to fiddle with. "It means that those who go around looking to start fights end up dying in them. What you're dealing with, it's just… being human. It haunts you because you're a good man."

"Pfft, yeah."

"You are, Simon."

Simon's jaw muscles tensed. "Maybe it's better this way. I don't deserve peace."

Ray dropped the piece of grass and turned towards Simon, his expression serious. "Simon, I'm saying this with as much care as I could, but stop moping around."

Simon blinked and looked up at him.

"I can't even pretend to imagine what you're dealing with, but I can tell you that this mentality isn't going to do anything for you. It won't earn you any kind of atonement or peace. It's just going to keep ripping into you until there's nothing left. Now, I think I know your real hesitation regarding women. Tell me if I'm wrong. You're scared that you'll jump into a bad relationship just to make the nightmares stop. It's even more difficult now that you're a Christian, because you'd have to be married to get a woman in the same bed as you, which is a commitment you can't easily get out of, no matter how bad the relationship is."

Simon swallowed. "It doesn't matter. Paul also said that just having sex is enough to set up a spiritual connection. Jesus said that to have sex with a divorcee is adultery."

"Adultery is grounds for divorce, according to Jesus. He doesn't say that spouses who are the victims of such a divorce can't remarry. Not to mention the prophet Hosea. Did he commit adultery by marrying the prostitute Gomer? If so, God told him to sin, which would mean that the entire Bible is bunk. You're the prostitute in this metaphor, Simon. You weren't Christian when you were having sex. It was wrong, sure. But if a woman is willing to move past that with you, it's a new relationship, so long as you're honest with her about it." Ray watched Simon carefully for a moment. "You're hiding behind a false sense of holiness, Simon. If you just don't want to be in a relationship and have a wife, if you really just want to focus on God, then by all means do so. But if it's an excuse to avoid having to face your fear… then you're doing a great disservice to the woman who's out there looking for you. And one day she's going to find you."

————————————

As she listened in on this conversation, Mary's thoughts went back to that mysterious woman Hailey had mentioned. Yanah.

After a time of silence, Mary took in a breath and rounded the corner. "Hey!"

The two men looked back at her and Mary held out Ray's phone.

"You left this in your office," she said.

"Oh, thank you." Ray accepted the phone.

"And I need to talk to you about something, Ray, if you don't mind."

Simon stood up. "Thanks for the talk, Ray." He gave Mary a nod and the faintest of smiles before leaving them to it and walking off towards the main house.

Ray turned to Mary. "So what's going on?"

FORTY-TWO

SIMON WALKED UP to the main house and entered. Shelby smiled at him from the kitchen. "Hey sweetheart. Your friend Mary is here."

"Yeah, I saw," Simon replied as he walked in. "Want help with lunch?"

"That'd be wonderful." Shelby set some vegetables to the side for him to cut. "Mary seems nice."

"She is." Simon started cutting the vegetables.

"And pretty."

Simon nodded wordlessly.

Shelby was about to continue when Ray, Bethany, and Mary came into the kitchen. The usual pleasantries were exchanged and soon enough Mark and Hailey joined them as well.

Once the food was prepared, they all sat down for lunch. Mary chose the chair next to Simon, infrequently glancing at him as lunch and the conversation played out.

Shelby noticed the glances between the two. "So, Mary, what do you do?"

Mary's face flushed behind her makeup. "I help out with the church and members of the church. Cooking, cleaning, checking in... that sort of thing. My parents left me enough to live off while I do that."

"That's wonderful," Shelby said warmly as the meal came to an end. "Not many young people would spend their time and money that way."

Mary shrugged and looked down at her empty plate. "I just want to help people. Considering how my life has gone, I've been able to do it."

"Hmm..." Shelby's gaze flicked between Simon and Mary a few times. "Well, I'm going to start cleaning up. Mary, would you mind helping me out?"

Mary stood and joined Shelby in cleaning the kitchen while the rest moved to the living room. Simon tried to listen in on Mary and his mother's conversation, but he couldn't make out the words over the talk of his father and Ray.

Shelby cleaned the dishes while Mary packed away the leftovers. "Do you have a boyfriend, Mary?"

Mary swallowed and shook her head. "No, I don't."

CHAPTER FORTY-TWO

"So you and Simon aren't…?"

"No." Mary flinched as she realized how quickly she'd responded. "No. Simon and I aren't together. Just friends."

"Mmm." Shelby continued to clean the dishes. "That's the best way to start."

"It's not going to turn into anything more," Mary said, disappointment creeping into her voice.

"Why not? I saw the glances you were giving him over lunch. He likes you."

"It wouldn't work."

"I know Simon's been through a bit, but it would probably be very good for him—"

"I said no." Mary went still upon realizing how loud she'd gotten.

Shelby froze, confusion and shock written across her face.

Mary cleared her throat. "I'm sorry, Mrs. Fletcher, but I need to go."

Shelby shook herself out of it as Mary swiftly left. "Mary—"

Simon stood up as Mary walked out. He followed after her. "Hey."

But she didn't stop.

He had to hurry to catch up and only barely got his hand on the door handle of her car when she reached it.

"Mary, what's going on?" Simon asked.

She turned on him. "I can't be with you!"

He calmly watched her as tears touched her eyes.

"Everyone thinks we need to be together somehow, except for you and me, because you can't trust anyone anymore, and I—" The thought clenched her throat. "I–I'm going to—"

She couldn't hold back the tears.

Simon gently pulled her into an embrace and she cried into his shoulder, the last nearly two decades of fear, anxiety, and dread finally spilling over. She clung to him, unable to let go. Simon held her until she had no tears left.

She sniffled and took a few deep breaths. "Thank you, Simon." Her voice was soft, almost broken.

Simon gave her a gentle squeeze. "You're welcome."

Mary sighed and let go of him. "I'll see you later."

"Mary?"

"Yeah?"

"Get tested."

She frowned. "There's no way to really test for my condition."

"There is if it's hereditary, and sometimes it skips a generation."

She shook her head as she tried to wipe away her tears, her makeup a mess. "Even if it skips me, I can't pass that on to my kids."

"Then maybe there's someone who is fine with not having kids. Or adopting. There are plenty of kids who need parents." He had a slightly pained yet hopeful tone in his voice. "And there are perfectly safe surgeries to ensure you don't have to worry about accidentally getting pregnant. There are options."

Mary was quiet, everything inside her railing against his words. She didn't want to feel any hope. Yet a small internal voice reminded her that she did have a chance. There was something she could do.

She tried to drown out the voice.

"Mary, please. At least go to the doctor and see what your options are. The worst that can happen is that the doctor just confirms what you already think."

When she looked up at him, her makeup was ruined. "Could you ever trust again?"

Simon looked off to the side. "I'll try. But even if it's not me, you are an amazing woman, and I don't think you should give up just yet."

"I can say the same to you."

He offered a hollow smirk. "Well, I'm not a woman."

"You know what I mean."

He nodded. "I'll try. You should probably go freshen up before you leave."

Mary blinked a few times, then looked at her reflection in the car window. "Oh. Thank you."

They went back into the house and Mary stepped into the bathroom. Simon stood by the front door, waiting for her. When she came back out without any makeup, she smiled and hugged him.

"See you."

He returned her embrace. "See you."

After Mary left, Simon went up to his bedroom to change his shirt.

Shelby knocked on his doorframe. "I messed up."

"I'm aware," he called.

She opened the door and came in, immediately noticing the shrapnel scars and burn marks on her son's torso.

She swallowed. "I didn't mean to..."

Simon buttoned up his new shirt. "Hence it being a mistake."

"Is she okay?"

"I don't know. We'll see."

"I'm sorry."

Simon finished buttoning up his shirt, then hugged his mother and kissed her forehead. "I forgive you. Next time you see Mary..."

Shelby nodded. "I know. Thank you."

"Mmhmm." Simon gently squeezed her. "Love you, Mom."

She leaned into him. "I love you too, Simon."

FORTY-THREE

SIMON PULLED UP to Hailey's school. He'd been dropping her off and picking her up for three days in a row. He got out of his truck, Delta at his side, when a young woman approached him.

"Mr. Fletcher?"

"I am," Simon said hesitantly. "You are?"

She held out her hand. "Emily Fern. I'm Hailey's teacher."

Simon shook her hand. "I'm Simon, technically her adoptive brother."

"Oh." Emily frowned and looked off. "I see…"

"Is there a problem?"

Emily nodded. "Hailey's been having trouble with the other kids."

Simon crossed his arms and leaned against his truck, his eyes sizing up the woman before him. "What kind of trouble?"

"She's avoiding the other kids and she won't talk to me about it."

Simon sighed. "I remember teachers not being able to help me deal with bullies and other kids."

Emily narrowed her eyes. "Well, we here actually care—"

"It's not about how much you care, Miss Fern." Simon cracked his neck. "I had teachers I deeply respected who cared a whole heck of a lot. But telling a teacher only makes bullying worse when the teacher tries to do something about it."

"I still want to help."

"Yeah. But your job is to teach the curriculum and only intervene when you see something." Simon took in a breath. "It's my parents' job, and by extension my job, to handle the rest. Thank you for letting me know."

Emily watched Simon for a moment, then nodded. "You're welcome."

Simon spotted Hailey, who'd witnessed him talking to Emily. The girl ran up and hugged Delta.

"I'm ready to go!"

"All right." Simon opened the passenger door for her and Hailey climbed in. Delta jumped in and sat at Hailey's feet. "See you, Miss Fern."

Emily gave a nod. "See you, Mr. Fletcher."

Simon got into the truck and started driving. "How'd school go?"

"Okay." Hailey's tone was dismissive as she played with Delta's ears.

"Learn anything new?"

"Some math. Multiplication. And fish. Salmon live in the ocean but lay eggs in rivers."

"Mmhmm." Simon checked the time. "Wanna—"

His phone started to ring and he checked the contact on the truck's display.

"Hey Mary," he answered. "What's up?"

"My car's totaled. Could you pick me up?"

His adrenaline kicked in. "Are you okay?"

"I am." Her frustration came clear through the speakers. "I was in the grocery store when it when it happened. I'm over on the corner of Denninger and Juno."

"I'll be there shortly." Simon hung up. "We'll be making a detour."

Hailey just continued to play with Delta's ears.

Simon drove to where Mary was waiting for him by her small car, which was parked on the side of the street. The side of the car was caved in, the driver's door pushed halfway across the seat. The frame was bent and Simon noticed the front bumper of a pickup truck on the ground beside it. It seemed the offending vehicle had already been towed away.

Hailey and Delta quickly got out and moved to the back seat.

As Mary transferred some groceries from her shopping cart to the back of his truck, Simon noticed that Mary had covered up her birthmark again. She climbed into the passenger seat.

"Thanks a million, Simon."

"No problem," he said. "Where to?"

"Home."

"You got it." Simon started driving towards Mary's house. "So what happened?"

"Someone cut off another driver while travelling at high speeds, and that second driver careened right into my parked car."

"Yeah, I never cared much for city driving."

"That's one thing to call it..." Mary sighed and looked over her shoulder at Hailey. "How was your day?"

Hailey looked up from petting Delta. "Better than yours."

Mary giggled. "I bet."

They pulled up in front of Mary's home.

"Why don't you two stay for dinner?" Mary offered.

"Please!" Hailey said quickly, her eyes practically shining at Simon.

"Sure." Simon got out and grabbed the groceries from the back.

When they had gone into the house, they slipped off their shoes and started walking towards the kitchen.

"Wanna help me like at church?" Mary asked, eyeing Hailey.

"Uh-huh!"

As Simon followed them, he saw the girl quickly set to doing what she could with the vegetables.

"Did you get an appointment?" Simon asked.

"It'll be two weeks before a specialist is available."

"I'm proud of you."

Mary blinked a few times. "Well, like you said, the worst that can happen—"

"Still takes courage," he said.

A ghost of a smile touched Mary's lips.

"And I imagine you'll need a ride for doing your rounds?" Simon added.

"I couldn't ask you to do that."

Simon smiled. "I'm happy to help. Haven't got too much to do these days anyway. I'll just have to stop in at Ray's house to check on progress at some point."

"Okay. Thank you."

"Mmhmm."

They worked in silence for a bit before Mary glanced at Hailey. The young girl's eyes were locked on the onion before her, but her expression betrayed the turmoil underneath.

Mary leaned in close to Simon and whispered, "Is Hailey okay?"

Simon shook his head. "No. She's having some trouble with the kids at school. I've been trying to figure out how to broach the subject."

"Want me to?" Mary asked softly. "I've got some experience in that area."

He considered her offer.

Mary noticed the fatigue in Simon's eyes and lightly touched his elbow. "Go ahead and lay down for a bit. Hailey and I got this."

"Nah, I'm—"

"Simon. You've got to be able to drive home after this." She lowered her voice. "And it'll give me a chance to talk to Hailey."

Simon watched her for a moment, then nodded. He washed his hands and went off to the quiet living room where he texted Shelby to give her an update. He lay down on the couch and stared up at the ceiling, afraid to close his eyes. But eventually his fatigue dragged his eyelids closed.

Meanwhile, Mary and Hailey continued making dinner.

"Is Simon okay?" Hailey asked.

Mary glanced back at Hailey for a moment. "He just needs a rest."

"Because he doesn't sleep?"

A frown took hold of Mary. "He doesn't sleep?"

Hailey shook her head. "He wakes up a lot, really upset and not breathing right. I think it's because he misses his baby."

Mary's gaze fell. "That's part of it. He's got quite a few things going on, and he can't... well, he's having a hard time working through them."

"Can you help him?"

"I've tried, but I can only help keep things from getting worse. I don't know how to make him better."

Hailey brought over the onions she'd peeled and the celery she'd broken apart. "That's okay. Yanah will know what to do. She's real good with people and knows how to help them."

Mary accepted the vegetables and started cutting them up. "Sounds as though you like her a lot."

"Yanah's awesome!" Hailey said, careful to keep her voice low enough that Simon wouldn't hear. "She's a good cook, she's super sweet, and she's also a soldier... like Simon was. She's real pretty and sings real nice. I wanna be like her when I grow up."

"Sounds like..." Mary trailed off for a moment. "Simon's pretty lucky. Does he know she likes him?"

Hailey shrugged. "Yanah says she told him she'd marry him once she was old enough, but it was a long time ago."

"So Simon either forgot or Yanah was young enough that he didn't take it seriously," Mary murmured. "How old's Yanah?"

"Twenty, I think."

"Hmm... thank you."

"For what?"

"Telling me these things." Mary finished making dinner, feeling more relaxed than before. "It's helpful to know that someone will be there for him. So how's school?"

Hailey wouldn't meet her gaze. "Fine."

"I remember school being real hard for me." Mary set a pan with meat sauce in it to simmer and stirred the pasta in a pot before she leaned against the counter.

"Really?" Hailey asked.

Mary nodded. "Yeah. Remember my birthmark?"

Hailey nodded.

"I got bullied a lot because of it. Got pushed around and called a lot of mean names."

"That's not fair."

"No, it wasn't. But I had a real good friend who helped me deal with it."

"How?"

Mary smiled. "She listened. I was able to tell her anything, and even just talking about it helped me a lot. Do you have someone like that?"

Silence held Hailey's tongue for a bit and she finally shook her head.

"I can listen if you ever need to." Mary grabbed a sticky note from the counter and wrote a phone number on it. "Here's my number."

Hailey accepted the sticky note, carefully folded it, and stowed it in her pocket. "Thanks."

Mary checked the food, then took in a breath. "Well, dinner's ready. Could you go wake up Simon?"

"Uh-huh."

Mary watched with curiosity as Hailey grabbed a throw pillow from the couch and walked off towards the room Simon had disappeared into. She took one step in and threw the pillow.

Mary frowned as Hailey came back.

"He's up," said the girl.

"Why...?"

Hailey tilted her head. "Why what?"

"The pillow?"

"Simon asked me to never surprise him, because he sometimes reacts without meaning to. So I threw the pillow at him."

Mary stared at Hailey for a moment, then smiled. "Very creative of you. Now let's get the table set."

FORTY-FOUR

MARY PREPPED DINNER at her place, absently stirring a pan of fried rice. She suddenly jumped as her phone rang and fumbled with it for a moment. She saw the caller ID and her heart skipped a beat.

No, she thought. *Yanah's coming. I need to let him go. Especially with my condition.*

She took in a breath and answered. "Hey Simon, what's going on?"

Hailey giggled. "It's Hailey."

"Oh." Mary paused. "Hey, what's up?"

Hailey was quiet for a moment. "You said I could talk to you."

Mary smiled as she resumed stirring the rice, careful to ensure none of it burned. "Of course."

In the ensuing silence, Mary had to glance down at her phone's screen to see whether the call had dropped.

She smiled and put the phone to her ear. "Hailey, sweetie? I'm here."

"Kids at school are mean."

Mary's gaze fell.

"They say… they say—!" She sniffled. "They say it's my fault my mom and dad died! That I'm adopted by Shelby and Mark because nobody wants me! That… well, they saw Simon and say I got adopted by him because Mark and Shelby didn't want me!"

Hailey broke down in tears.

"Oh, sweetie…" Mary sighed. "I'm so sorry, Hailey."

Hailey continued to cry. "I want my mommy and daddy!"

Mary didn't have the words. All she could think of were her own years of self-harm, but she hadn't known what she needed to get out of it. She knew Hailey wasn't there just yet, but her heart couldn't stop imagining the same kind of future for the girl.

"I'm so scared!" Hailey managed. "I–I don't… I…"

"Hailey, sweetie?"

Hailey's sobbing continued.

"Could you do me a favour?" Mary asked.

CHAPTER FORTY-FOUR

Hailey brought her sobbing under control just well enough to respond. "Uh-huh."

"Could you go and hug Simon for me?"

She heard Hailey get up and run through the house. Simon's voice faintly came through the speaker, followed by a grunt. Hailey's sobs redoubled and Mary's heart broke. She then heard Simon comforting Hailey, and after a while there was silence.

Simon picked up the phone. "Hey."

"Hey," Mary responded softly. She explained the situation to Simon.

"Okay." He sighed. "Thank you."

"No problem. See you tomorrow?"

"Yeah," Simon replied. "See you tomorrow."

Mary hung up and looked down at her dinner, her stomach in knots. No longer hungry, she packed the food away and put it in the fridge.

FORTY-FIVE

SIMON LOOKED AROUND at the greenery as the Middle Eastern sun beat down on him. He was in Israel but didn't wear a uniform. He sat in front of a laptop, in the middle of a video call. Heather was giggling on the screen.

"I miss you too, Simon," she said. "One of these days you'll spend Thanksgiving with my family, if I have to tie you up and drag you here myself."

Simon smirked, feeling a sense of longing and loss. "I'd like to see you try."

"Oh yeah? Well saddle up, cowboy. I've been practicing with a lasso lately." She yawned. "I'm gonna go to bed. Love you, Sye."

Simon kissed his fingers and pressed them to the camera. "Love you too, Heather. See you soon."

When Heather ended the call, Simon's gaze fell. He knew what he was going back home to when this was over. He knew what was going to happen in a few weeks.

"This is a dream," Simon murmured. Tears struck his eyes. "Please, God, don't make me wake up. Just take me home. Take me to her!"

Simon broke down, his body racked with sobs.

"I can't—!"

But then he felt hands on his shoulders and his whole body went still. He looked up to see a young Israeli woman standing over him. She looked familiar, but older than he remembered. Her dark green eyes watched him with concern, her mahogany hair tied back in a ponytail.

The woman knelt and slid her arms under his shoulders and silently hugged him. He trembled and slowly returned the embrace.

"I'm going to lose her!" he said.

The woman held him tightly.

"She's going to kill herself and I can't stop it!"

"I'm sorry," she said quietly into his shoulder.

"I didn't see the signs. It's my fault!"

She simply nodded. "I see your pain."

He held onto her tightly.

CHAPTER FORTY-FIVE

"I'm here for you, Simon." She squeezed him. "I'll always be here for you. No matter how far apart, no matter how much time passes."

She pulled back and looked into his eyes. Her dark verdant gaze gently held his as she cradled his jaw and caressed his cheeks with her thumbs.

"Always, and forever." She kissed his forehead...

...and he woke up.

Simon stared at the ceiling, his heart shattered. He reached up and felt the tears that wetted his cheeks. He slowly got up, not noticing that he had somehow avoided being struck with a panic attack.

He got dressed, affixed his prosthetic, and looked back at his bed. His eyes settled on the sweat stains and he sighed. He grabbed his cot and set it up on the other side of the bed with a sleeping bag.

As he went for his morning jog, he passed the cowboys doing their job like usual. He noticed a new man riding amongst them. A second later, he smiled in realization.

"Morning, Eggsy," he said when the cowboy rode up to him.

Eggsy smiled. "Good morning, Sye. I, uh... wanted to thank you."

"For what?"

Eggsy rubbed the back of his neck. "For getting me clean again. And Clyde told me I have a job here if I want it."

"Clyde got you clean. I just brought you here."

His friend looked down. "I'd be dead a few times over without you, Sye."

"I'm just glad you're doing better. And the job offer was from my dad."

"Take some credit where it's due, will ya?"

Simon smirked. "All right, all right. You're welcome. So you gonna stay here then?"

Eggsy glanced away. "I'd like that. It'll keep me away from all that mess."

"Okay. I'll let Winston know."

"Thanks, Sye."

Simon shifted his weight. "You're welcome. I'll let you get back to it."

"Oh, and Sye?"

"Yeah?"

"Daisy gave birth to her pups last night."

Simon smiled. "Nice. I'm sure that was quite the experience."

"Yeah."

He watched Eggsy's expression for a moment, then patted his knee. "You're doing really well, Eggsy. It's not about how many times we fall..."

"It's about getting back up," Eggsy finished for him.

Simon gave a single nod. "I trust you, Eggsy. I know you can do this, and I'm proud of you."

Eggsy's jaw clenched and his lips tightened into a thin line. "Thanks, Sye."

FORTY-SIX

WHEN SIMON DROVE up to Mary's home, she quickly came outside. She hurried down the driveway, her arms hoisting a couple of bags full of groceries.

"Good afternoon," she said once she'd gotten in.

"Afternoon. To Neil's, right?"

She nodded. "Yep."

"All right." Simon started driving. "Thanks again for helping with Hailey. She opened up to me and I was able to talk her through some things."

"You're welcome," Mary said warmly. "She's a sweet girl. She cares a lot about you."

Simon smiled. "Yeah. The feeling's mutual."

A few minutes later, a call came through and he glanced at the number. There was no ID.

"Hello, Simon speaking."

"Simon!"

He blinked a few times. The woman's voice was familiar.

"It's Yanah," she said.

Simon cleared his throat. "Yanah? How'd you get my number?"

"From your mom. I need your help."

"I'm back home right now. I'm not sure how I can help you in Israel."

"That's the thing," Yanah said sweetly, the excitement clear in her voice. "I'm at the airport and I need a ride."

Simon stopped at a red light, his mind racing. "You're here?"

"I am. Could you pick me up? Please? Pretty please?"

Mary noticed a slight smile touch Simon's lips.

"Yeah. I'll be there in…"

Mary patted his arm and whispered, "Pick her up first. Trust me."

He watched her for a moment, then nodded. "About twenty minutes."

"I'll see you soon!" Yanah hung up.

"Yanah?" Mary asked.

Simon nodded. "Yeah. She's the youngest, and only, daughter of some family friends in Israel. My family always spent Thanksgiving out there. Her mandatory service must be up… wait, she's twenty-one. Her service should've ended last year. I guess she served an extra year."

"And she flew all the way out here. You two must have a pretty special bond."

"I don't know about that," Simon said, gripping the steering wheel. "She's seven years younger than me, so the last time I saw her I was eighteen and she was eleven. I knew her older brothers better, but she did follow us around a lot. I suppose she was a little clingy."

"Clingy?"

Simon nodded. "In a cute way. If I was taking some time to just sit down, she'd come over and sit with me. Wouldn't even say anything until I did. And then she'd just take off talking on one subject or another. She was a real sweet kid. Even sweeter than Hailey."

"Don't let Hailey hear you say that," Mary said with a chuckle.

Simon smirked. "I'm sure they've met. Oh, the two of them together… that'd be something to see."

Mary watched Simon's expression closely. "You seem a little less tired today."

Simon nearly flinched, but he managed to keep himself relaxed. "Yeah."

"No nightmare?"

He shook his head. "It wasn't a pleasant dream, but I didn't wake up in a panic attack."

"That's good," Mary said. "I hope they only get better from here on out."

Simon was quiet for a moment. "So do I."

When they reached the airport, Simon got out of his truck. Mary moved to the back seat and watched as Simon looked around the arrivals area. People were running to and fro.

Suddenly, he heard Yanah's voice calling his name. He turned just in time for the woman from his dream to reach him. She dropped her bags and jumped up, colliding with him. She wrapped her arms around his neck and her legs around his waist, holding tight.

"It's so good to see you!" she cried.

As Simon slowly recovered from the shock, he smiled and returned the embrace. "Good to see you too, Yanah."

She gave him another squeeze and then dropped to her feet. She looked up at him with the sweetest smile.

"You've grown," he remarked.

She giggled and hugged his arm as he grabbed one of her bags. She grabbed the other. "That does tend to happen."

He led her back to his truck and noticed that Mary had moved to the back seat. Simon opened the passenger door for Yanah and put her bags in the back.

"Yanah, this is Mary, a good friend of mine. Mary, this is Yanah."

Yanah turned in the seat and held out her hand.

Mary shook it. "Shalom, shalom."

Yanah's eyes lit up. "Shalom, shalom!" Then she said something else, something in Hebrew presumably.

After that, Mary glanced between them, not really knowing what else to say. "I, uh… don't really know Hebrew."

"Oh." Yanah giggled. "I was just asking you how you're doing."

"My car was recently totalled," Mary explained. "Hence why Simon's chauffeuring me around. But otherwise I'm fine."

Genuine concern took hold of Yanah. "Are you hurt?"

"No. I wasn't even in the car when it happened."

"Thank God for that. Car accidents can do some real damage." Yanah got a slightly far-off look for a moment, but a moment later she seemed to return to the present.

She and Mary talked as Simon drove. The two women got to know one another, bonding over their mutual connection with Simon.

Eventually Simon reached Neil's house and he got out to open Mary's door for her. As Yanah waited in the truck, Simon helped Mary bring in the groceries. He also took the opportunity to greet Neil.

But a few minutes later, he was back in the truck next to Yanah. They drove off together.

———————

Neil stood by the living room window, watching as Simon drove away.

"Who's the young lady?" he asked.

"Yanah," Mary replied.

"Yanah…?" Neil murmured. "The name sounds familiar."

Mary explained Simon and Yanah's connection.

"Ah. Heather must've mentioned her in passing at some point." He looked back at Mary. "Are you okay?"

"Hmm?" Mary picked up the groceries that had been left by the front door and carried them towards the kitchen. "Why wouldn't I be?"

"Yanah's going to take Simon away from you."

Mary flinched but smiled. She set the bags on the counter.

"I know," she called. "I'm not going to live too long anyway, so I'm going to get to know Yanah and make sure she's up to my standards for him."

Neil walked into the kitchen with eyes full of empathy.

"Neil, I'll be better knowing that he's got someone with him."

"What about your doctor's appointment?" he asked.

Mary shook her head. "It won't change anything. They won't be able to tell whether I have my mom's condition or not."

Neil sighed, then coughed. "Well… don't give up so quick."

"I'm not going to try to come between Simon and Yanah."

He coughed some more, then shook his head. "I'm talking about life, Mary. Don't give up on your life so readily."

Mary's gaze fell. "I'll go to the appointment."

"Good."

FORTY-SEVEN

"I REALLY WANT a cowboy hat," Yanah remarked, staring out the window at the passing scenery as they drove through the suburbs on their way into the countryside.

Simon blinked a few times. "A cowboy hat?"

"Look at me. I stick out like a sore thumb here."

He chuckled. "You look perfectly fine. Flannel shirt and jeans? You fit right in."

"I still want a hat." She leaned towards him, her eyes big and sparkling. "Can we stop somewhere so I can get one?"

Simon sighed. "All right, we'll get you a hat. Looking for something authentic, or something for city folk?"

"Authentic all the way." Yanah adopted her version of Simon's accent. "I ain't no cidiot."

Simon raised an eyebrow. "Was that supposed to be me?"

"Mmhmm. I think it was pretty accurate."

"Unfortunately, I became a cidiot over the years."

She gasped and covered her mouth. "Say it isn't so?"

"I'm afraid it is, Yanah. I'm getting back to my roots now, though."

She playfully punched his arm, her touch gentle. "You better be. Self-loathing and hatred isn't healthy."

His amused expression wavered, but he kept it together.

His phone started to ring.

"Hey Winston," Simon answered. "Yeah, it's about Eggsy. He won't be coming back. I recommend that Roman step into the position permanently. Good. Thanks, Winston. The Torrington project is going well. We'll be in the touch-up phase by next week. Talk to you later, boss."

Simon hung up with a sigh.

"What's wrong?" Yanah asked.

He glanced at her, meeting her jade gaze. "Just some work stuff. You didn't fly out here to listen to that."

"I came here for you, problems and all."

CHAPTER FORTY-SEVEN

Simon brushed it off. "One of my guys at work had to quit due to personal reasons, so we're shuffling some people around, promoting others…"

Yanah studied his face. "But there's a deeper issue."

"My guy quitting, especially in the way it happened, reflects poorly on me since I convinced my boss to hire him. He let me promote him in the first place."

Yanah's eyes flashed. "But you've always been a hard worker. It might reflect poorly on you, but it wouldn't be enough to put your job in jeopardy."

Simon narrowed his eyes. "Did my mother tell you anything about what's going on?"

"No." The word was so soft and simple as it tumbled from her lips.

"So you've just gotten good at reading people?"

"Nope." She shook her head. "I've just always been able to read you."

He pulled up in front of a small storefront. He hopped out and opened the door for her. She smiled brightly and stepped out into the sunshine.

"Welcome to Wrangler Crown Headwear," the young shopkeeper greeted them from behind the counter. "Can I help you two?"

"Just getting my friend here a hat," Simon said.

The clerk came around to meet them. "Might I suggest a Drifter Grey for you, ma'am?" She picked up a hat and held it out to Yanah.

Yanah put it on and didn't even look in the mirror. She turned to Simon. "What do you think?"

Simon smiled. "Looks good."

Yanah narrowed her eyes, then took off the hat and set it down. She whispered something inaudible to the clerk, who in turn glanced at Simon and smiled.

A moment later, the clerk walked away to look over the shelves.

"What did you tell her?" Simon asked quietly.

Yanah shrugged, her gaze scrutinizing the selection of hats on the wall in front of them. "That's a secret."

Simon raised an eyebrow.

Yanah grabbed a hat and put it on his head.

"I don't need a hat," he insisted.

"But you said you became a cidiot. So much that you don't even bring your hat with you in your truck anymore. That means you need a new one."

Simon shook his head. "My hat is back home in my closet."

"You left it there for how long…?"

"Ten-ish years."

"It's the one your dad got you at fifteen, right?"

"Yeah…"

"Then it's too small. I mean, your head is just so big now." She giggled and took the hat off his head before trying another one on him.

"You tryna start something?"

She giggled again and gave him a mischievous side glance as she took off the hat and looked for another. "Who, me? I'm a sweet little angel."

"That halo's looking a little crooked there."

She gasped and put her hand over her heart. "Simon! How could you?"

He chuckled. "Very, very easily."

She lightly bumped his shoulder with hers as she stepped around him in a circuit. "You're just a grumpy old meanie."

"You can call me grumpy and mean, but I ain't old yet."

"You're already twenty-eight. I, on the other hand, am the picture of youth at twenty-one."

"Well, if I'm a grumpy old meanie, I suppose I should just leave you here and head home." Simon started to walk towards the door. "After all, a youthful young woman like you wouldn't want to hang out with an old guy like me."

She ran back to him and hugged his arm, in the process draping yet another hat onto his head. "Don't you dare. There's no other grumpy old meanie I'd rather spend my time with."

"You're way too easy."

Her eyes lit up. "You little manipulator."

"Who, me?" he asked, chuckling. "I would never."

"Uh-huh." She smiled and took a step back. "That's the one."

He raised an eyebrow. "What's the one?"

"The hat."

The clerk was on her way back, with a hat in hand destined for Yanah's head.

"I think this one will look best." The clerk held up the cowboy hat and Yanah took it from her.

Yanah set it on her head and once again didn't bother looking in the mirror. Instead she eyed Simon. "So whatcha think?"

Simon quietly held her gaze, then almost imperceptibly swallowed and nodded. "That's the one."

FORTY-EIGHT

SIMON AND YANAH sat across from each other in a booth at Vera's Diner. The waitress came over to take their order after a few minutes.

"Sorry, Simon," said Emma. "Busy day. What can I get you?"

"Iced tea for me, and a beef dip."

Yanah glanced up at the waitress and smiled warmly. "I'll have what he's having, but double."

Emma's eyes narrowed, but she nodded. "You got it." She looked under the table, surprised not to see the dog waiting there.

Yanah tilted her head in confusion.

"Delta's home today," Simon explained.

"Gotcha," Emma replied. "I'll hold off on the breakfast sausages then. Be right back with your drinks."

Once they were alone, Simon drummed his fingers on the table. "Still packing it away, huh?"

"I practically starved in the military." She glanced past Simon at the waitress, then resettled her gaze on him with a brief, pensive look in her eyes.

"What?"

A playful smile graced her lips. "Looks like I've got even more competition."

Simon stiffened slightly and he realized what today was about. "Yanah—"

Emma came back and set their drinks down. "Food will be ready in a few minutes."

"Thanks," Simon replied.

Emma smiled and walked off.

"You were about to say?" Yanah asked sweetly.

Simon sighed. "I'm not on the market."

Yanah flinched, but her smile remained. "Mary?"

He looked off to the side and shrugged. "That's a complicated situation."

"You're either with her or you aren't," Yanah said simply, a twinge of hope and disappointment swirling in the undercurrents of her tone.

"It's not that simple, Yanah. I'm not even sure I want to be in another relationship."

"What?"

Simon took in a breath. "I'm not in a place to be in a relationship. I'm just—"

"Just…?"

He looked away. "The man you're looking for is gone."

Yanah reached out and took his hand. "No, he's right here. I came here for you. Past, present, and future."

Simon swallowed. "Yanah, I just can't."

"Is it Mary?"

"I already said—"

"You avoided the question." Yanah's thumb caressed his knuckles.

"She and I help each other a fair bit. I think that if we could, we would. But we can't."

"And you're afraid that dating somebody else would hurt her?"

Simon was quiet.

"Is there something else?" Yanah prompted.

"I'm too broken."

She frowned, an expression that had clearly only become more common in recent years. "Broken how, Simon?"

He shook his head, unable or unwilling to answer.

"Please let me in," she said. "I don't have a key."

When he replied, he couldn't look her in the eye. "Paul wrote that marriage is a means of sexual purity. I've already had sex. With a few partners. So that ship has sailed." He cleared his throat. "And in Matthew, Jesus said that people commit adultery when they have sex with a divorced person. And Paul wrote that merely having sex establishes that bond. Jesus also said there are only two reasons for divorce: infidelity, or if it's initiated by a non-believing partner."

"Simon…"

"Since our spirits are immortal, they reach outside of time," he continued. "That means that people are spiritually connected and married from the moment they have sex. So I've cheated on my future wife, if I have one, with seven different women."

She squeezed his hand. "You're not going to scare me away with this. Your ex has probably had sex with another man by now. If you haven't been with anyone since then, that means she committed adultery and you can 'remarry.'" She studied his dejected expression. "Jesus didn't say you had to get a divorce over infidelity, either. With you already being spiritually married, if your wife can move past it, then you have to trust her judgment and live up to her standards in that regard." She smiled gently. "Besides, why would God want you to be alone? I'm sure you've been punished enough. You shouldn't be punished for what your ex did. What any of your exes have done, for that matter."

"I have nothing to offer you." Simon's voice was quiet, almost broken.

Emma came back with their food and set it down. In the process, the waitress noticed Simon's dejected body language.

"You all right, Sye?"

CHAPTER FORTY-EIGHT

"Yeah. Thanks for the food."

"Need anything else?"

He shook his head. Emma glared at Yanah, as if she'd done something to Simon.

"All right," the waitress said. "Just holler if you change your mind."

"Will do."

Emma gave Yanah one last accusatory look, then walked off.

Yanah kept her gaze on Simon but let go of his hand. They finished their meal in silence.

FORTY-NINE

THE DRIVE ON the way to the ranch was quiet. When they pulled up to the main house, Simon got out—but before he could get the door for Yanah, she jumped to the ground and walked towards the front door.

Just then, Delta sprinted out and jumped up on her.

Yanah laughed and caught him. "Hey boy. You're Delta, aren't you?"

Delta barked and licked her.

Simon watched the interaction, masking his confusion and surprise. "Delta. Down."

Delta sat and held up a paw to Yanah.

She shook his paw. "It's all right, Simon. He's a dog."

"Until he jumps someone who can't take it."

Yanah tutted at Simon, then looked at Delta. "You wouldn't hurt anyone who didn't deserve it, would you, boy?"

Delta barked and nuzzled her hand.

"You're such a good boy."

Hailey was the next to come running from the door, moving as fast as her little legs could carry her. The girl collided with Yanah.

"Shalom, Yanah!"

Yanah hugged her. "Shalom, qatan echad."

Hailey giggled. "I'm not that little!"

"You are getting big," Yanah remarked. "You should lay off the sweets. Simon's been spoiling you, hasn't he?"

"Not that kind of big," Hailey shot back. "You're a meanie!"

Yanah giggled and cuddled her. "Aw… can you forgive me?"

"Maybe…" Hailey pouted and Yanah tickled her. The girl started to giggle uncontrollably. "I forgive you, I forgive you!"

Yanah laughed. "Good. Can you show me around? Simon has to go help his friend Mary."

"Okay."

Yanah grabbed her luggage from the back seat. "See you later, Simon."

He offered a single nod and got into his truck. Delta jumped into the passenger seat.

Simon looked down at the dog for a quiet moment, then sped off the ranch.

———————

Yanah's gaze fell as she watched him go, but she put on a smile. She sat down on the front steps next to Hailey.

"Did you two have a fight?" Hailey asked.

Yanah shook her head. "No, not a fight. We just disagreed on some things."

"Oh. Simon's in a lot of pain."

"His leg?"

"He misses his baby."

Every thought in Yanah's head stopped dead in its tracks. "His what?"

"His baby," Hailey repeated. "I also heard the grownups talking about some other kids, but I don't know what that's about."

Yanah's gaze fell and she sighed. "I moved too fast."

"What?"

"Just… I didn't take time to see how Simon was doing before I… I mean…" She shook her head. "It's okay. You don't have to worry about it, Hailey."

"But I want to help."

"Has he been spending time with you?"

Hailey nodded. "He even drives me to school and picks me up a lot."

"Then you've probably been helping him a lot."

"Ray might be able to help you."

"Ray?"

"Yeah. He's Simon's pastor. He's staying in a trailer in that barn over there." Hailey pointed to the barn.

"I'll keep that in mind, thanks."

"Uh-huh." Hailey grabbed her hand. "C'mon, I wanna show you around!"

———————

Meanwhile, Simon pulled up to Neil's house and got out with Delta.

"How's everything going?" Simon asked as he walked into the man's living room.

Neil looked up from his chair. "Simon! Doing well enough." In that moment, he was struck with a coughing fit. It took a while to regain control. "Mary's just out getting some groceries using my car."

Simon sat down. "Gotcha."

Delta settled at Neil's feet, and the man started to pet him.

"So who was that Middle Eastern beauty in your truck earlier?" Neil asked.

"Yanah," Simon replied simply. "Family friend. She just finished her mandatory service in Israel."

"Oh. And she chose to celebrate by coming out here to see you?"

Simon shrugged. "Seems so."

"You really plan to spend the rest of your life alone, don't you?"

"I've got friends."

"Sure." Neil slowly nodded. "Friends are good to have. But those friends will have partners of their own. Who's going to be there for you when they can't be?"

Simon's jaw tensed. "I'll handle it."

"Not to be a jerk, but how well has that gone for you so far?"

Simon paused.

"Seeking companionship for the sole purpose of staving off the nightmares?" Neil continued. "Falling apart because no one understands what you're going through, because you can't let them in that deep?"

"I try!" Simon snapped. He flinched and then forced himself to calm down. "I try to let them in, but everybody just…"

Simon looked down at his hands as if they were covered in blood. "It doesn't matter if I let them in or not. It doesn't change a thing."

"Even Mary?"

"Even Mary. I still feel this crushing weight. It's like my chest is being pressed in and ripped apart at the same time. Last night was the first night I woke up able to breathe."

Neil raised an eyebrow and kept petting Delta. "What was different about last night?"

When Simon looked away, Neil narrowed his eyes.

"You don't have to tell me anything, Sye. Just know that I'm here for you in whatever way I can be. And…"

Neil had another coughing fit and Simon got up to pour him a glass of water from the kitchen.

"Thanks," Neil said a couple of minutes later, taking a sip. "I'm lending Mary my car until she finds a new one. So you don't need to drive her around."

Simon's gaze fell. "All right. Then I guess I should head out."

"Sye? Keep your heart open. There's someone out there who deserves you. Don't let them down."

He stared at Neil for a moment, then walked to the door and snapped his fingers. Delta jumped up and followed him out of the house.

Simon had just walked down the steps to the driveway when Mary pulled up in Neil's car. She got out and smiled at the man and his dog.

"Hey, I was going to text you that I don't need a ride," she said. "Neil's lending me his car."

"Yeah. He let me know."

She tilted her head. "Everything go well with Yanah?"

Simon swallowed. "Well enough."

CHAPTER FORTY-NINE

They stood in silence for a moment.

Mary walked up to him. "Simon, I have a big favour to ask." She took a deep breath. "When I start to decline, I'm going to inject myself. I don't want to be locked up—or worse, end up hurting someone."

His heart shattered.

"I want you to handle the funeral and all that stuff for me please," she said. "I know it's a lot to ask, especially after Heather, but… I trust you."

Simon found his voice. "What about your meeting with that specialist?"

She shook her head. "There's no guarantee. I'll just have to wait and see. I need to know you'll handle this for me, and that you'll be okay too."

"Me?"

Mary gently placed her hand over his heart. "Don't let your heart harden, Simon. No matter what happens, keep it soft."

He reached up and held her hand, his gaze having fallen. "I'll try."

She smiled and squeezed his hand. "See you Sunday."

He nodded as she withdrew her hand, her fingers lingering. "See you."

Mary grabbed the groceries from the car and brought them into the house as Simon got into his truck and drove away.

FIFTY

RAY STOOD OUTSIDE barbequing some sausages when he heard footsteps. He looked over his shoulder to see Bethany coming out of the trailer with Annabelle cradled in her arms.

"Hey babe. Meat's almost done."

His wife nodded and quietly leaned against him. He put an arm around her shoulders and kissed her head.

"Love you."

She sighed. "Love you too."

"How's Anna doing?"

"Fed." Bethany yawned. "I was thinking that if she stays asleep tonight, you and I could have a little…"

Ray smiled and kissed her. "Sounds like a plan."

A voice suddenly interrupted them: "Do you do nothing in North American churches?"

They both went still and turned to see Yanah walking towards them from the main house.

"I'll go get the rest of dinner prepped." Bethany kissed Ray's cheek. "Good luck."

Ray nodded and turned his attention to the woman who had almost reached him. "Can you explain what you mean?"

"A member of your congregation is in pain and doesn't think he has value. And you just let him go on believing that?"

Ray's brow furrowed. Then his eyes lit up with recognition. "You're the young lady from Israel, the one Shelby mentioned would be coming…"

"Yes."

"I assume you're talking about Simon?" Ray flipped some of the sausages as Yanah nodded. "Why do you think he believes he has no value?"

"Because I know him." The frustration was clear in her voice. "He's still the same man I knew. He's not happy, though. He said he has nothing to offer. He's defeated."

"We're praying for him."

"So you just pray and hope God will come in and fix him?" she asked. "Have you not read the Bible? God uses people to help people all the time. You sit back and pray for God to intercede when he gave us each other. We're supposed to pray for guidance and the words to speak, not sit by for God to do it for us." She let out an exasperated sigh. "Or are you Mother Teresa, telling children who only need very basic medicine to pray for their own healing while you go to the best doctors in the world for a cold?"

"I'm aware of how he feels," Ray said calmly. "We've talked about it. I've told him about his worth to God. Paul wrote that it's better for a man not to have sexual relations, and only to marry as a means of sexual purity. God is enough."

"Immediately after that, Paul also wrote that each man should have a wife, and each woman a husband, because of sexual temptation. And remember that God saw man was alone and thought he would be better off with a woman, just as he'd paired off everything else."

"And Eve brought Adam away from God, did she not?"

Yanah paused.

"I'm not saying you shouldn't get married," Ray said. "But you should consider that Simon may not be the man you should marry. Paul gave a concession, writing that if a man or woman isn't tempted sexually, he or she doesn't need to marry. If anything, it's better that he doesn't, so his attention isn't split between God and his wife. Now, I don't know whether Simon is no longer tempted—but if he isn't, who are we to interfere?"

Yanah looked down and swallowed, her fingers curled into fists. "God promised me."

"What?"

"He called me to serve in the IDF for an extra year, in the most dangerous areas. I didn't want to. I really, really didn't want to. I planned to serve in logistics, or some other noncombat role." She sniffed. "But he wanted me there. I told him I would do it on two conditions: that he keep my heart soft and he bring me and Simon together." Tears started to roll from her eyes. "He kept my heart soft. It made my service even more difficult, because I couldn't close myself off from the suffering. I felt it all."

She choked on a sob and covered her mouth with her hand.

"Now I've come to Simon. I'm here for him. My family knew of this and are going to come here because of it." She swallowed. "They all believe that the Lord will do this thing, that he will uphold his promise."

Ray was quiet for a bit. "God didn't necessarily make a covenant with you. You answered his call, and he protected your heart. But Simon? God won't force Simon to be with you. He has given us all free will. And he did bring you two together."

She squeezed her eyes shut. "This isn't what I wanted."

"That may be true, but you now have time to spend with him. You said that God gave us each other for him to work through, and you accused me of waiting on God to do all the work."

She sniffed. "I'm sorry."

He shook his head. "Perhaps you should consider whether you aren't doing the same thing here."

"What?"

"You asked for God to bring you together." Ray took the meat off the grill and set it on a plate. "He's brought you here to Simon. Maybe you should let God work through you on him, instead of hoping that Simon will change his mind. Maybe he'll change his mind, and maybe he won't. Maybe he'll change his mind and choose someone else." Ray let out a breath. "The thing of it, Yanah, isn't to seek what you want, but what God wants. He wants for Simon what he wants for all of us: to grow closer to God, and to grow as people, following the example of Christ."

He looked past her as Simon drove up to the house.

"It always works out better when we set aside our own desires and focus on him," Ray finished.

Yanah followed his gaze and watched as Simon parked his truck. "Okay. Thank you, Ray. I'm sorry for coming at you so aggressively."

"Someone you care for deeply is in pain," Ray said gently. "You felt that the people who are supposed to help him were neglecting him."

Yanah took in a breath. "Pray for me."

"Consider it done."

Yanah walked off towards the house as Ray returned to his barbeque.

FIFTY-ONE

SIMON HAD RETREATED up to his room after dinner that evening to read from his Bible when Shelby's voice called out to him.

"Simon?"

He bookmarked the Bible and went downstairs, where he encountered two soldiers in dress uniform standing in the entryway. Simon narrowed his eyes, dread building in his chest.

"Gunnery Sergeant Simon Fletcher?" the taller of the two asked.

Simon nodded. "Yeah. What's this about?"

"I'm Sergeant Sam Flynn, and this is Corporal Frank Janzen. We served with Master Gunnery Sergeant Donald Relna."

Simon went completely still. "'Served'?"

"Don was caught in an—" Sam paused when he saw Hailey at the top of the stairs.

"Let's take this outside," Simon said, gesturing for them to step out onto the front porch. When they had gone out and closed the door behind them, he took a deep breath. "You were saying?"

"An IED, sir," Sam said. "He died. Near instantly, the medic claims."

Simon's hands clenched into fists.

Frank held out a folded flag. "We're sorry you missed the funeral, sir. He had no next of kin and his will was misplaced. It took some time to track you down."

Simon accepted the flag.

"His personal effects are also yours, sir." Sam gestured to the pickup truck with a travel trailer attached, parked in front of the house. The sun was setting right behind it. "Conveniently he kept a travel trailer to store his things. You just need to sign a document, and we'll take care of the rest. Transfer of ownership and all that."

Simon nodded slightly. "Thanks."

Frank approached the military vehicle they'd arrived in, opened the door, and reached in to grab a document that seemed to have been kept in the glovebox.

"May we see some ID please, sir?" Frank asked when he returned.

Simon took out his wallet and showed the officers his driver's license. Frank used his phone to snap a picture of it, and then Simon signed the document. Frank took a second picture, this time of the signed paper, and put his phone away.

"We're sorry for your loss, sir," Sam said.

Simon looked up as they saluted, and he returned the salute. "I'm sorry for yours."

"Sir?"

"Hmm?"

"How did you know Don?" Sam asked. "You were Marines. He was Army."

"We met in the field," Simon said. "Ended up working together a lot, and he led a team…"

"Understood, sir." Sam cleared his throat and handed Simon the keys to Don's truck. "Then I'm glad he left it all to you, sir. He is buried at Abilene."

"Thanks," Simon replied as he gripped the folded flag in his hands.

Sam and Frank each offered one last salute, then got in their vehicle. Simon stood on the deck and watched them drive away. It felt like a metal claw gripping his heart as his gaze finally fell to the flag in his hands.

After a time, he got into Don's truck and moved it to the side of the house. The sky was dark by the time he entered the trailer and looked around the messy interior. Tears clung to his eyes as he started to sort through Don's belongings.

He eventually heard a knock on the door and looked up to see Yanah.

"Can I come in?" she asked softly.

When he nodded, she climbed in and they both sat on the edge of the bed.

"Don was the man who saved you from those terrorists, right?" Yanah wrapped her arms around him. "It must hurt. Having so much taken away from you."

Simon felt the claw around his heart loosen.

"You should come inside and sleep," she suggested. "This will all be here tomorrow. I'll help."

She took his hand and led him back into the main house. Soon she had brought him to his bedroom, giving him a final hug at the doorway.

"I'm so sorry, Simon."

He returned the embrace but couldn't muster any words.

She squeezed him. "Good night."

"Good night."

Getting those words out took every ounce of strength he had.

Yanah walked into the guest room and started preparing herself to sleep. She was just about to lie down in the bed when she heard a soft knock at the door. Opening it, she found Shelby and Mark.

"We have a favour to ask," Shelby said quietly.

CHAPTER FIFTY-ONE

Yanah gestured for them to come in. "Sure."

They entered and Yanah carefully closed the door behind them.

"I never served," Mark said. "There are things I will never understand about my son. But you… you understand. Please help him through this."

"He's been through so much already," Shelby added. "Mostly by himself."

Yanah smiled. "I'm not going to let him grieve alone anymore."

The couple relaxed and then both gave her a hug.

"Thank you, Yanah," Mark said. "You're a godsend."

Yanah returned the embrace. "It's my pleasure."

FIFTY-TWO

SIMON OPENED HIS eyes to find himself staring up at a panelled ceiling. He was in a hospital bed. Bandages covered his whole body. On the wall, signs appeared in both Arabic and Hebrew. He tried to focus on them but couldn't read the words.

He finally slumped back just as a man in an IDF uniform came into the room with a nurse.

"Gunnery Sergeant Simon Fletcher," the man said. "I am Colonel Hassan Almachmud, IDF. What do you remember?"

Simon shook his head to clear out the cobwebs. "I was on patrol around the embassy..." He frowned. "There was an explosion."

"Correct," Hassan said as he sat next to him. The nurse began to conduct an examination of Simon. "Your attackers got close to you. Do you remember their faces? Anything they were saying?"

Simon struggled to focus. "I... it was... I can't. My ears were ringing, my vision blurry. I couldn't make out any of it."

"That's all right." Hassan patted Simon's knee. "Some of the other members of your squad were taken. I was hoping we could find them before the enemy got any intel out of them about the embassy."

Simon flinched at Hassan's touch and looked down. His heart leapt into his throat as he saw that everything below his left knee was mangled.

He started to hyperventilate. "Oh God..."

"Simon, you need to calm down," the nurse cautioned.

"My leg!"

"We are trying to save it, Simon. It's a new treatment. It takes time. Just remain calm."

"My—" Simon choked on his words.

"Gunnery Sergeant Fletcher!"

Simon snapped his gaze to Hassan.

"You need to calm down," the man ordered as the nurse injected meds into his IV.

Simon scowled. "No, wait... where's Major Johnson? Why's the IDF here, but no Americans? Who are you?"

"I am Major Hassan Almachmud of the IDF," Hassan said again. "I have already contacted your commander and informed him—"

"There should be a U.S. soldier stationed outside my door. It's protocol. Where is he? Bring him in…" Simon's words began to slur.

"I'm afraid I can't do that, Simon." Hassan's voice was soothing yet condescending.

Simon struggled to keep his eyes open. "You bastards…"

———————————

Simon woke up in a cold sweat and fought to regain control. A memory flashed across his mind—Yanah embracing him. He closed his eyes and focused on that. Slowly his breath came back to him and he calmed.

He went through his morning routine and eventually found himself back in Don's trailer, sorting through everything. Delta climbed in behind him and started sniffing around.

The dog looked up at Simon and whined.

"He's not here, bud."

Delta sat in front of him and whined again.

Simon sighed and hugged him. "He's gone."

Delta's ears flattened and his tail stilled, mourning his former master.

Simon knelt and properly embraced the dog. "I'm sorry, bud. He's dead."

Delta nuzzled and licked him as he held on tight, as much for Delta as for himself.

He felt the trailer rock slightly underneath him and glanced up to see Yanah come in. She knelt down and embraced both him and Delta.

After a while, Simon let go of Delta and the dog went back to sniffing through Don's possessions. Before long, he found a doggy bed in the corner and pawed at it.

"It's yours, bud. Lemme help."

Simon grabbed the bed and moved it closer to the door. Delta lay down on it.

As Simon set about the work of inventorying Don's things, Yanah worked quietly right alongside him.

She held up a magazine and frowned. "I imagine you don't want this?"

Simon looked over and his eyebrows shot up. "Huh. They usually remove stuff like that before sending it to the family…" Simon glanced at the laptop peeking out from the corner of a half-opened cardboard box. "I'm almost worried to crack that open."

Yanah shook her head and put the magazine into a garbage bag.

Meanwhile, Simon opened the laptop and turned it on. The main screen wasn't password-protected, so he started sifting through the folders. He deleted a fair few of the ones he found.

Yanah glanced over at the computer. "He, uh… was quite a lonely man."

"Well, you take what you can find when you're starved for connection and intimacy, no matter how hollow it is." Simon's expression betrayed his own experience in the subject.

Yanah pulled another box out from under the bed. "He had good taste in beer, though."

Simon flinched.

"At least my brothers would say so. They love this brand." She pushed the box back out of sight. "It'll be great for when they come out here."

Simon nodded, then paused when he started to understand what she'd said. "What?"

"My family's coming out this way for Thanksgiving," Yanah said nonchalantly.

"Then I guess we should hold onto it for them…"

Yanah studied him for a moment before pulling the box of beer back and setting it by the door. "Okay."

Simon finished his cursory sift through the laptop, then closed it as Yanah examined a large footlocker.

"Any keys?" she asked.

Simon passed her a set of keys he'd found underneath the laptop. She tried them while he started sorting through discarded clothes.

She cracked open the footlocker and suddenly cleared her throat to get his attention.

"What?" he asked.

She motioned for him to come over. When he joined her, he saw that the lid of the footlocker had all kinds of pictures of Don with different soldiers he'd worked with. Inside the footlocker itself was a heavy rifle and ammo.

Simon picked up the weapon. "Well, he always did like big guns."

She took out a semiautomatic as well. "I see."

He rummaged around in the footlocker and found a combat handgun, a fully kitted-out assault rifle, and the registration for each of the firearms.

"That makes this easier," he murmured as he stared at the paperwork. His eyes couldn't focus.

Yanah gently touched his arm. "What's going on?"

"I'm losing everyone."

Her expression softened and her eyes fell on the paperwork.

"Neil's got a cough. He acts like it's just a little thing, but he wears a metal hospital bracelet. Now Don's gone. And my parents were already pretty old when they had me, so who knows how much longer I've got them?" He stirred. "Then there's Mary…"

"What's wrong with Mary?"

"It's not my place to say, but… she's probably only got a few years…" Simon's grip tightened on the paper and tears clung to his eyes. "Heather killed herself, and Sue killed our—" Simon choked on the truth. He felt surrounded by death. "She killed our b–b—"

Yanah gently set down the semiautomatic, took the paperwork from his hands, and embraced him. He closed his eyes tightly as tears broke free.

"I'm sorry." Her voice was tender and soothing as she spoke into his shoulder.

"I can't… I'm not—" His chest tightened, his breath shortened. His heart felt crushed, ripped apart, his lungs deflating…

CHAPTER FIFTY-TWO

"I see your pain."

Those four words brought everything to a grinding halt. He remembered his dream...

"It hurts to lose those you care about," Yanah continued. "It hurts more when you feel responsible. And even more when you can't do anything about it."

A wisp of air made it to his lungs and he reached up with shaky hands to cling to her as she nuzzled him. She started to sing a Hebrew lullaby, her voice softly massaging away the crushing weight and slowly releasing his lungs and heart.

He finally broke down, letting the well of sorrow and pain overflow. She held him through the storm, a rock amidst the waves. She rubbed his back and held the back of his head.

Eventually his tears ceased and his breathing slowed.

"I'm here for you, Simon." Yanah squeezed him. "I'll always be here for you. No matter how far apart, no matter how much time passes."

She pulled back and looked into his eyes. Her dark verdant gaze gently held his as she cradled his jaw and caressed his cheeks with her thumbs.

"Always and forever," she finished.

Simon stared into her eyes, desperate to believe it, but terrified as well. She smiled gently and pressed her forehead against his.

FIFTY-THREE

MARY DROVE DOWN the country roads to the Fletcher ranch. As she pulled up, she saw Simon and Yanah step out of a small travel trailer parked next to the house. Simon was on the phone. Yanah then gave him a hug before walking inside.

Putting it out of her mind, Mary walked over to the barn and found the trailer housing the Torringtons. She knocked on the trailer door and Bethany answered.

"Hey Mary! What's up?" the pastor's wife asked.

"Thanksgiving is weekend after next. I wanted to go over our plans for the event the church is hosting."

"Gotcha. I'll get him up."

Mary walked back outside the barn and sat down in a foldout chair that was pushed up to the wall. Soon enough Ray joined her.

Ray took a sip of coffee. "Aren't we doing the same outdoor potluck and games as years prior?"

"Yeah, that's the general plan. I just wanted to confirm and go over inventory and numbers. We may need more tables than last year, since the church has grown. We'll also need to rent the bouncy castle for the kids, and all that stuff…"

Mary handed him a piece of paper with all the budget items laid out.

"We should be ready for it. We made sure to set aside money…" But when Ray looked over the numbers, his eyebrows shot up. "This is more than expected."

"Inflation," Mary said with a sigh. "And higher taxes. The cost of everything's gone up."

"Death and taxes…" Ray let out a grunt. "It's already Monday. It'll be difficult to ask people for a little extra at this point…"

"I know. I should have addressed this two weeks ago."

He shook his head. "It's okay. We all forget things… We'll just have to work something out. For now, start calling around for the rentals and see if we aren't too late. I'll see if I can't scrounge up some more money."

As Ray walked back to the trailer with his empty coffee mug, Mary started making calls. In the process, she couldn't help but notice that Simon was still on his phone. And Yanah had come back outside too. He eventually hung up and the two of them got to work moving boxes out of that mysterious travel trailer.

On the yard nearby, Delta was sprinting away from the bunkhouse as Hailey chased after him, trying to grab him by the collar.

Mary couldn't help but smile. The four of them looked like a family.

The realization felt like a needle sliding into her heart.

She shook her head and returned her attention to the task at hand—making calls to arrange the party rentals.

She hung up just as Ray and Bethany walked towards her. Annabelle was cradled in Bethany's arms.

"Everyone's all booked up, unless we use a rental company that's a lot further away," Mary said. "But then we're paying through the nose."

Ray grumbled. "Well, I secured the extra money… but I guess that's useless if nothing's available to rent this last-minute."

They heard a horse neigh and all three of them looked up to see the cowboys herding the cattle through the adjacent field.

Bethany's face lit up in a smile. "Maybe…"

"We've already imposed too much on Mark and Shelby," Ray said dismissively.

"It can't hurt to ask," Bethany pointed out. "And you just said you got the money. We could pay some."

Ray frowned and considered the notion. "All right. I'll ask."

Mary approached Simon and Yanah as Ray walked off towards the main house. Delta and Hailey had run off by this time.

Yanah noticed Mary first and smiled, offering a small wave. "Hey!"

Simon glanced up from the boxes he had in his arms. "What brings you all the way out here, Mary?"

"I had to meet with Ray about the Thanksgiving event we host every year," Mary explained. "We kinda forgot to start planning it with everything that's been going on."

"Gotcha," Simon murmured. But his gaze had shifted back to the travel trailer behind him.

"I could actually use some help," Mary said. "Sorting through the decorations in storage, getting some more tables and other supplies…"

Simon opened his mouth to speak, but Yanah put her hand on his arm and turned her green gaze to Mary.

"I'm free," Yanah said. "Simon's got to get this trailer taken care of."

He made a move to protest. "Yanah—"

She gently squeezed his arm. "If you don't do it now, you might never get it done."

"I should finish later today," he acknowledged with a nod. "I'll be able to help tomorrow."

"Can we borrow your truck, Simon?" Yanah asked.

He took out his keys and took off the one that would start the truck. "Don't forget it's diesel."

"Got it." Yanah smiled, hugged Simon, then turned to Mary. "Shall we go? We can come back for your car, unless you want to drive it to the church?"

"I'll drive it there."

Simon watched as the two women left before climbing back into the travel trailer.

Yanah followed Mary to the church. After parking it, she got out of Simon's truck and looked up at the humble structure.

"It's not very big," Yanah remarked as she and Mary walked up to the front doors.

Mary smirked. "No, it isn't. But it's intimate and everyone knows everyone."

Mary unlocked the doors and stepped inside. She held it open for her companion to come in right after her.

"What is this Thanksgiving event?" Yanah asked.

"Thanksgiving is a holiday here in America—"

"I know what Thanksgiving is," she said sweetly. "I mean specifically what I'm here to help with."

"Oh." Mary blushed a bit. "It's a community event we host. A potluck, games, that sort of thing. People from the area, and even some outside of it, swing by. We hold a fundraiser for some charities, and a bit of the money goes towards covering our costs."

"You make money?"

Mary shook her head. "No, we generally lose money. We only take enough to cover excess expenses, which are determined after it's over. We raise money to pay for Thanksgiving dinners for families who can't afford them."

"I see..." Yanah murmured as she followed Mary down a set of stairs into the church basement. "You do a lot for this church."

Mary smiled as she turned on a light and opened the door to a storage room. "I do my part."

The room was packed with boxes filled with seasonal decorations. Mary started sorting through them while Yanah moved some of the heavier items out of the way.

"You're very strong for your size," Mary said.

Yanah shrugged. "I was active combat for three years. I might be stronger than Simon now, if he hasn't been keeping up with his exercise."

"Oh, he keeps up with it." Mary remembered how strong his arms had felt. Her ears burned as she turned to Yanah. "So you've known Simon a long time?"

"My whole life. He's very special to me."

"He's a very special guy," Mary replied as she pulled out the Thanksgiving decorations.

It took a few minutes, but together they succeeded in moving the boxes out of the storage room. They stacked them up at the bottom of the stairs.

"He cares deeply for you," Yanah commented. "I may know who he was, but you know who he is. I want to help him."

Mary went quiet. A part of her wanted to keep Simon to herself, to hold onto him until her time came. Her lips parted to speak, but then she saw the look in Yanah's eyes—the earnest, hopeful, determined look of a woman who would fight tooth and nail to love and live.

Mary's gaze fell slightly as she realized she'd already lost. "Simon doesn't sleep well. It helps when he has someone with him."

Yanah's eyes flashed. "How do you know this?"

"I overheard him talking with Ray."

After a moment, Yanah looked away. "Well, I can't just join him in bed… but that does give me a starting point. Thank you, Mary."

"Mmhmm. Could you help me bring these decorations upstairs, please?"

Yanah nodded and got to it.

You don't get to be jealous, Mary thought to herself as they worked. *He's not yours. And all you've done is help manage his symptoms, not actually heal him. Yanah has a chance to heal. She may be what's best for him. You can't stand in the way of that.*

As Mary went down for the last box, she found herself alone for a moment.

"You don't get to be jealous," she murmured, repeating the sentiment.

With that, she turned off the light and went upstairs.

Yanah met her halfway to the top. "Where are these all going to go?"

Mary's heart raced as she realized that it was possible for Yanah to have overheard her. But she swallowed her feelings and got back to work, pulling out the decorations and deciding where they should go.

FIFTY-FOUR

AS SOON AS Yanah and Mary sat down in the booth at Vera's Diner, Emma came by. Confusion was written across the waitress's eyes to see the women without Simon accompanying them, but she set down the menus.

"What can I get you two?"

"Tomato soup and grilled cheese for me," Mary said. "And just a water to drink."

Yanah looked up at her and smiled sweetly. "I'll get the same as last time, please."

Emma nodded and walked off.

Yanah started to giggle and Mary couldn't help but smile at the sound.

"What's so funny?" Mary asked.

Yanah leaned forward. "Emma has a crush on Simon. But she's seen him here with both of us, and now here we are together."

Just a few moments later, Emma returned and placed their drinks down. Without another word, she bustled off to take care of the other tables.

"Emma thinks Simon is with you and having an affair with me," Yanah said, her eyes following Emma's movements around the diner. "So when she sees you and I here together…"

Mary blushed. "Simon and I aren't… I mean—"

"I know."

"And how do you know what Emma's thinking?"

"I don't," Yanah said. "It's a game. It's like people-watching, coming up with stories about random strangers. Except this is an educated guess. I feel like a detective."

Mary allowed herself to chuckle. "Okay, that is kind of funny. But next time, preface it with the fact that this is just a game. I don't like rumours."

"Gossips destroy churches," Yanah said solemnly. "If a gossip doesn't stop, they should be kicked out. That's what the Bible says." She smiled. "This is just a fun little thought experiment between you and me. So I presented the scenario. What do you think?"

Mary glanced back at Emma and watched her go about her work. "I think she thinks Simon is just friends with both of us."

Yanah's eyes narrowed. "Well, I don't actually think she thinks Simon's a cheater."

CHAPTER FIFTY-FOUR

"But you—"

"It's a game. I suppose Emma simply seemed confused. She hasn't come to a conclusion yet. But she'll come to one of only two conclusions."

"What're those?"

"She'll either be shy and give up her crush on Simon, seeing him as too entangled, or she'll ask one of us, or Simon himself, for the truth and realize she can't compete."

Mary blinked a few times as Yanah sipped her iced tea. "Can't compete?"

"For Simon."

Mary swallowed. "I don't see why she wouldn't be able to."

"Because he has you and me in his life already." Yanah twirled her straw. "And she only has a crush. You and I know Simon. We see what he's dealing with and can help him. We're both thinking of what's best for his life, not just having a relationship with him. We both love him."

Mary's heart raced. "Yanah, I'm not—"

Yanah quietly sipped her drink, waiting for Mary to finish her sentence.

"—I'm not going to live long enough for that."

Yanah's already gentle gaze softened further.

Emma came over with the food. "Can I get you two anything else?"

"No, this is perfect," Yanah said. "Thank you."

The waitress nodded and walked off.

Yanah returned her attention to Mary, who went on to explain her medical situation. Yanah listened intently.

"I'm so sorry." Yanah took Mary's hand and squeezed it. "It must be terrifying."

Mary looked up at Yanah, and for a moment she was reminded of the moment when Simon had held her after she'd met his parents for the first time. "It is."

"But you said you're going to see a doctor this week?"

"Yes. They may or may not be able to tell me whether I'm going to end up like my mother."

Yanah closed her eyes and held both of Mary's hands. "Father in heaven, I pray today for you to guide the doctors to find out whether Mary has this affliction or not. If she does, then I pray for healing—for you to guide the doctors and bring her health. If it's not your will, then I pray for peace and acceptance, and for her to know and experience your love like never before, for this world is temporary, but after this world is an eternity with you. Amen."

Yanah opened her eyes and smiled at Mary, whose own eyes had misted over.

Mary held onto Yanah's hands tightly. "Simon is yours."

"What?"

"Simon is yours," Mary repeated, dropping her gaze to the table between them.

"He's a man, not a possession. Only he can give himself away. And I didn't do all this to prove anything. I did it because Simon cares about you, and you're a pivotal figure in his life. I want to know you and befriend you, regardless of what happens with Simon and me."

Tears rolled down Mary's cheeks.

"All I ask is for permission to pursue him," Yanah said.

"You don't need my permission."

Yanah shook her head. "As I said, Simon cares for you dearly, and you him. Regardless of your situation, I would ask, because I consider you a friend."

"We've only really gotten to know each other today…"

Yanah shrugged and offered her the sweetest smile. "I make fast friends."

Mary took in a shaky breath. There was a part of her that wanted to deny Yanah the permission she sought. But just as quickly, she felt an overwhelming peace wash it all away.

"You have it, Yanah. On one condition."

Yanah looked at her eagerly.

"You love him recklessly," Mary said.

Yanah stared at Mary for a moment, then giggled. "I have loved him recklessly ever since I knew what love was. But I do promise to continue to do so."

Mary relaxed, a twinge of longing still tugging at her heart. "Then I know he's in the best hands he could be in."

FIFTY-FIVE

SIMON OPENED HIS eyes and found himself back in a hospital. He immediately struggled to get out of bed. He swung his left leg over the edge but quickly collapsed to the floor. He cried out in pain as his stump struck the linoleum and panic set in. He looked down at where his left calf should have been and his breath came short and quick.

The door opened and he glimpsed a pair of IDF-issue boots stride towards him. He grabbed the IV, ready to rip it from his arm.

The officer in the room with him cursed under his breath. Then Simon's head began to swim. The whole room spun as he tried to comprehend the soldier's words. His eyes lost focus and he blinked to try reorienting himself.

When next he opened his eyes, the man had grabbed him and pulled him back up to the bed. Simon ripped out his IV and reared back his arm to try stabbing the man in the eye with it.

He stopped just short, his eyes wide. "Lavi?"

The older IDF officer stood completely still and swallowed. "Simon."

Simon blinked, then let go of the IV.

Lavi helped him settle back onto the bed. "You were rescued, Simon. You're safe now."

Simon stared, hardly able to comprehend what he was seeing. "H–how?"

"With the help of the Americans, Mossad discovered the safehouse and executed a raid."

Simon frowned. "Where's the American liaison?"

"There wasn't time—"

Simon started to breathe heavily again and the room once again spun. The walls seemed to crumble, and the image of Lavi began to melt away…

"No!"

Before his eyes, Lavi transformed into a Middle Eastern child holding an AK-47. Simon looked down and saw the gun in his own hand—

His training kicked in—

There was a flash—

He suddenly sat up and realized he was in his own bed, at his parents' home. His body wracked with sobs and tremors as he struck his leg with his fist, a confusing mass of complicated emotions boiling over.

The thought of Yanah holding him helped to bring his breathing under control.

Simon grabbed his prosthetic and went down to the living room, where he sat on the couch for a long while, just staring at the floor. Everything within him raged against his latest dream. He ran his fingers through his hair and gripped tight. The sobs threatened to return.

He sank deeper and deeper into misery and his heart twisted in his chest as though trying to escape the crushing weight and pressure bearing down on him.

A hand suddenly touched his shoulder and he grabbed the wrist and dragged the person over the couch. The owner of the hand let out a yelp but grabbed him and wrapped her legs around his arm and used her weight to force him to the floor.

He broke free of her grip and was about to strike her when she wrapped her arms and legs around his torso, holding tight.

He went still as he recognized her. "Yanah?"

"Yes, Simon?" Her voice was soft as she buried her face into his neck.

"I could've—"

"I can take it." Her breath was hot on his neck. Her arms and legs tightened around him.

He started to break down again.

As she got her legs underneath her, she pushed him back up onto the couch. She sat on his lap and held him tight.

"I'm here for you, Simon. Always and forever. I see your pain."

Simon cried freely into her shoulder while she petted his hair and kissed his head.

"I can't escape it!" Simon managed to get out.

"Escape what?"

"Any of it! The nightmares. The children I've killed. Heather. The torture. My own—"

"Your own what, Simon?" Her voice was as soft and soothing as a cool stream on a hot day.

He closed his eyes tight and shook his head.

"Simon, you need to let this out."

"My own—" He halted again, everything inside him screaming to claw it back inside, desperate to keep her from seeing the depths of his pain. "My own..."

He struggled as the truth finally breached the surface.

"My own child!"

Yanah kissed the top of his head. "Was it a boy or a girl?"

He shook his head.

"How did you lose them?"

"My ex abort—" He stopped and took a few breaths. "She aborted them. With my money. And tried to hide it."

"I'm so sorry, Simon. To lose a child is a special kind of pain."

He nodded silently.

CHAPTER FIFTY-FIVE

"Did you have names?" she asked quietly.

He swallowed. "She'd talked about not wanting to know the gender, so we planned for versatile names, like Alex."

"That is a wonderful name. Can you do me a favour, Simon? Take a moment and think of everything you want to say to Alex. All your hopes and dreams for them, all your fears."

Simon closed his eyes tight and conjured up the moment in his mind. He was kneeling in front of the mother of his child, his ear to her belly as he whispered. He said all the things he needed to say…

…and then opened his eyes.

"Now…" She stroked the back of his neck. "Ask God to pass that on to Alex in heaven."

Simon's vision blurred with tears as he did what she asked. He felt his heart loosen up and relax. A tender smile graced her lips and she rested her head on his shoulder. He finally wrapped his arms around her and held her close.

FIFTY-SIX

THE SMELL OF bacon filled Simon's nose and he stirred. He looked up at the living room ceiling, his eyes slowly focusing. He stared straight ahead, almost concerned that his breathing was so normal and he wasn't covered in sweat.

That's when he felt the weight on his chest and looked down to find Yanah snuggled up to him, his arms enclosing her. He watched her sleep, trying to remember what had happened the night before.

The memories slowly came back to him and he let his head fall back onto the armrest of the couch. He subconsciously drew circles around Yanah's shoulder with his thumb, his mind wandering.

Mark entered the living room and set down a couple of cups on the end table for them, one with coffee and the other tea, then sat down with his newspaper and his own mug.

Simon felt unsure what to do. No words came to mind, no excuses or explanations. When he tried to sit up, Yanah only cuddled into him more. He settled back again but managed to snag his cup and take a sip of coffee.

"Sleep well?" Mark asked softly.

Simon swallowed and nodded.

Mark turned the page. "Good."

Simon continued to lay there, quietly holding Yanah.

"She loves you," his dad said. "Has loved you since forever."

Mark's face held an expression Simon remembered all too well from the years when he had dated Heather.

"I know." Simon's voice was soft as he watched Yanah sleep.

"I'm not sure she'll ever be able to let go of you, Sye." Mark's voice was almost grim.

"I can't."

"What about that Mary girl?"

Simon shook his head.

Mark let out a sigh and set his paper down. "Sye, it's time you learn to let go. Clearly I can't help you with what you're going through, as much as it pains me. But I can still point you in the right direction. You feel responsible. You've had to do some horrible, horrible things to protect others. Things that will haunt you for the rest of your life. But that young woman in your arms right there…" Mark sighed and shook his head. "She's been through hell and back, Sye. She understands your pain better than the rest of us, and she's struggling with it too. But look at her."

Simon looked down at the serene expression on Yanah's face.

"She's been sleeping as poorly as you since she got here. Yet now you've finally found rest and peace together. Don't throw that away because of your pride."

A frown took hold of Simon as Mark finished his coffee and left.

Eventually Shelby came in and smiled at them. "Breakfast is ready."

Simon gently shook Yanah. "Hey."

She groaned and buried her face in his chest.

"Yanah, it's time for breakfast."

She shook her head and gripped his shirt.

"Yanah… I'm gonna leave you on this couch alone if you don't wake up."

"No…"

"That's it."

Simon gently dumped her on the couch.

Her eyes snapped open. "Simon!"

She reached for him but he stepped away.

"Breakfast is ready."

"You're mean."

He smirked. "Yeah, yeah… what else is new?"

She sat up and he gestured for her to fix her hair. She ran her fingers through it, but then gave up. "I'll just go brush it…"

She yawned, stretched, and then, as Simon turned to walk towards the kitchen, she darted forward and hugged him from behind.

"Thank you for last night, Simon. I really needed it."

He swallowed and patted her hand. "Same."

She smiled and nuzzled his back.

When Yanah finally let go and walked around him to head up the stairs, he went into the kitchen and quickly ate his breakfast.

"I see you and Yanah are back to napping together," Shelby remarked.

Simon raised an eyebrow at her.

"I remember when you used to go off to recharge. She would join you and often nap on you."

Simon blinked a few times, then looked down at his empty plate as memories flooded his mind. "I forgot she used to do that…"

"Really?" Shelby smirked. "I remember that her brothers would give you a hard time about it. Called you her—"

"Kariyt," Simon finished for her. "Her pillow."

Shelby giggled. "That's right."

"I'm gonna go for a walk."

Simon stood up and walked outside. As he strolled around the house, he opened his phone and caught up on his calls and messages.

———————

Mary awoke to the sound of her alarm. She smacked it, yawned, and murmured a morning prayer before going through her morning routine. As she stood in front of the bathroom mirror covering her birthmark, her phone went off. She put it on speaker mode.

"Hello?" she said.

"Hello, this is Dr. Richard's office calling about your appointment today."

"Oh, right," Mary murmured. "I don't need it anymore."

"Ms. Alabaster, you should come for the checkup anyway. It's already scheduled, so we may as well get it done."

Mary sighed. "All right. I'll come in."

She hung up and finished her morning routine.

Just over an hour later, she arrived at the doctor's office and checked in at the front reception. A member of the staff brought her into an examination room where she waited for several minutes.

At last the doctor came in.

"Hello, Ms. Alabaster," he said, closing the door behind him. "I'm Dr. Lenall. Dr. Richards asked me to come in because you were concerned about early-onset mental degradation. Is there a reason you believe this is going to happen?"

"It happened to my mother."

"Your mother…" Dr. Lenall started looking through the files in his hand. "Apart from her, do you know of any other cases in your family?"

"Not that I'm aware of."

The doctor frowned. "Ms. Alabaster, do you recall when your mother's condition began?"

"When I was in Grade Seven. I was twelve."

"I seriously doubt that your mother's condition was genetic."

Mary blinked a few times. "H–how do you…?"

"Your mother seems to have suffered a head injury around that time. It wasn't enough to cause concern, but it could have led to a slow brain bleed that was missed until it was too late." Dr. Lenall sat at the desk and turned the computer screen to her. "I can run some tests just to be sure, but Ms. Alabaster… you should be perfectly fine."

Mary stared at the screen, her eyes wide as she tried to comprehend what was being presented to her. Tears built up along her lower eyelids, then slowly broke free and rolled down her cheeks.

"I… I'm not going to…?" Her tears flowed freely. "I thought—" She took a few breaths and brought herself under control. "How did… how did this never come up?"

"You've not been to see a doctor since you were a teenager, Ms. Alabaster. It says here in your file that you haven't shown up for any checkups."

Mary took in a shaky breath.

"Like I said, I can still take a blood sample and run some tests to be sure there isn't anything else."

Mary swallowed and nodded. "Doublecheck, please."

FIFTY-SEVEN

MARY DROVE HER car to Neil's place and went inside. The older gentleman was seated in the living room, like usual, as she stepped in. He watched her quietly take off her shoes and jacket.

"You seem different," he remarked.

"Hmm?"

"Lighter, yet more conflicted."

She swallowed and looked away. "I'm fine."

"I'm old, not blind. Yet."

She walked into the living room and sat down across from him. "I know, Neil. I'm saying… I'm *fine*."

His brow furrowed, until understanding flashed across his eyes. "Just to be clear, you mean…?"

"I'm not going to go crazy."

"And this isn't good news?"

"I've been living my life like I'm doing to die!" Mary blurted out.

"Most people live like they have all the time in the world," Neil said gently. "You've made the most of your time."

"But I haven't!" Tears burned her eyes. "I've missed out on so much! There are so many things I could've…"

Neil waited a moment before speaking. "You mean Simon? He is your biggest regret now. Had you known, he'd be yours."

Tears broke free from Mary's eyes and she nodded. "I already gave up. Yanah asked me for permission to pursue him, and that's what I did."

"That doesn't mean you can't compete."

Mary shook her head. "She's a wonderful woman, and she'll do better for Simon than I can."

"Simon doesn't need Yanah to get better." Neil rose to his feet. "He can get that same help from any number of veteran support groups. He just has to set aside his pride and attend one. What he needs is someone to hold him through the night to stave off the nightmares. If even Susan could do that, then so could you."

CHAPTER FIFTY-SEVEN

Mary swallowed. "But I like Yanah. She's my friend now. I don't... I can't do that to her, give my blessing one minute and then start pursuing Simon the next. It would be a betrayal."

Neil embraced her and she stiffened.

"It must hurt," he said, stroking her hair.

She gripped his shirt and nodded through her sobs as her heart shattered.

———————————

Back on the Fletcher ranch, Simon sat on the porch with Ray. As the day passed, the pair of them watched the cowboys herd cattle through the field.

"I don't see the problem, Simon," the pastor remarked after a few moments of silence.

Simon glanced sidelong at the pastor. "I've already made my stance clear."

"Then push her away," Ray replied. "You can't keep saying you can't have a relationship, then lead them on. You've done this to both Mary and Yanah now. With Mary, I can understand. But there's no excuse for what you're doing with Yanah."

"Jesus said that it's adultery to marry a divorcee. Paul said that sex establishes a spiritual connection. That means I've been married seven times over now, and thus divorced seven times over."

"You weren't Christian then. And Jesus also said that divorce was acceptable in the case of sexual immorality. I'm almost a hundred percent sure all your past partners have moved on—not to mention the fact that *you* have moved on. As far as those relationships go, they're shot—"

"Jesus didn't say that it was okay to marry a divorcee if the divorce was the result of sexual immorality," Simon insisted. "He simply said that it's adultery."

"You're wrong. Matthew 19:9 says, very specifically, the following: 'And I say to you: whoever divorces his wife, except for sexual immorality, and marries another, commits adultery.'"[1] Ray looked at Simon pointedly. "The Greek has a double meaning here. The woman such a man marries is committing adultery as well. The verse means that you have been divorced from all those other people, since the relationships were immoral. That means you're free to marry. It wouldn't be sinful."

Simon didn't know what to say.

"I can pull up the verse if you like," Ray suggested.

Simon just looked away. No one spoke for a long time. Their eyes continued to follow the work going on in the nearby field.

"What do you actually want, Simon?"

"What I want doesn't matter."

"Considering how tightly you clung to an erroneous reading of that verse and refused to doublecheck whether you were understanding it correctly, it seems to me that it matters a great deal. Otherwise why would you intentionally skew the Bible to protect yourself from having to face the world around you?"

———————————

1 ESV.

Simon paused. "What?"

"You're lying about the Bible as an excuse not to pursue the lovely young woman who's pursuing you."

Simon went quiet.

"What about the prophet Hosea?" Ray asked. "You know, God told him to marry a prostitute. We've talked about this before, but really listen this time. In your case, you are the prostitute. God did that to make a point to the Jews of the time, but ask yourself this: when did God ever tell any of his people to do something that would otherwise be a sin? This wasn't a test, such as with Abraham and Isaac."

Simon's brow furrowed.

"Whether you remarry or not is entirely up to you. I can't say if it's right or wrong. That's between you, this woman, and God. But the Bible is clear that it isn't a matter of sin. Yanah is pursuing you with godly intentions, and I know that you would pursue her back with the same intentions. So ask God about this. Don't just put your nose in the book and close it. Have a conversation with him."

Ray looked past him to see Yanah approaching from the bunkhouse.

"You're in an enviable position, Simon," the pastor added. "Few women pursue men at all, let alone as doggedly as Yanah is pursuing you."

When Yanah arrived, she stopped right in front of Simon. "Come with me. There's something you should see."

Ray smiled. "Hi Yanah."

She smiled back. "Shalom, shalom, Ray." She returned her gaze to Simon. "Please? It won't take long."

Simon took in a breath and stood up. "Sure."

FIFTY-EIGHT

YANAH LED SIMON across the ranch.

"What are you going to show me?" he asked.

Yanah squeezed his hand. "To see a miracle."

He frowned but let her lead him.

When they reached the bunkhouse, she opened the door only for Delta to run outside and leap onto Simon.

"Hey bud, what's the…?" His eyes widened when he saw Daisy and all the pups on the floor.

Yanah gently pulled him into the bunkhouse and knelt next to Daisy. Delta sat beside her, looking up at Simon proudly.

"You helped make this happen, Simon," she said.

Yanah gently picked up one of the pups and held it out to him. Simon remained still at first, but then Yanah took him by the hand and carefully placed the pup in his palm.

Daisy sniffed Simon first, then Yanah. Then Delta sniffed the pup in Simon's hand and nuzzled him.

"I didn't," Simon protested.

"You did. You played an important part in this miracle of life, Simon. Without you, Delta and Daisy never would have met. If they hadn't met, these pups wouldn't be alive." Yanah leaned into him, looking down at the pups. The pup in Simon's hand squirmed. "You helped bring about a miracle."

Simon's eyes started to mist.

"These hands are the hands of a guardian. This heart…" She placed her hand over his chest. "It beats for others. You shoulder such horrible trauma so others won't have to. You are a good man. Your pain is proof of that." She wrapped her arms around him. "Your pain is yours. It belongs to you and you alone, Simon, just as my pain is mine and mine alone."

Simon looked at her, not sure what to say.

"I don't know your pain as intimately as you do, but like you I have taken the life of a person far too young to be in war."

His breath caught in his throat. "I'm sorry."

She smiled gently.

"It must hurt," he added.

"It does." She rested her head on his shoulder. "But last night I slept without fear. Without guilt or pain."

Simon swallowed. "So did I."

She searched his eyes. "Can you hold me tonight too, please?"

He looked away. "I'm not sure that's appropriate."

She gently guided his eyes back to her. "King David had a woman just to keep him warm at night. Regardless of whether anything else happened during those nights, the purpose was to help him sleep. There was no sin in that purpose."

"Yanah—"

She waited for him to finish his thought and then gave him a squeeze when he couldn't.

"There is no sin in our purpose either," she said. "We can sleep on the couch, where we can be held accountable. I am aware of your exes, but they required sex. Perhaps you wanted it too. But the purpose was to bring peace to your nights. Let us bring peace to one another."

He swallowed. "I need to think about it."

She rested her chin on his shoulder. "Okay. Take your time." She smiled. "And I met your friend, Eggsy."

"Oh yeah?"

"You should speak with him. He looks up to you like a big brother." Yanah gave him one last squeeze. "I'm going to head out."

"Need my truck?"

Yanah shook her head. "Mary's going to pick me up."

Simon nodded and carefully placed the pup back with the others.

Together Simon and Yanah walked out of the bunkhouse. Simon walked to the pasture to get a horse while Yanah disappeared into the main house.

He was in the middle of saddling a horse when he heard a car engine. He looked over his shoulder and saw Mary pull up in front of the house. She waved at him.

"That's a beautiful mare," she remarked when she walked towards him.

"She is." Simon petted the mare. "Yanah helping out with the Thanksgiving event?"

"Yeah. We're setting up today."

Simon frowned. "It's Friday already?"

Mary nodded. "Yeah. Must be easy to lose track of time out here."

Simon took in a breath. "It sure is… either way, Ray and Bethany will be able to move back into their place next week. The painters are just finishing up."

"That's wonderful to hear." Mary beamed. "I'm sure they're excited."

"They are." Simon looked over at the barn that held the travel trailer. "But I'm gonna miss having an on-call pastor."

CHAPTER FIFTY-EIGHT

Mary giggled. "Yeah, I imagine it's been convenient having him here. But…" She looked back towards the house just as Yanah stepped outside. "Your life is moving forward, Simon. You don't need Ray here anymore. It's time for you to grow in a different direction."

Simon followed her gaze. "Mary…"

"Pursue her."

"What?"

"Pursue her." Mary met his gaze. "She loves you so, so much, and I know you feel the same for her."

Simon swallowed. "I don't want to lose you."

She smiled. "You will eventually. Besides, Yanah and I are friends. Being with her doesn't mean you can't be friends with me."

He let out a shaky breath. "You'd be okay with it?"

"I'd be over the moon," Mary said. "She's a great woman, and she loves you. It'd actually help me to know you will have her with you when I'm gone."

"I have nothing to offer her."

"You have plenty. Even if you didn't, you would still have yourself. And for her? That's more than enough." She smiled. "She asked for my blessing to pursue you. If you need it too, you have it."

Simon kept his gaze on Yanah as she approached. "Okay."

Mary smiled warmly. "I'm proud of you, Simon. Don't let her go."

"I won't."

When Yanah reached them, she gave Mary a big hug. "I'm ready to go." She let go of the embrace and glanced at Simon. "See you."

Simon paused for a moment before reaching in for a hug. "Have a good day. Be safe."

Yanah practically glowed at his touch. "I will. You too."

FIFTY-NINE

SIMON RODE HIS horse out into the fields wearing the hat Yanah had chosen for him. He tracked down the cowboys and worked with them for a while to herd the cattle.

He came alongside Eggsy. "Afternoon, Eggsy."

"Afternoon, bruv."

Simon looked out over the herd and leaned against the front of his saddle. "How're you holding up?"

"I'm doing good, Sye." Eggsy sniffed. "The fresh air, the animals, and guys who can relate and will help keep me straight." He sighed. "Not exactly what my old man wanted for me, but it's better than the alternative. You keep saving my life, Sye. I owe more than I can ever repay."

"I don't do it for debts, Eggsy. I do it cause you're my brother."

"Not by blood…"

"I will cut my hand right here and now."

Simon's tone caught Eggsy off-guard and he looked over to check Simon's expression. "That, uh… won't be necessary, bruv. I get it."

"Good. Here's what you can do for me. Stay clean and work hard. Help keep the other guys clean when they're having a hard time. And here's one final thing, the most important thing."

Eggsy looked away, knowing what was coming.

"Call your sister and parents," Simon finished.

"Mum disowned me."

"Your dad and sister still care, Eggsy. Call your sister and have her get in touch with your dad. This is the last step you've avoided for years. It's time to take it."

Eggsy finally nodded, the conflict clear in his body language. "Okay."

Simon clasped his shoulder. "Good man. I'm proud of you, Eggsy."

Eggsy started to smile, but he tried to hide it.

"Let's get this herd over to field three," Simon said with a smirk.

As Mary and Yanah worked alongside other members of the church, making preparations for the Thanksgiving event, Mary couldn't help but notice that Yanah was making fast friends.

When the group took a break to share a late lunch, Mary and Yanah sat together. They noticed some of the young men whispering amongst each other while glancing their way.

After a few minutes, one of those men stood up and approached the women.

"Mind if I join you?" he asked.

Mary opened her mouth to speak, but Yanah spoke first. "You may."

"I'm Asher." The man sat down next to Yanah.

"Eliyanah," she replied. "Pleasure to meet you."

"You're from Israel, right?"

"I am." Yanah finished her meal and turned towards him, giving him her full attention.

"Did you serve?"

"I did."

Asher cleared his throat. "Did you see combat?"

"I was in an advance combat unit that specialized in clearing urban areas and tunnel networks."

Asher's brow furrowed as he tried to consider the implications. "I can't even imagine…"

"No, you probably can't." Yanah smiled sweetly. "And I hope you never find yourself in the place where imagination meets reality."

Asher swallowed. "Well, what brings you out here to the U.S.? Do you and Mary go back?"

"She's not here for me," Mary said as she finished her meal.

"I'm here for Simon," Yanah clarified. "I just happen to have made friends with Mary and offered to help out."

Disappointment flashed across Asher's eyes. "And you and Simon are friends?"

Mary spoke quickly. "They're dating."

Yanah looked sharply at Mary, the shock clear on her face. Mary smiled and winked.

"I came here with the intention of courting Simon," Yanah said. "If things don't work out, I'll go home."

"What if you found someone else here?" Asher asked.

Yanah shook her head. "That's a bridge to cross once I reach it. But as things stand, I'm here for him and him alone. I won't let anyone or anything pull me away from that."

"I see," Asher murmured. "Well, it was nice getting to know you, Eliyanah."

"It was nice to meet you." Yanah offered a single nod.

She and Mary watched as Asher went back to the other young men.

"He was crushing on you pretty hard," Mary remarked.

"I'm aware. That's why I let him sit here."

Mary raised an eyebrow.

"The young men would've found out tomorrow that I'm pursuing Simon," Yanah added. "I thought it best to shut it down now. Asher will tell the others I only have eyes for Simon. If this were any other setting, I'd have politely told him to leave me alone without letting him sit down.

But this is Simon's church, and I imagine it may become my church. I wouldn't want to cause problems before I even officially join."

"Huh."

"Why did you say that he and I are dating?"

Mary shrugged. "He's yours, Yanah. And you're his. I figured you'd use the phrasing you did, which could have left room for this guy to feel some false hope. This way they know, in no uncertain terms, that you're off-limits."

Yanah considered Mary's words, then looked down at her plate. "I understand your reason, but Simon and I are not yet dating. I can't condone you saying that we are."

Mary gathered their plates and cutlery and stood up. As she did, she glanced up towards the front door just as Simon stepped into the foyer, Hailey in tow.

Her heart ached to tell him that she was fine, that she wouldn't lose herself to her mother's insanity. But when she saw how his eyes settled on her, she steeled her heart. She couldn't tell him. Not yet. Not until she was no longer an option.

"Then go ahead and ask him," Mary suggested.

Yanah jumped up and ran over to the door. She gave Hailey a hug, reserving an even bigger one for Simon.

"Hey Hailey," Mary said as she walked up. "Could you come with me a sec? I could use your help."

Mary winked at Yanah before taking the girl and leading her away, sparing Yanah and Simon a few private moments together.

When Yanah and Simon were alone, she felt a pit in her stomach. She took in a deep breath, but mid-breath she felt Simon pat her shoulder. All her anxiety disappeared.

"Hey Sye."

He smiled. "Hey."

She swallowed and glanced away for a moment, then let out a breath and settled her gaze back on his. "I want to restate my intentions."

He gave her a nod and waited for her to continue.

"Simon, I have always loved you. I promised you that one day I would marry you. While I'm unsure whether that promise will bear fruit, I want to plant the seed for that tree together. I came here to do just that. I understand that you have things you need to work through, but… I'm here, Simon. I'm right here, to work with you and help." She looked down and closed her eyes tight. "And I will stay here until you tell me you don't want me."

Yanah squeezed her eyes even tighter, her whole body going rigid as she waited for his response. Her heart pounded in her ears. Her chest felt like it could explode at any moment.

Only a few seconds passed, yet it felt like an eternity.

She had just started to open her eyes again when she felt those familiar strong arms wrap themselves around her. His scent filled her nose and her eyes widened. She smiled broadly and snuggled into his chest.

"This better mean you want me to stay, or you're being real cruel right now." Her voice was soft, barely reaching his ears.

Simon kissed the top of her head. "I want you to stay."

"And...?" Trepidation filled her voice.

He swallowed. "And I want to plant that seed."

She nuzzled him, then placed her hand on his chest and looked up at him. "So we're together now?"

He nodded and she went on the tips of her toes to kiss him.

www.ingramcontent.com/pod-product-compliance
Lightning Source LLC
Chambersburg PA
CBHW031228260626
47169CB00007B/2205